Banjo Man

*To Debbie
Enjoy journeying with
Susanna
June*

June E. Titus

JUNE E. TITUS

Copyright © 2020 June E. Titus
All rights reserved
First Edition

Fulton Books, Inc.
Meadville, PA

Published by Fulton Books 2020

ISBN 978-1-64654-321-2 (paperback)
ISBN 978-1-64654-322-9 (digital)

Printed in the United States of America

Dook

Willson's Cove, North Carolina, June 2009

Dook, a hound of some various mixed origins, was the Seventh Dook of Willson's Cove. Anytime someone came, he greeted the guests as royally as he knew how. He sniffed the feet of those he rarely saw and wagged his tail and barked as friendly as he could to those more familiar. He even let his fractional beagle ancestry shine in his lovely roar.

Today he was more excited than usual; more guests than usual. All this had begun eleven months before when Susan, one of his very favorite subjects, had brought a nice fellow to pay homage. The man had shared his ham sandwich.

Now there was promise of far more than a ham sandwich from the delightful scents coming from the casseroles being carried into the house of his dookdom. It was a wedding feast.

CHAPTER 1

Susan

Boone, North Carolina, July 2008

John "Mac" McBride, seventy-year-old retired surgeon, sat on the ground in front of Jones House,[1] in Boone, North Carolina. Every sense in his being was focused on the haunting melody the petite lady with a mop of white curls was singing, unaccompanied by any instruments. She sang "Barbry Ellen." He had never heard this version of the popular ballad before.

The pathos of her melody and rich voice brought goose bumps to his tanned arms. He couldn't take his eyes from her. She sang another one that was equally beautiful: an old mountain hymn, "My Lord, What a Morning." He ran his fingers through his gray-tinged sandy curls as if to ward off that morning of retribution.

Jones House hosted free concerts every Friday evening during the warm summer months. This evening, several groups were performing bluegrass, old-time music, folk songs, and ballads. The woman had played banjo and did vocals with one of the bluegrass bands. She was good on the banjo, but she was struggling, wiggling her fingers at every opportunity. Mac murmured, "Arthritis?" But now she was singing without the instruments.

"I want to meet this lady."

The music went on for several hours. Audiences came and went as they wished, but if Mac hoped the woman would sing again, he would be disappointed. She didn't. Later, when he looked behind where he was seated on the ground, she was seated on a blanket directly back of him.

Mac more than glanced at the woman. He watched how she twirled a snowy curl with a finger, absorbed in the music. She was apparently alone, although he noticed her blanket had room for two. He got up from his spot on the ground and went to where she was seated.

"May I join you?"

She shrugged and patted the blanket. "Sure. Plenty of room."

"I never heard such a beautifully haunting sound as you gave us with your a cappella songs. Thank you. You made the program worth hearing. Oh, I'm Mac McBride from Macon, Georgia."

"Howdy, Mac McBride. Thank you. Songs my grandpa taught me. I normally play the banjo when I sing, but my hands were cramping. Those songs do well without instruments. I am Susan Reese from Willson's Cove, a little community west of here. What brings you to Boone?"

The music had changed from bluegrass to rockabilly. It was a bit difficult to hear each other over the booms and twangs, so Mac suggested going across the street to Our Daily Bread for a cup of coffee.

"Good idea. My ears are getting tired of the noise. They aren't that good to begin with. My ears, not the music!" Susan laughed at her "punny."

Mac offered to carry her banjo. Despite his stocky Scottish build, when he picked up the case, he understood why her hands must have been cramping while she played.

Susan saw him looking at her hands. "Yeah, a little bit of osteo-arthritis in my right pickin' hand." She was otherwise very fit and looked younger than her sixty-nine years.

"This banjo's heavy!" he said.

"Yes. I'm going to sell it. Too heavy for me with the resonator. I need a good old mountain "banjer" like my grandpa used to make."

They drank decaf coffee, ate sandwiches, and talked without concern for the time.

"You here in Boone to get away from Georgia heat?"

"Partly. I just turned my surgical practice over to my son, Jack, a few months ago. I have always enjoyed vacationing here. In fact, back when the children were in their teens, we came up here for the Scottish Games on Grandfather Mountain. I've dabbled in the bagpipes and enjoy playing but not in public. Bob, my youngest son, tried bagpipes, but that was not his best talent either. He is a lawyer in Savannah now and good at that. The oldest son, Jack, the doctor, is a runner and runs the races at the Scottish Games.[2] He was great in track and still comes here every July and runs. He was with me here last week with his entire family. Then Jessica, my daughter, well, she used to come along for the vacation, but she and her mother were more into the shopping. Ha. I doubt if you would ever see her at the Highland Games of her own accord."

Susan shook her head, causing her white curls to bounce. "You know, I've lived here all my life and never went to the games. I love hiking at Grandfather Mountain, and I used to take my school students to the mountain every April when they have free admission for locals. We would hike, but I never went to the big festivities."

"So you are a schoolteacher?"

"Retired. I taught at the little country school in the '60s after I got out of college, but they closed the school. I got a job teaching here at Watauga High School then and taught till I retired in 2000. Wonderful career. I taught English and literature. I've been enjoying playing with our little string band ever since."

Mac nodded. "I liked it. I'm not a great fan of bluegrass because it all seems to be the same, yet your band is a mix of bluegrass and old time."

"You were a surgeon? What variety?"

"General surgery, appendectomies, gallbladders, stuff like that. Guess I did okay since I never got sued."

Susan's giggle reflected her perpetual youthfulness. "I guess that's a good criteria."

"And yes, this is partly a vacation and partly looking for a place to buy. I'd like to live here except for the real cold winter months. I still have my home in Macon, but Jack and his family are talking about moving in my place. They are outgrowing their home. It'll be a good place for me to go when the weather gets cold, and even if they move in there, they'll still have room for me."

"Winter here isn't that bad. It snows, the wind blows, it warms up in the daytime, and the snow melts. So where are you looking?"

"I have looked in Banner Elk, too remote. Linville, too small. Boone and Foscoe, meh. And Blowing Rock, which so far I like the best. My realtor is looking for the best fit for me. It needs to be big enough to host my family and small enough that I don't have to hire a housekeeper."

Susan cocked her eye and laughed. "I can't imagine letting someone else clean my place. I take it there is no Mrs. McBride anymore."

"She passed away two years ago. That's when I decided to retire. I wasn't able to be there for her much of the time when she was so sick, and now she is gone. Is there a Mr. Reese?"

"He was killed in Korea. We hadn't been married a year. We didn't have children, so I have had hundreds of wonderful children as students instead. I have my music, my extended family, lots of cousins, a host of friends, and lots of good memories. I still have an aunt who lives by herself at age eighty-six. But she told me a few weeks ago she has her name in a retirement home in Banner Elk."

When the waitress at Our Daily Bread approached with a cleaning cloth in her hand and told them the store was closing, they were surprised. They had been chatting for an hour and a half, and it seemed as though it had only been ten minutes. Yet on the other hand, it seemed they had known one another for years.

Over the next couple of weeks, Mac saw Susan every day. Although she lived a half hour away from Boone, they met either in Boone or some other place that either he wanted to see or she wanted to show him.

One day she got behind the wheel and didn't say where they were going. Winding curves to gravel roads and shifting into four-wheel drive up a country lane and mountainside. She took him to Willson's Cove and showed him the old family home, although they did not go inside since her cousin Mike wasn't there. Dook, the mixed-breed hound, greeted them with a bit of jumping and tail wagging. He recognized Susan's car. Mac shared his lunch with the dog.

Then Susan took him to her own house, the place her daddy, Harvey Willson, built when he and her mother had married. They stayed long enough for her to show him the house and raid the refrigerator.

Last but not least, she took him back a rocky track to visit her Aunt Carrie.

Aunt Carrie was delighted to see them. "Well. Hope you don't mind if I don't get up and make y'all coffee, but seems I'm a-windin' down these days." She patted her walker. "Got my name in over at the retirement home in Banner Elk. You won't forget to come and visit, will ya?"

"You know I won't, Auntie."

Carrie put her stamp of approval on Mac by pulling him down to her ear. She whispered something, but Mac never told Susan what she said.

One day they hiked the easy trails on Grandfather Mountain. Susan had no trouble keeping up with Mac. She was in great physical condition. She told him she worked out at a fitness club in Banner Elk.

"What better way for you to get acquainted with the high country than to visit the places of local interest with a local," Susan said.

Mac laughed.

Does he know what I'm thinking? She really meant get acquainted with each other.

Mac had to return to Macon for some business, but before he left, he purchased a great place in Blowing Rock. He gave her more than a hint that he wanted more than a few weeks' vacation in her company.

Does he have something permanent in mind?

Mac first met Susan on the third week of July. After going to Macon briefly, he returned to Blowing Rock and remained in the area until October, enjoying his new house in Blowing Rock and Susan. Bob, his son, and his family from Savannah; and Jessica, his daughter, with her family visited late in August. All the family met

Susan, and she seemed to fit into their idea of a suitable consort for Mac. Jessica, however, made her feelings known.

"Dad, I am glad you found someone you enjoy being with. Just remember that no one, but no one can replace my mother. Be careful. That's all I'm saying."

At Thanksgiving, Susan joined Mac in Macon for a family get-together, and everyone hit it off well enough that even Jessica grudgingly admitted that Susan brought the best out of their father.

In December, Mac came to the high country supposedly to ski on Beech Mountain. He did not get much skiing done but spent most of his time fifteen miles off the slopes, in front of Susan's fireplace. It was there that he proposed.

After a few trips back and forth between his place in Blowing Rock and Macon, Mac returned for the summer of 2009, and on a Saturday afternoon in early September, they had a private wedding ceremony at Susan's little country church in Willson's Cove. The only ones attending were Mac's children and grandchildren and some of Susan's first cousins who lived nearby. Susan insisted that Aunt Carrie Vance should come and asked Aunt Carrie's daughter, Gladdie, to bring her mama.

There was a nice reception at the family home with foods provided by some of the cousins. It was a simple, low-key ceremony with the two families getting to know each other. Aunt Carrie was almost as lauded as much as the bride and groom.

The bride and groom took off the next morning for a honeymoon in Apalachicola, Florida.

Chapter 2

Susan

Apalachicola, Florida, September 2009

Susan stood glued to the floor at the entrance of a storefront. *It couldn't be. But it is. It is like his ghost!* Banjo music was floating out the doorway, and it was coming from a white ponytail with holey blue jeans. He was playing Willson's Cove songs the unique way Grandpa always played, and the sound was exactly the same. And it was Grandpa's voice. *Almost makes me believe in channeling.* Once she got over the shock of the sound, she ventured inside.

Mac, having been in another store, came and stood beside her and handed her a glazed doughnut. "We need to go across the street and make reservations for this evening's dinner. You come with me?"

"No. I need to talk to this fellow. He has given me a jolt!"

"Jolt?"

"I'll explain later."

Susan approached the man as soon as he took a break from playing. "Hey. Where did you get your banjo? Who taught you to sing that way, those versions? What is your name?"

"Whoa! One question at a time. I am Harry Harvey from St. Petersburg, Florida. And you are?"

"Susan Re—I mean, Susan McBride from North Carolina."

"Well, Susan McBride, my dad taught me, and he learned from his mom. She, in turn, learned from my grandfather. The banjo was one he gave Dad when he was a little boy back in the 1920s."

"May I see your banjo?"

Harry grasped the neck and held it out to her.

Susan grasped it with one hand supporting the head and the other hand on the neck, like it was going to get away from her. She peered inside, scrutinizing all around inside. She hoped to see if there were any markings that would tell who had made the instrument. *Could this be one?*

Susan had been looking for one of Grandpa Willson's banjos for more than twenty years, but they were illusive as the fogs on Grandfather Mountain's nose on a sunny day.

She gasped. There it was: "lw-1919."

"May I play it?"

He jerked his neck back, somewhat surprised, but with that much interest, perhaps this person did know how to play. "Sure. Try it out."

Susan sat on a stool and played the banjo. Her fingering was good, but her intonation was off since it was a fretless banjo. She played "Sourwood Mountain" almost the same as Harry had played it moments before.

Meanwhile, Mac had returned from making reservations for dinner and stood, listening to his wife on a borrowed banjo. He hadn't heard her on the banjo since last year. She had sold hers when her arthritis had gotten too bad to play. This was a much smaller wood-constructed banjo without the heavy resonator on the bluegrass banjo she had played. He didn't interrupt her.

Once she finished, Harry reached for the instrument. He nodded appreciatively. "I can tell you play, but you aren't used to this little gem with her unimpeded fingerboard. Where did you learn?"

"Music is in my family. I studied the violin when I was in school, but my, well, I was advised to learn how to fiddle. I pooh-poohed the idea until I realized the advice was right on and took up the banjo. My uncle Roby taught me then. By the way, this is my husband, Mac McBride.

"And you? You say your grandmother was the source of your banjo style and versions of ballads and folk songs?"

Harry nodded. "Yeah. She played on up till about a year before she died. When I was, what? Twelve, I guess. Dad learned from her, and the two would play together, switching off between banjo and fiddle. I don't play the fiddle, but Dad still does at age eighty-seven. He can't remember anyone's name, but he remembers how to play his fiddle."

"Does he live here?"

"In a retirement home in Tampa now."

Susan snapped her blue eyes, trying to imagine the old man playing those old tunes perhaps the way her uncles would play when she was a girl. "I'd like to hear him someday, if I ever get to Tampa. So your grandfather, did he play as well?"

"He was out of the picture, I guess, before I was born. But Grandma said she learned from him. That's all I know." Harry acted as though he was getting uncomfortable with the direction of the conversation and feigned another appointment. "Nice talking to you, ma'am. I need to get going. Pressing matters."

As Susan and Mac went their way, she said, "This might be an interesting honeymoon!"

Chapter 3

Luther

Willson's Cove, North Carolina, October 1921

Music was practically what Willson's Cove was all about. It was almost like an enclave of the Willson family; the clan had been there for several generations and were all kinfolk. There was probably no one, even in the extended family, who was not musical. Pickin', singin', and cloggin'. They did it all. Luther Willson was not only well-known for his great singing voice and picking the banjo—"banjer," he called it—but his musical instruments were renowned as far away as Georgia and Florida for his superb handcrafted quality. He was a luthier extraordinaire.

*****

Luther picked up the small grip with the few clothes Susanna, "Zanny," had fixed up for him. She was a good seamstress, and he could proudly wear anything she made for him. He would wear his suit and his snazzy derby hat.

He had crated up the instruments; six banjos and two fiddles were in a wheelbarrow that two of his children, Rancie and Harvey, took turns pushing.

As they walked along, Luther didn't have much to say, but Zanny did.

"I'll miss ye, Luther, this winter more'n ever."

Zanny was beginning to show. She was carrying their ninth child, and it would be due before he returned in April.

"Too, the church is 'thout a preacher, and who'll fill in the preaching each Sunday with ye gone? Who'll be a-visitin' the homebound, prayin' with the sick? But the money ye kin make in Florida." She understood that both with the sale of his instruments and the money he got from singing in restaurants and churches, they could not afford to do without. "Ye gotta go, Luther. I know it. It's jes harder ever' year."

Luther looked straight ahead, and he put his hand over his heart. He readily told Zanny every day how much he loved her. She was a sweet, trusting soul. Seeing him leave was torture for her. Yet he knew that she would see to it that life would go on.

Getting to Luther's destination was torture, too. The narrow-gauge railroad to Johnson City, Tennessee, then to points south: Chattanooga, Atlanta, Jacksonville, and on to Tampa and St. Petersburg. It was an agonizing trip, but he would make some money on his musical instruments; enough to send money back to Zanny and the children and have some left for his time in the sun. With his "weak" lungs, he would benefit from warmer weather of Florida. He wouldn't need to hire a room. There were "friends," he told Zanny. (But none he would introduce to his family.)

When Zanny tearfully, but without complaint, voiced her disappointment that he needed to be in Florida for six months, he shared his reasoning. "Why, Zanny, all them rich folks from the north winter in Florida. Half of the population in St. Petersburg are people with money to spend from their businesses up north. If I don't take advantage of their desire for somethin' new—they love mountain music—I'd be amiss. In the long run, it'll mean more for you and the young'un. And another big reason, and I hate to admit it, I need the warmer weather for my health. This cold weather in these here mountains gonna kill me if I stay another year!"

Now he had to leave.

Five of the eight children still lived at home, and they went to the station with him, along with Luther's dog, Dook II. They all formed a circle with their mother around Papa. He prayed with them, kissed the children, pulled Zanny as close as her pregnant belly would allow, and gave her that kiss that always welcomed him back, even if she had suspected his philandering. He boarded the train.

As the train pulled away, Luther saw Zanny scratch behind Dook's ears as she watched the train. Little Delphy was in the empty wheelbarrow, and Harvey had already started to push her toward home. Not Zanny. She'll watch until the train disappeared around the mountain heading down to Tennessee. He knew she would refuse to cry and hold her head high. He visualized her following the wheelbarrow and leading the other children on foot the three miles back to Willson's Cove.

As they walked, she would point out different trees and quiz them on what they were. They would pick up the pretty leaves to keep so they could show Papa when he came home in the spring. They would dip them in hot "parry-fene" wax to preserve the color. They would stop by the spring house and pick up milk to take to the house, and when they got inside, she would give them milk and cornbread.

He could see her at night, every night that he was gone and after the children had gone to bed, reading her Bible and praying. *Zanny's not a good reader. I taught her to read and write, but she doesn't always understand what she reads. Sticks to the Psalms, the book of Proverbs, and the Gospels.* If Luther were to look in her Bible, he would see where teardrops had fallen on the pages of her well-worn King James Bible.

Zanny loved her family and her god. Luther knew that prayer came easily, more easily than reading. He had heard her prayers; they were the same night after night, praying aloud beside their bed. She would pray for each of her children, beginning with the youngest and on through to the oldest, telling God her hopes for the child, and asking God to lead the child the right way, help them be all they should be, and show her how to be a good mother to them. If one or more of them was sick, she would claim God's promises to heal them. Particularly, she prayed for strength for eleven-year-old Coliah because she was sickly. Then she prayed for her two older sons, that they wouldn't get mixed up with some of the riffraff around the mountains, like moonshiners and bad girls. He was confident that she would pray long prayers for him, too. Sometimes these prayers would go for a long time; so long that sometimes Luther would wake up and she had fallen asleep on her knees.

Luther knew that although her reading skills were limited, she would look forward to his letters. *Back before the war, I'd send one letter while I was away, and one time, I got home before the letter got there. Dad-ratted slow and far-scattered post offices in these mountains!* He fingered the case in his coat pocket that held his fountain pen. *Now that I'm staying all winter and into the spring in Florida, I'll write more often.*

I wonder what she thinks about me being in St. Petersburg. I know how she likes to speculate. She doesn't have time during the day, but when the young'un are a-bed, I bet she thinks I'll be playing in some church by the end of the week. I told her about Tampa Bay and folks that stroll alongside. She knows I play for them. She'll woolgather till she falls asleep.

After several days aboard trains going south and changes in Chattanooga, Atlanta, and Jacksonville, Luther finally arrived at the station in St. Petersburg.

So in October 1916, Luther began his routine of six months in Florida and six months in North Carolina. And now in 1921, five years later, he was on the southbound train. Luther's destination was St. Petersburg, Florida, but once there, he billed himself not as Luther Willson, but Luke Harvey. He claimed that he was in Florida to sell banjos from a famous mountain luthier. Luke had met Martha Lindsay in January of 1916. She was a well-off widow who was raising her teenage daughter, Maggie. Martha was fascinated by his music and by the man himself. She made it a point to find out where he would be playing, and she would be there, leaving her daughter with the servants for an evening. *What speakeasy? Which bayfront café?*

Martha Lindsay had been widowed when Maggie's daddy, Paul Lindsey, had disappeared in 1914. He had been sailing solo in the gulf beyond Tampa Bay. A storm blew up; not as violent as a tropical storm or hurricane, but it was enough to capsize his ketch. His body had never been found. Maggie was only nine. The late husband had come from money, leaving the widow with a guaranteed income.

One evening, an attractive, well-dressed lady came into the speakeasy and sat alone at a table near the stage. Luke noticed her right away. She looked to be in her late twenties or early thirties. The first thing that Luke noticed after he eyed her face and form was her choice of beverage: lemonade. *Well, I'll be. Must be here to listen to me!*

More than that, Luke Harvey determined to meet her. He zeroed in on the fact that she was a well-off widow. It must have been a stroke of luck that led him to her. Who wouldn't want a handsome young widow with money, a big house a couple of blocks from Tampa Bay, and servants, Jesse and Georgie? Yes, the widow Lindsay would be well worth courting, not because of the amenities, but because she evidently liked what she saw in Luke Harvey; and he ate it up like candy.

The first time he visited her, Georgie served them tea and little cakes.

"You have a maid?"

"Oh, I don't consider Georgie a maid. She's part of the family, Mr. Harvey. Why, Georgie's family has been with mine since before the Civil War. They have stayed through the generations. Now Georgie and her husband, Jesse, their own children grown and living elsewhere, they live in that cottage out back of my house."

Luke wooed Martha with little effort. Well enough that she was swept off her feet. After a courtship of letter writing after he had returned to North Carolina, when he got off the train in October of 1916, they went directly to a "preacher" Martha had introduced him to on his last trip and got "married." Did the thirty-year-old bride wonder if it was a real marriage? Did she suspect that he had another family in the mountains? Luther told her he was a widower with grown children back in the mountains. Martha told Luther that the few months each year that they were together was the happiest she had ever known.

"Luther, even when Paul was living, it wasn't as sweet as being with you. He tended to drink a bit much, and we often argued. I like it that you don't drink," Martha had told him.

The closer he got to St. Petersburg, the less he thought about Zanny and the more he thought about Martha. She was a great lover and companion for a man away from home. Did he love her? He didn't want to think about it. Their relationship just was.

He thought about Maggie, too, her daughter. I'll bet Maggie will be just as anxious to see me as Martha.

Indeed, Maggie was with her mother at the train station awaiting the 4:15 in from Jacksonville. "Momma, I sure am glad it's time for Papa to come home. I was thinking about him last evening as the sun was setting. I remember when we walked along the water and he told me of colors in the sunset I never knew existed. I love it when he plays his music and sings, but when he recites poetry, I just swoon!"

"Swoon, is it? Maggie Lindsey, where do you get such words? It's time. I miss him, too. But since he isn't able to tolerate the heat of summer, we only get to enjoy his company when it is cold up in the mountains."

"I wish he could stay here year-round. I love him so." Maggie swooned again. At sixteen, she and her girlfriends always talked about swooning over someone, particularly Rudolph Valentino and Douglas Fairbanks.

"Maggie, you swoon over everything. What would Papa Luke say if he heard such nonsense?"

And there he was. Luke's flamboyance made him bigger than life. The great shock of white hair beneath a derby hat, penetrating blue eyes, trim mustache, immaculate black suit, and hand-carved cane made of mountain ash, and he was standing tall and erect. As always, Martha's heart melted, and the agonizing months of his absence melted away with her heart.

After a tender embrace, he noticed Maggie and broke into song.

"Little Maggie sittin' in her cabin door, combin' back her raven black hair."

The song was his version of an ancient ballad. He had so many ballads, and his people had reworded and retuned them to fit in with their mountain image.

Maggie giggled as he tickled her under her chin. "My, but you've grown into a real lady, Ms. Maggie, since last April. I'll swan! I think you are plumb grown-up. D'ye have a feller come a-courtin'?"

"No, Papa. I'm saving my love for someone just like you."

He gave her an extra hug and pretended he was going to bite her neck, but as he did so, he noted the pallor on Martha's face. Releasing the girl, he asked Martha, "Are you well, my dear? You seem a bit wan."

"Oh, I am fine. Just tired, I suppose. Shall we move along and get out of this heat? I have a cab waiting." And she knew it was more than "just tired," not just tired but fear. There was a lump in her breast, and she hoped he wouldn't notice. He will. She took a deep breath and shook off her fears. For now.

"Georgie has your favorite St. Petersburg cooking ready for dinner."

"Ah, shrimp and grits!"

Luke settled back into the routine of living by the bay and playing his music, not in churches and restaurants as Zanny supposed, but nightclubs or speakeasies where his derby would be filled each night. During the day, he would peddle his musical instruments.

Chapter 4

Susan

Apalachicola, Florida, July 2009

Handcrafting musical instruments in the early part of the 1900s was a means to a livelihood for some of the mountain people. They lived with the basics. Harry's banjo, if not built by her grandfather as she believed it was, was definitely one of those beautifully crafted mountain banjos.

After Susan and Mac left Harry to go to whatever pressing matters he had, Susan was troubled. She brought Mac up to speed on her family connection with the banjo and the music, and explained the jolt she had experienced.

"Mac, I have little doubt that banjo was made by my grandfather. I have been trying for twenty years to locate one of them since I first learned that he made them for peddling and took them south into Florida. Daddy was sure there were Luther Willson banjos and fiddles floating around South Florida, if none could be found in the North Carolina High Country. They have been as elusive as wind. Some of his fiddles and dulcimers are still around but not the banjos. But this banjo is the first one I've seen that adheres exactly to the pattern he used, and I know there has to be more. I memorized that pattern. After Grandpa died, Grandma had the three sketches of his instrument plans framed and placed over the fireplace. I know that banjo by heart!"

"So you are certain it is one your grandfather made."

"Yes. That banjo is in great shape and despite the fact that it was built ninety years ago. I was lousy at it but plays like a dream. I want one now more than ever."

Mac laughed heartily. "I knew about your family and music but not that someone was actually a luthier and balladeer. You probably told me, but it didn't sink in. Even though we have known one another for over a year, I love that I am going to get to know more and more about you. You are a good musician, I know, but I didn't understand about the ballads and folk music. I used to go to old-time jam sessions, but I know very little about the folk music scene. Now if it was the pipes, I might have gotten as excited as you are."

"Oh? Are your bagpipes a family instrument?"

"Yeah. They were my uncle's. He was really good at it, including the marching competitions."

"I want to hear you play. Promise me."

Mac gave her a big grin as they strolled hand in hand back toward their hotel, turning heads of those watching seventy-somethings as lovers.

"Mac, I want to hunt this Harry up again tomorrow. I think there is more to his story that he was reluctant to share."

"You may be right, Susan, but let's enjoy our honeymoon and get ready for our dinner tonight."

Back in their hotel room, they changed out of shorts to blue jeans and polo shirts. In Apalachicola, no one overdresses for dinner, even when making reservations. Laid back. Casual. They looked fine.

As they entered Tamara's, they were surprised that Harry was there to entertain, having moved up the street from the little storefront where he had been earlier. The hostess took them to a table in a quiet spot, Mac having suggested that this was their honeymoon.

"Miss, could we have a table near the banjo man? Would it be too much to switch?"

She eyed Mac and then smiled when he nodded his approval.

There was a table directly in front of where Harry was playing. He barely acknowledged them and went on playing and singing. "Crawdad," "Johnson Boys," "Little Maggie," and song after song from Willson's Cove. Susan noted that he had another banjo, one with frets. It looked like a Vega White Ladye, open back. Not a cheap instrument. She knew she could play it every bit as well as he played the fretless. *Do I dare ask? Since the weather has cooperated with my arthritis this week, I think I can play.*

They ordered their dinners of the surf and turf Mac had wanted. Susan wasn't hungry and only ate the redfish. She gave her steak to Mac. Nothing shy about his appetite. Amazingly, his waistline did not reflect his hearty appetite. It paid off for him to routinely work out.

When Harry took a break, she made her move. "Harry, are you going to let me play your White Ladye?"

"White Ladye, eh? You really do know your banjos, don't you? Yeah, maybe you won't scare the customers away, but after your performance on the fretless—" He laughed, but it was more derisive than joyful.

"Try me." It was a beautiful instrument and only needed a little tweaking to tune it. Despite age-related hearing loss, Susan Willson Reese McBride still had perfect pitch.

She started in playing "Barbry Ellen," even singing along. Mac loved it. His favorite. The song that hooked him when he first saw her. He hadn't heard her sing much since that night over a year ago at Jones House and never with the banjo. She claimed that her voice had aged too much to sing in public. He had never heard her singing with the banjo.

She went from one tune, to another, to another, singing with some of them. She never repeated those Harry had played. Her style was much different from his, more Southwest Virginia than North Carolina. Yet she still sang the Willson's Cove songs the Willson's Cove way. It seemed that finding what she had no doubt was a banjo her grandfather had made had given her a renewed voice. Harry was both surprised and fascinated, as were her audience. Mac was captivated. Again.

After dinner, they lingered, listening to more of Harry. He sang some of the songs she had done, but with the fretless, it was different. On his next break, he offered for her to play the White Ladye again, but she declined. "No, thank you, Harry, but I have arthritis too bad to keep at it. I may need for my husband to doctor my hands."

Harry shrugged.

"But, Harry, can we get together again to talk about your banjo? I'd like to know a bit more about your family and how they got the banjo in the first place."

"Breakfast. Eight. Caroline's."

Susan looked at Mac and rolled her eyes. *A little terse!* "Done. Caroline's. Eight. Breakfast."

Back in their hotel room, Susan told Mac what she knew about her grandfather and his banjos. "Grandpa, back as early as 1900 made his mountain banjos, fiddles, and lap dulcimers. He would sell them in the mountains and over the mountain in Johnson City, Tennessee. I doubt if he made enough money to cover his costs. But around 1910 or 1911, the story goes, somebody from Florida had gotten hold of one of his instruments and wrote to him. Evidently, he offered him more money than he ever made before, and the letter was something to the effect that he could make money by peddling them in Florida. He had the connection and made arrangements to go to the vacation destinations of America. St. Petersburg, Miami, or Key West. He settled on St. Petersburg.

"Up until right before World War I, he would make his trip right after Christmas, stay through January, and come home the beginning of February. In October of 1916, he changed his pattern and stayed in Florida longer, six months. I always heard that he claimed the cold weather in the mountains was bad for his health. He got home just a few days before the US entered World War I. Meanwhile, Grandma had her eighth child, Aunt Delphy. Despite f the war, he continued his trips, but he helped Grandma with her gardening and chopping wood for the fire for the winter. Then as soon as the leaves turned, he left again for Florida. That is what my daddy told me."

Mac shook his head as if to shake the notion of a man who could leave his growing family and stay away for months at a time. "Gee whiz! It was really big of him to help her chop wood and follow the mule! Susan, I think he must have had a girlfriend in Florida.

Had to." Mac snickered. "Sounds like he was a man of passion, given that he left your grandma pregnant each time he left."

"Well, maybe not every time, but that's the rumor."

The honeymooners forgot about Grandpa Willson as they pursued their own passions. The next morning, they were up early for a walk by the bay and then to meet Harry at the Chowder House for breakfast.

Chapter 5

Susan

Apalachicola, Florida, July 2009

Susan and Mac were already enjoying steaming cups of coffee when Harry showed up. The banjo man was obviously a regular at the restaurant, and the waitress brought him his coffee without asking.

As soon as Harry walked into the restaurant, he saw Susan and Mac and greeted them. He was direct, a quality Susan was beginning to get used to with the man.

"I'm a bit mixed up about you. There are things I have questioned and didn't think I wanted to know the answers, but on the other hand, you might be able to relieve what has nagged at my brain for years."

Susan cocked her eye at him but said nothing. *He'll get to it, I suppose.*

The three ordered their breakfast; while waiting, Harry launched into the story of his banjo. "Seems like this salesman from the mountains, representing who he termed as 'a famous luthier' would come to Florida every year, stay for a while, and then return to get more instruments for the next year's sales. His name was Luke Harvey. I think it was right before the First World War that he met my grandmother. This is where my story sometimes doesn't make sense. Supposedly, they got married, but what I never understood was that Grandma's last name was not Harvey. It was Lindsay. She was real young, maybe sixteen or seventeen, when Dad was born in 1922, so she would only have been twelve or thirteen in 1916. That's the creepy part. Although I remember her well, she died when I was twelve, and I never asked her about Luke Harvey or any of that history. She didn't talk much about him, other than the fact that he taught her to play the banjo and sing the songs. She taught Dad, and then he taught me."

Susan glanced at Mac. He had a smirk on his face that she would like to wipe away. She wanted to know more. "Harry, is your dad lucid, good memory? Would it be appropriate to visit him?"

"He has more long-term memory than anyone I know but forgets people's names. He calls all the women good-lookin', and guys, he calls brother. He even calls me brother sometimes. As far as short-term memory deficit, it isn't terrible. I notice the confusion if he's tired or when he first wakes up. But yeah, I think he would love to talk to you, especially if you play banjo for him."

"I don't even have a banjo anymore. Sold it last year. I could probably get one at some pawnshop and fix it up. But Harry, if I'm going to play, I need a lightweight instrument. I had a resonator on the one I sold, and it was too heavy for me. That's why I got rid of it. Even if I had removed the resonator, it would have been too heavy for me."

"You did well on my White Ladye last night. But I'd never sell that beauty. I have another mountain banjo, much lighter, that you might be able to play. It's fretted. I picked it up a couple of years ago. It isn't old. Probably made in the last twenty years. I would be willing to sell it to you, if you are interested."

"Have to see it and play it, of course. Mac?"

Mac shrugged. Although they had only just gotten married, he had already learned that when Susan had something on her mind, it would be useless to try and stop her. "How much are we talking about, Harry?"

"Two-fifty."

"We'll see."

"I can pay for it myself, if it's what I want!" Susan snapped at her groom, giving him the eye.

Mac grinned at Harry and shrugged.

After breakfast, the three walked back to Harry's rooms. Susan was pleasantly surprised that his pad was neat as a pin, not a reflection of his appearance. *Wonder if there is a Mrs. Harry. Does he have a girlfriend?*

She asked. "A wife, Harry?"

"Not anymore." End of conversation.

The banjo in question was similar to her grandfather's work, but it was obviously a newly built one. She looked inside and saw that it was made by Hatfield, a Kentucky luthier. The work was good; it was easy to handle. She tuned it and played it as though she had been made for it and it, made for her. She dived into a vigorous rendition of "Cripple Creek."

"Wow! I thought my banjer pickin' days were over. Not with this little jewel!" She dug into her purse and handed him the two-fifty he'd asked for and hugged her new baby. Just like that.

She looked at Mac, and he was obviously pleased. "Good deal, babe. You got your banjo."

As the newlyweds left his rooms, Harry looked after them. He muttered to himself, "Maybe I should go to St. Pete and look at birth records. Assuming is not enough. That woman has stirred up a pot I didn't know was on the stove. And why did she have to ask if I'm married? Don't like to think about it. Thinking of Gloria's death rubs a sore spot that just doesn't want to heal."

CHAPTER 6

Luther (aka Luke)

St. Petersburg, Florida, October 1921

Luke was in his element with his beautiful family, the balmy weather, and knowing he would live like a king the next several months. A willing "wife," Georgie's cooking, and mingling with the flapper set in the clubs. As the train slowed down coming into St. Petersburg railroad station, his heart gave a flip. *The excitement of seeing Martha, mixed with my deep love for Zanny, should give me a heart attack, not just a couple of flip-flop beats, but I can't help it.*

After he got his luggage and the crates of musical instruments from the baggage car, they piled it in the cab Martha had hired. He sat between them in the back seat. The ride to her home was short, and the cabbie helped him unload his crates of banjos and fiddles.

When Luther was in North Carolina, he spoke like every other mountain person, but as Luke, he had developed a cultured speech his own children would not recognize. Luther Willson was a consummate actor.

"Well, Ms. Martha, do you think I should be able to sell my wares for my supplier in the mountains? He only sent these six banjos and two fiddles this time. Had some family difficulties and did not have the time to build anymore of them."

The truth was, he had the busiest summer he'd had in years. Crops were good, the community wanted a real church, and he was a good builder. If he could craft beautiful musical instruments, he could build houses all the same. Why not a church? But he didn't want to tell Martha the real reasons. That was Luther, not Luke. His thoughts went to Zanny telling him that with no current preacher, he would not be there to fill in. *Don't think about it.*

"Oh, you'll sell them, Luke. I've talked to people who have heard you play, and there is still a definite interest. Maggie and I have been working on the songs you taught us. She is a lot better at it than I am. She has a real talent, Luke. I hope you will encourage her."

"Does she have a sweetheart? I have noticed when a youngster thinks they are in love, they put more heart and soul into their music."

"No. I have tried to keep her from thinking too much about boys, but she is at that age when girls are in love with love. She told me that even you make her swoon!"

They laughed together about it. "Sounds like we should have a merrymaking and invite all the young folks about. Get her interested. How is she doing in school?"

"Good grades, but she says she doesn't want to go next year. She will get her two-year secondary diploma in the spring."

If the truth were told, Maggie swooned over someone who was more than a boy. Her declaration of love for Papa alone was a ruse. But her mother was totally unaware of it. She only saw the blossoming of her daughter's womanhood and enjoyed watching her grow up.

Once Luke was settled in, he went to the customary places to sell his instruments. As usual, buyers had to do the typical dickering with him over a period of days before he dropped the price to what they were probably worth.

His spiel often went like this: "You need to understand not only the skill of the luthier, but consider the time-consuming hours he puts in to produce these beautiful instruments. Each one is specially crafted and bears the remarkable touch of amazing talent. Truly an art. The woods, harvested from the north side of the trees, produces a sound that you may not find in any other instrument." It was as though he could brag on the skills of someone else, if he pretended they had not been his own construction.

Several evenings each week, he and Martha would make certain Maggie had something to occupy her time and that Jesse and Georgie were home, in case she needed something. They went to speakeasies where he would entertain. He would put his derby hat on the stage in front of him, and customers would toss in coins and bills. Some nights he would come home with little, and the next time there might be a couple hundred dollars or so.

Often he would be urged to drink the bootlegged liquor, but he was adamant that he never drank or smoked. "If I were to start, I might never stop. No, I'll keep myself clean." Luther Willson knew what high price alcohol could exact from those who never thought their first drink would jump start a lifetime of misery. Back home there were family members—his own brother, in fact, among them— who had their own still way up the hollow and suffered from it along with their families. No, he wouldn't drink as either Luther or Luke. Some of his folk songs reflected the misery of demon alcohol, but the speakeasy patrons didn't care. They drank anyway.

Luther Willson had a postal box as a means to keep in touch with Zanny and the children. He would check it twice a week and write a monthly letter to them. Right before Christmas, he received a letter from Zanny.

> The baby come early, Luther. I was afeared she would be too small, but I birthed a healthy little lassie. Named her Carolina.

He shipped a box of oranges and grapefruit to Zanny, and little gifts of candy and nuts for the children. He included a silver baby rattle for baby Carolina.

Christmas in St. Petersburg was a festive affair with lots of good food, friends coming by to share the holidays, and of course, lots of music. In 1921, Luke decided it should be a party for Maggie, who had decided she liked cooking. She would be in charge of refreshments. Boys and girls from her school would be invited and several adult couples. The house would be filled with gaiety. He and Maggie would play and sing, entertaining the guests. They practiced together, and Martha put her stamp of approval on her daughter's ability to play banjo.

"You are really good at it. With talent like that, you should be able to catch a young man without trying."

Martha had never learned to cook and depended entirely on Georgie, but Maggie wanted to cook. Georgie was more than happy to teach her. But along with cooking, the girl began to put on the pounds. Of course she had to eat all the wonderful things she had learned to cook. When Martha chided her about gaining weight, she did the typical teenage girl thing and ran to her room crying.

Luke laughed, almost slipping and telling about his teenage daughter, Rancie, at home. "That's what Ra—uh, re-really what all young ladies go through, Martha. Let her be."

Preparations for the party were going according to plans, and Georgie had covered all the culinary bases with Maggie's help. "Yo' gwine be a baker when yo' grow up, gal, making fancy cakes fo' parties, weddings, for all dose fancy folks. Dat's de troof!"

The party, on Saturday, the week before Christmas, was a great success. Ten of Maggie's friends and their parents came; twenty-three people in all. Music, food, and lots of good fun. No booze.

Then on Christmas Day, Martha had a special Christmas surprise for Luke. She whispered in his ear that she was in a family way. He was shocked. They had been together since even before the war, and she had never conceived.

"Are you certain? Could it be the change?"

"I'm only thirty-five years old! Of course I'm not going through the change. I know what it feels like to carry a baby. I am delighted, and I hope you are. I hope I will have your son, Luke. A son!"

That seemed to satisfy him, but he would not be there when the baby came. It would not be due until July.

The baby grew in her, but so did the lump in her breast. He had noticed it at first when he came in October. Now Luke could tell it was growing. Martha went to the doctor regularly, but she neglected to mention the lump. Finally, Luke intruded into that delicate area and point-blank asked her about the lump. *I have to talk to her about this.*

"Martha, I know you have a lump in your breast. I hope you have told the doctor about it. You need to have it taken care of, even if you are with child."

"I hoped you wouldn't notice. No, if I tell him, he will want to remove it. I couldn't stand to lose my breast, Luke."

She refused to tell Dr. Morgan, but in his routine examination on her next visit, the last one before Luke would be going back to the mountains at the end of March, he did examine her breasts. Before examining the breasts, he explained that if she wanted to breastfeed her baby, he needed to make certain all was well.

It was not. Not only did he note the large mass, but there were smaller ones in the other breast and in her arm pits. Dr. Morgan urged her to have both breasts removed immediately. She refused.

Dr. Morgan said he was surprised that Martha was even able to conceive a child with the cancer already metastatic. He expected it had already spread to the ribs, lungs, and maybe the liver. "But Mrs. Harvey, this is cancer, and you will most certainly die if we do not remove your breasts. Think: who will raise your baby if it even survives to the end of term. There will be a fair chance that you will have a miscarriage if you do not have surgery."

Luke was torn up in shreds. Martha would die; the baby would die; the good life he had made for himself in St. Petersburg would come to an end. He thought about Zanny and the new baby back in North Carolina. Suddenly, he felt his world being ripped apart. *My sins are about to catch up with me.* He didn't know whether to remain in Florida with Martha until the baby arrived or to go home. He had to make a decision.

Just like the post office box Luther had in St. Petersburg, when he was in the mountains, Luke Harvey had a post office box in Johnson City, Tennessee. He would take the train there on a regular basis, ostensibly to buy supplies needed at home, which was at least partially true. But the real truth was, he received mail from Martha. Sometimes there would a half dozen letters from her. But now, what to do? Luke pondered and stewed for days. Letters would not suffice.

Meanwhile, Maggie, oblivious at this time to her mother's illness, was learning the technique of playing the fretless banjo. Her ear was good, and she seemed to be born to it. Her memory was keen, and she learned the words just the way Luke taught her. But Martha was not doing well. As she became obviously more ill, Maggie noticed and asked why. Luke knew he had to tell her the truth.

Luke was frank with her. "I'm sure you can see that your mama is not healthy. Yes, she is in a family way, but she is not well. She is not only going to have a baby, but she has—she also has cancer." He patted his own breast.

Maggie grasped her own breasts with both hands. "Her bosom, Papa? Oh no! Can't Dr. Morgan cut it out?"

"Sweetheart, your mother has known for a long time. She knew she had a lump, but she didn't tell Dr. Morgan. She didn't tell me, either, but, well, we are, uh."

"Papa, I understand about husbands and wives. You found it."

"Yes." His face reddened, but he had to pursue it with Maggie. "You mother wouldn't let Dr. Morgan operate, and it has already spread. She may not even be able to keep the baby, and she could even pass away before the little one is born. She needs your comfort and your help. Can you do this for her?"

Maggie sobbed, hiding her face against his chest. He did his best to comfort the girl, but she cried and cried. Finally, when she had expended all her tears, she told him she was committed to caring for her mother. "Papa, I will even give up my new love of cooking if it means Momma will have it easier."

By the end of March, at five months, Martha was not gaining weight as she should with her pregnancy, and she was weak. But the baby seemed to be growing despite her. Luke liked her to be with child, and Maggie was ecstatic that a little brother or sister was on the way. But at the same time, they were both worried sick over her Martha's health.

But now Luke had to make a decision: go home to Zanny or stay with Martha till the end. Although she wouldn't admit it, he knew she was dying. If she died before the baby was far enough along, it would die with her.

He would stay. But what would he tell Zanny? He stewed and pondered some more. Maggie had a lot to say about it.

"Papa, you can't leave her the way she is. I know you always go back to Tennessee in April, but not only is Momma going to have a baby, she is going to die. I know it. You have to stay. If you don't, much as I love you, I'll hate you."

That did it. He knew what he had to do. I'll send Zanny a telegram that I have taken ill and will remain here until I'm well enough to travel. She will believe it. After all, I do come here for my health.

Chapter 7

Susan

Legacy at Highwoods Preserve Assisted Living, Tampa, Florida,³ July 2009

Martha's baby would come early and be healthy despite his mother's cancer. Today, eighty-seven years later, that baby was enjoying his life at Legacy at Highwoods Preserve, one of the finest assisted living facilities in New Tampa.

As Susan dialed the home where Luke lived, she was so excited her fingers tingled. She was going to meet Junior Harvey. She had called the home to see if Mr. Harvey was up to having company. "I know his son, Harry, and he thought the old fellow would like to hear me play my banjo."

Mac couldn't come with her. He had to make a trip to Macon for some legal matters related to turning over his medical practice to his son a year earlier. He flipped through a pile of legal forms. "You would think by this time the paperwork would be a done deal. Sheesh!" he complained. "I will miss you. Call me every night, okay?"

Susan missed him. She did call him every night and gave him a running detail of her day. It had been the first time since they were married two months before that he had not been with her. But Susan knew she had to meet the old man to pick his brain. There were too many unanswered questions. Was his father really someone named Luke Harvey, or could it possibly have been Luther Willson? *You know, it fits! Daddy's name was Harvey, a family name way back. Luke or Luther.* But what could Junior reveal, especially if he had memory issues?

As she walked down the hallway to his room, carrying her little banjo, she was unusually nervous. His door was open, and she saw him seated at a card table playing solitaire. Seeing him in a typical retirement home setting calmed her nerves. She knocked on the doorjamb. When he turned to face the door, her heart jumped. *Grandpa!*

"Come on in, good-lookin'! Are we gonna go jammin'? See ya brought yer banjer!"

Susan was put at ease by the old man's country lingo. "Got yer fiddle tuned up, Mr. Harvey?"

"What's this mister business? Just call me Junior. And yeah, I was playin' just a bit ago. The fiddle is in fine fettle." He laughed at his alliteration. "Just let me get it out, and then we'll go a-jammin'. I have forgotten your name again. My memory is terrible when it comes to names, but I can remember details from eighty years ago. Figure that one out. Forgive me if I call you good-lookin', but you are."

Susan played along with the forgetfulness. "Oh, it's okay if you can't remember my name. It's Susan. I was named for my grandmother, Susanna Willson." She purposely mentioned the name Willson to see if it raised any memory. *Was the flicker of his eyebrow an indication that the name means something?*

"I learned about you from your son, Harry. Thank you for seeing me today, Junior."

They went to the common room together. Junior almost jogged down the hallway, and Susan did well to keep up with the spry eighty-seven-year-old. He still sported a fine shock of straight, white hair, like all the men in her family. He was tall and lean but not unhealthy in appearance. And yes, there was more than a resemblance to Grandpa Willson. She looked at his hands. Not gnarled with arthritis, well-cared-for nails, but with veins standing out beneath thinning skin and several minor bruises, indicating the fragility of aging skin. He wore loafers without socks, and his baggy pants were held up by old-fashioned black suspenders. Once seated facing each other on straight chairs, they tuned together.

"You'll hafta tell me if it's in tune. My ear isn't as keen as it once was. We Harveys got music in us, but gettin' older plays tricks on the ears and eyes. Can't see well enough to read much either, but well, I know all the old ballads.

"Where'd you get that mountain banjer with frets? Sorta like the one Papa gave me, but that'n didn't have frets. My son, Harry, has it now. You need to meet him some day. He actually makes money playing his banjer. Oh, that's right, you said you know him."

Susan grinned. Not as forgetful as Harry suggested.

Susan told him she was from North Carolina and knew all the old tunes from there. "Could we start out with my favorite, Junior? 'Little Maggie?'"

"Oh my! Yes. You know that was Mom's song. Her name was Maggie. And she said Papa always sang it as her song."

At that, he began the fiddle playing, with a slide up the A string, and then double stops. She caught up with him, and they were lost in the music. Two oldsters, seventy and eighty-seven, feeling their youth surge with flying fingers and oblivious to the little audience that gathered, residents and personnel alike. A few people were tapping their feet to the music or clapping their hands in time.

Junior would suggest one song, then Susan suggested the next one. They played for thirty minutes without a break. He was enjoying himself so much; she didn't want to stop. But her hands were hurting, and after all, she came not as much to pick her banjo as to pick his brain.

He had already forgotten Susan's name. "Got lots more songs, good-lookin', but maybe we can find us a cup of coffee and some doughnuts before we start up again. I don't think this crowd will pay well, anyway. My papa used to lay out his derby hat for people to throw money in it. Sometimes he'd make nothing. Sometimes come home with a couple hundred dollars."

There was coffee on the counter and some tables where they could sit, chat, and have their coffee. An attendant, having heard Junior mention doughnuts, brought them two plump glazed doughnuts. "Why, thank you, good-lookin'." Harry was right. Junior used that name for every female.

Susan chose a table away from where others might hear the conversation. "Junior, what can you tell me about your mom. Harry, your son, tells me that she taught you the songs and fretless banjo. Did she teach you the fiddle, too?"

"Little Maggie. That's what Papa called her. But you know, she wasn't my real mom. She told me she had to bring me up after my mother died."

That was significant news. Harry didn't even know that. He had mentioned that he was confused about her last name being Lindsay.

"My real mother had cancer and died when I was too young to know her. It may have been as soon as I was born. Her name was Martha Lindsay Harvey. Mom always said I was a miracle baby, destined to be born a musician. Yes, she taught me fretless banjer, and I kinda picked up the fiddlin' on my own. Tried to copy how Papa would play. Papa had a nice fiddle, but he was a banjo man. My fiddle was his. He played in the speakeasies back in the '20s, but he never drank alcohol."

That settled one question for Susan. "You say Luke Harvey played in the speakeasies? What else do you remember about him?"

"He wasn't around very much after I was old enough to remember things. I only recall seeing him in the late '20s, before the Depression. He would come to St. Pete right after Christmas, sell what banjers and fiddles he brought, and then go back to Tennessee. Every afternoon he would play either the banjo or the fiddle. I was named after him, you see, Luke Harvey Jr., and that's why I'm called Junior."

"Makes sense."

"Papa. I remember his great shock of white hair and a neatly trimmed white mustache. He was tall like me. I guess I look like him. I see him in the mirror every morning. He would sing and play the fretless for hours, entertaining me. But with the stock market crash, no one had money to buy musical instruments, so he didn't ever come back. It was like he plumb disappeared off the face of the earth. At first he would write to us, but then that stopped, too. There was one final letter that made Mom real mad. I don't think Mom tried to locate him after that. I think he's the reason she never got married."

Whoa! Tennessee? Reason for not marrying? "Junior, are you certain Luke Harvey was from Tennessee? I thought Harry said he brought instruments from a luthier in North Carolina."

"You know, that's kinda funny. He talked about the man who made the instruments in North Carolina, but when Mom wrote to him, the address was in Johnson City, Tennessee. We just assumed he was from there."

Susan knew this might be a touchy question, but she barreled ahead with it anyway. "Why do you think Mom didn't marry because of him?"

"Oh, a couple of reasons. In the first place, she was madly in love with him, not that they were, well, you know. I don't want to be indelicate. She used to say he spoiled her for any other man. Then, I recall a young fellow used to show up when I was only three or four years old. He was nice enough, if I remember, but Papa was there once when he came, and after that, we never saw him. I guess Papa ran him off."

"What was your life like during the Depression? Did you and Mom have difficulty making ends meet?"

"Not too bad. Evidently, my real mother was well-off enough to leave a substantial house, and her money wasn't tied up in the stock market or some bank that fell." Junior shook his head with the memory. "When she died, it all went to Mom. We had servants when I was little, but Mom had to let them go. Eventually, the money in the bank dwindled to the point that we lived on what I call 'Depression food.' Dried beans and garden vegetables. Once in a while, she would get meat for us, but we survived and were healthy despite the shortages. When she died, I got the house, and now Harry has it."

"So what did you do for your lifework, Junior?"

"Ha, ha! I was into fish. I started out on a fishing boat for the Jones Fish Company back as soon as I got out of the Navy, while getting a college education. I eventually worked my way up to vice president. I retired after Stella died."

Susan had run out of questions to ask, but she thought, *I probably know more than I think I do.* She would try to put it all together before she drew any conclusions. She wondered: *Will Grandma Zanny be looking in vain for Luther in heaven?*

Chapter 8

Luther (aka Luke)

St. Petersburg, Florida, 1922

Luke could see that Martha was failing, and Maggie mentioned it to him. Sometimes she couldn't get her breath. Was it because the baby was pushing against her lungs, or had the cancer spread to her lungs? When the baby moved or kicked, Martha would complain that it hurt, especially under her right rib cage. *Will she live to have this little baby? I hope so, but how?*

Luke had announced that morning that he had sent a telegram back home, telling them he was planning to stay at least until summer. Meanwhile, he had sold all the musical instruments he had brought. All he had to play was the banjo and fiddle he had given Martha when he came back in 1918. Those were the ones Maggie played for her momma. Sometimes she would play the fiddle, while Luke played the banjo. It seemed to calm Martha to hear the music. He didn't go to the speakeasies anymore.

"Papa, thank you for deciding to stay, at least till the baby comes. Momma needs you, and I do, too."

"Maggie, I don't want you to be burdened with all this. But I don't see how I can remain after the baby is born. I have children yonder in the mountains, and they need me to help them with the gardens and harvesting. I think they will be fine till July. That's when the vegetables begin to get ready. There will be canning and drying of foods for the winter, digging potatoes, burying cabbages. It has to be done by the time I return here. As soon as I know the baby is going to live, I need to hop the first train and get back to the mountains."

"You have children my age? Older than me? Do they take care of younger ones?"

Luke had never divulged how many children he and Zanny had. But now it was nine, with the newborn girl. Zanny had sent a letter just last week telling how little Carolina was growing. But Martha and Maggie had no idea he was getting mail at a post office box.

"My oldest son is married and lives next door. His wife is a big help to his younger two brothers and sister at home." That was partly true. His oldest son, Luther, did live next door. Only four children? The lies piled one on top of another. But Luke was believable.

The school year was winding down for Maggie. She would graduate from the two-year high school, and then she would be home to take care of Momma and the new baby. Graduation day was sad for her. Her mother couldn't come. Luke was there and tried to encourage her.

St. Petersburg had just opened a beautiful new public library. When she got home, she went to the library and signed books out on how to raise babies. She devoured them more than she ever had with her algebra or literature books. Often, she sat around for hours nibbling on a cookie or piece of cake Georgie had taught her to make and reading about babies.

Luke shook his head. To him it was gluttony, and gluttony was just as bad as drunkenness. But he said nothing.

By the time school was out the middle of May, Martha was weaker than ever. She could barely get out of bed. The baby looked like it took up most of her frail body. She tried to eat more, but it was difficult to swallow sometimes because she was nauseated.

Luke could see that Maggie was the ideal nurse. She was compassionate, knew just how to move her momma into a comfortable position, and was very patient with her. She offered her small amounts of food every waking hour, putting a tiny bit on the spoon and feeding what she could take. Not much, but enough to keep her going. She made her get out of bed and walk through the living room, dining room, and back to her bedroom twice a day, until she was too weak to get up.

The first of June arrived, and the baby was still active and appeared to be growing normally, but Martha's body could no longer sustain a pregnancy. She went into labor. The doctor wanted her to go to the little hospital where he was on staff, Augusta Memorial Hospital,[4] but she refused. She would have her baby at home.

Luke or Luther, back in North Carolina, despite having nine children, had never actually been present when any of them had been born. He left Zanny to the midwife. When Martha went into labor, he went fishing.

And Maggie had never witnessed the birth of a baby, but she had read all about it. Dr. Morgan came and brought his nurse with him. Maggie, along with Georgie who had done her share of midwifery in her day, remained at Martha's side.

Maggie was available to supply anything the doctor might need that he did not bring. Otherwise, she sat by Martha's head, rubbed her temples, and let her squeeze her hand as the contractions increased. Since the baby was preterm, it might be a short labor, but with Martha's weakened condition, would she have the strength to push? Maggie encouraged her with calm words to help her through the process. Georgie's calmness calmed Martha. She labored from midmorning until seven in the evening. Dr. Morgan left twice during that time to tend to other patients, leaving Georgie to time her contractions and the nurse to check her for dilation.

Morgan returned in the nick of time to welcome the tiny boy. Although the baby was a month early, he was lively. He weighed four pounds and came into daylight hungry. He would grow. Because of the breast cancer, he would be a bottle-fed baby. Maggie was ready to take charge of "her boy."

Where was Luke during all this? He spent the entire day fishing in Tampa Bay. He didn't catch anything worth taking to Georgie to cook.

Jesse came to the pier where Luke was fishing to tell him the baby had come. "Mistah Luke, dat baby be hyar. One lusty boy from de soun' o' his lungs. Georgie say you betta show yo' face soon or she gonna come down hyar and whap yo' on de head wif dat fishin' pole. An' missus, she ain't doin' good 'tall."

He left faster than when he came to the docks. He handed the fishing pole to Jesse and took off in a trot, leaving Jesse in his wake.

Georgie was washing the baby and showing Maggie how to get all the white cheesy stuff off. She didn't know it was called vernix, but she said, "Dis ol' white cheese is what keep de baby's skin from getting sore while he in de womb. Gotta wash it all off, gentle like, yo' see."

Luke appeared at the door and saw his little red-faced son. "Ah! What do you think, ladies? Is he not a handsome boy? We'll call him Luke Harvey."

"No middle name, Papa?" Maggie asked. "I thought everyone had to have a middle name."

"Well, I don't. If I want him named Luke Harvey, he will have to be Luke Harvey without a middle name."

"We will call him Luke Junior, then," Maggie announced. And Junior became his name.

Martha was terribly weak; she knew she would not live. She hardly paid attention to her baby, and she gave him into the care of Maggie and Georgie. The next day, she grew weaker and lapsed into a coma.

But Luke needed to return to Willson's Cove and his family. He dreaded it more than ever because now he had a son in Florida. Maggie, however, encouraged him to get on the road. "Papa, you have been so good to stay by me through this. I know your children have missed you, but I needed you here. Thank you. I know you love us, and that is what is important. You go on, now."

The next morning, Martha was dead. Luke and Maggie made burial arrangements, and then Luke left, not even staying for a funeral. Junior, only days old, was motherless, and his father boarded the northbound train.

Normally, when Luke left for North Carolina in April, he would have some oranges and grapefruit to take along. June was not the season for citrus fruits. But some of the lush Florida gardens were producing vegetables he knew his family wouldn't have yet and would travel well: sweet potatoes, eggplant, and summer squash. He took a crate from the market with him.

As he left the house, Maggie verbalized her thoughts to Georgie, "Will this be the last time we see him?"

CHAPTER 9

Susan

Willson's Cove, North Carolina, August 2009

The old family home in Willson's Cove was still standing and owned by Susan's cousin Mike. Mike lived there alone in the huge house. Mike did a good job of doing upkeep, repainting, repairing, tending to the grounds, and updating outdated things, like corroded water pipes. Every five years, Mike would host a family reunion at the old place. Next year, 2010, would be the next one. Grandpa Luther and his two oldest sons, Luther and Roby, had built the house in 1912, when the boys were hardly big enough to wield a crosscut saw together. It made tough men out of them before they were barely in long pants.

After her trip to Tampa, Susan had returned home to Mac in Blowing Rock, where they had their summer home, and the next day, she drove over the mountain to Willson's Cove. She so loved her mountains, but Mac was more a city boy. He conceded to living the warmer months in Blowing Rock, but he had told her it would be back to Georgia as soon as the leaves started to fall. She had put her house in Willson's Cove on the market and sold it within a week, to a second cousin, Jeff Willson, who wanted to return to his roots. It was with mixed feelings that she sold the house. It was the only home she had ever known, but at least kinfolk would be living there.

Susan had called her cousin Mike, the evening she got home, to see if she could go into the old house. She knew the attic was filled with boxes, crates, and trunks. What might she find to help her solve this mystery of Luther Willson? She declined telling Mike about her purpose. "I just want to get in touch with our ancestors a bit and think looking through the attic would be helpful."

"Y'ain't into see-ancies and ghosts, air ye?" Mike was the proverbial hick, a typical hillbilly.

Susan laughed, giving back to him in the same countrified lingo. "Y'ain't skeered of ghosts, air ye? If'n I find one, I'll send him yander t' you." Then she addressed him more seriously. "No, Mike, no séances or conjurers of the dead."

Dook announced Susan and Mac's arrival before they got to the house, knowing it was Susan. Mike, hearing Dook's announcement, was there in front of the house when she and Mac arrived. Some of the family had not yet met Mac, but Mike had been to the wedding. Even at that, he didn't know Mac well, so he looked his new cousin-in-law over closely. Evidently, Mac met his approval because he offered him a "Co-Cola" right off the bat.

Mac graciously accepted, although he wasn't much for soft drinks. He figured that was the price of acceptance in this family. As she left the two men exchanging bits of idle chatter, Susan headed for the attic, flashlight in hand, in case there was no electricity.

She was met with a preponderance of boxes, old furniture, trunks, barrels, and even some pieces of farm equipment. *Good grief! Where do I begin? At the back, most likely, since the oldest things would have been stored there first.* She snaked her way through the stacks of boxes, trying to ignore the combined smell of must, mice, and mothballs. There was enough light from a dim bulb in the ceiling to see where she was going and then some from a dirty window at the front of the cavernous room. She attempted to open the window, but it was stuck.

She spied an old trunk, circa 1890s, beside the window. She would begin there. Opening it, she smelled camphor. *No, moths.* Old clothes, baby clothes, maybe Grandma's wedding dress, and a few letters from names that meant nothing to her. Digging down to the bottom, there was nothing that suggested anything more than an old family with their normal history. She piled it all back in neatly and closed the trunk.

Her eye caught another trunk almost hidden back in the corner, peeping out from a pile of blankets. It looked more modern and much smaller. She retrieved it from the corner, scooted it over to the window, and tried to open it. The hasp was stuck but not from a lock. She was about to go see if Mike had some kind of tool to help her open it, when it suddenly popped open as she hit the top of the lid with her hand. Then she saw what it was: a small button that served as a release. *Ingenious!*

This one was filled with letters. *Bingo!* They were all addressed to Mrs. Susanna Willson. The first postmark was January 1911, St. Petersburg, Florida. The letters continued each year through 1915; and then from 1916, there were monthly letters for the six winter months up until 1922. Finally, at the bottom of the pile, letters were again yearly to 1929. She picked them up gently, like eggs she didn't want to drop and break. This was exactly the kind of thing she wanted to find. Letters. She looked for a place to sit and read them, but she didn't want to remove items that were stacked on the couple of chairs. She was just about to go ask Mike for a box or something to put them in to take them home when she heard Mac on the stairway. And Mike.

"Hey, up there. The spooks get you yet?" That was Mac.

"Yeah. Turned me into a zombie. Come on up but watch your head. Not built for you tall boys, just shrimps like me."

Mac stood in the middle of the floor, about the only place he could stand without hitting his head. He looked all around at the many decades spread before him. Mike, even taller than Mac, walked stooped over to the window where Susan held the packet of letters.

"What ya got, coz? I never paid no mind to this junk. I figured one day I'd cart most of it off to the dump or the Rag Shakin' over in Crossnore."

"These letters are a great discovery, Mike. They are old, going back as far as 1911." She decided not to tell him what they were. "I want to read them. And! Don't you dare cart any of this stuff to the dump or the Rag Shakin'! If you don't want it, at least let family come and see what they want. In fact, next family reunion, we could do an attic cleanup."

"Yessum, that might be a way to get some folks who tend to mooch on the rest of us to stay away, if they think they hafta work, yeah, I got a poke sack in the kitchen you can carry them letters in," he said this all in one breath, turned about, and left Mac standing in the middle of the floor and Susan sitting on the floor, giggling at her colorful cousin.

"Mac, we have a gold mine here. These are written from Grandpa to Grandma, 1911 through 1929, from St. Petersburg. I will take them home to read them."

"Why don't you take the time to go to the room where she used to sleep here in this house. Mike won't mind. You could read them while Mike shows me your grandfather's workshop. That's what we came up here to tell you. I'm interested in looking at some of his tools."

"You? Tools? I didn't know you were interested in tools."

"Yeah, I might embark on a second career: building banjos!" He raised an eyebrow and gave her a half smile. "After all, my hands have crafted more delicate things than banjos, with my surgeries. Why not?"

"I'm impressed, Mac! Go for it."

They heard Mike on the stairwell. "Here ye are. This oughta serve to cart them away. Keep 'em as long as ye want."

"Mike, how would it be for me to go down to Grandma's bedroom and read them while you men do your thing in the workshop? Would you mind?"

"Why not? The house is yours whenever yer here. You know that. I'm only the clan caretaker."

"Have you ever encountered any of these ghosts, Mike?" Mac asked, tongue in cheek. He gave Susan a wink as he asked the question.

"Well, I don't know. Sometimes there are mighty strange sounds around here. Both Grandma and Grandpa died in this house."

Susan tried not to laugh as she made her way to Grandma's room. She knew Grandma's room well. She would come and sit with her for hours when she was living. As she walked down the attic stairs, she thought of Grandma. *Grandma had the best stories ever. Not silly fairy tales, but mountain tales about hants and the Brown Mountain Lights.*[5] *Then she would tell about back when she was a girl and how they lived by the land. She'd talk about the hard winters when all they had was dried beans to eat. She was a wonderful storyteller. I think I learned storytelling from her and used it a lot when I taught school.*

Grandma's room was right beneath where the window was in the attic. Unlike the dingy attic, the room was filled with light, filtered by the lace curtains. A lingering essence of her grandmother remained in the room, possibly from the old perfume bottle on her chifforobe. Susan stopped by the old piece of furniture, picked up the bottle, and sniffed it. It was like Grandma was there. *Maybe Mike is right. Grandma's ghost.* She went to the window where Grandma's rocker still sat, where it always did, and sat in it to read the letters.

The first letter from January 1911 was rather what she expected. Grandpa wrote to Zanny and the children about how much he missed her and the children, his surprisingly good sales, his enjoyment of the weather, and that he hoped they would not have too much harsh weather. He admonished his sons to make certain plenty of firewood was brought in each night and his daughters to help Mama with doing housework, cooking, taking care of the little ones, keeping Dook the dog from running off, and being good children. Then at the end of each letter was a bit of flowery romantic language thrown in to Zanny, words that she would not have read to the children.

> Zanny, Zanny. How I miss ye so. I can barely wait till I get these banjers and fiddles sold and hop on the northbound train. I long to taste your kisses, feel your skin, feel your heartbeat against mine when I hold you in my arms.

Susan wondered if her grandmother felt the same way. He was most likely home by the time the letters would have even arrived, given the slowness of the postal system in the remote areas of the mountains.

The subsequent letters were pretty much the same until January 1916. That letter was abrupt.

> Dear Zanny and young'un,
>
> Good sales this year. Sold all eight banjers and a fiddle. Have a man lookin' at the other fiddle, and he is interested in the delcimore, too. Should be home by the time you get this letter. Love you all, Papa.
> The special note to Zanny was abbreviated to "Sweet Zanny, I miss you, and soon we will be in each other's arms.
>
> Love,
> Luther

When she got to the fall of 1916, there were several letters; monthly letters from November through March of 1917. These letters, although they were the same speech patterns as the previous letters, had a different tone. Although there still were personal notes to Zanny, Susan thought they were contrived.

Chapter 10

Glimpses into Grandma Zanny's Soul

Willson's Cove, North Carolina, 1916

As Susan read these letters from 1916, she felt as though she was touching Zanny's soul. The hurt, the courage, and the longing overwhelmed her.

*****

Mail service was always slow in the mountains. Although there had been a post office established in Boone in 1904, it might take a couple of weeks before it arrived over the mountain to Willson's Cove. The first one was written October 18, 1916, and postmarked November 1, 1916. Zanny penciled on the envelope November 21.

Susan could almost hear her grandma say, "La mercy! Hit took three weeks to git here. That's the longest ever."

Opening the letter, Zanny would have devoured it, hoping he would return to the sweet talk from his old letters. A tear dropped and blurred the writing in a couple of places. Susan wondered if Grandma was sad and angry because Grandpa chose to leave her for half the year. Or was she grateful and happy that he was well and making some money to send home? Another short one and not so sweet.

> Dear Suzanny and children,
>
> I got here safe and have a right nice place to stay. I'm taking board with a widder woman and her maiden daughter. They've been kind [smudged from tears?] to take in a travelin' feller. As soon as I got money to send back, I will. I know y'all need it. So far, I ain't sold nuthin', but I done met a feller yesterday who is mighty interested. The weather is good, although we are still alert for hurrycanes. Back in July, there was a biggun. I like bein' here this time of the year because the weather is so nice, and the sunsets over the bay are better than any I ever seen.
>
> Love you all,
> Papa

The remainder of letters from that year were all about the same: a paucity of romance. A few admonitions for the children and wanting to know how two-year-old Herbie was doing. He told her of sales he had made and that he had been asked to give mountain music concerts at a local restaurant. He went so far as to suggest that he was playing in church without actually saying it:

> They's lots of churches here too. One a few blocks from where I'm staying.

In another letter, he described the beauty of one of the churches, comparing it to the little log church where they met back home. Susan figured it would have been a relief to her grandmother, thinking he was going to church and maybe even playing his banjo.

Grandma used to say, "They's lots o' folk 'round here been saved cause of his playin' and preachin'."

Luther's letters came regularly but were always at least two weeks behind when they were postmarked. They were all the same tone. After Delphy as born, Zanny sent him a letter—one of the few in the pile from her to him—telling him of the event.

> Dear Luther,
>
> Done had our eighth young'un. Hit's another girl. Pretty as a picture with a full head of red hair. I named her Delphy after your aunt Delphy. I hope you like that as a name. I miss you so much. Wish I could go to sleep with you huggin' me next to yer chest. I'll be a-lookin' my eyes out till first of April. I heared maybe our country's about to get into the war in Europe. I hope Luther and Roby won't join up. They's old enough. Love you more than I can express. I cain't write those pretty words like you do.
>
> Zanny

His response to this letter was less than what Zanny had expected. The letter showed signs that it had been crumpled up and then smoothed out again. There were tear stains on it. Susan thought it should have infuriated her when she read it. *I'd have fled to this room and plopped right down on his rocker and rock like the dickens till I was calmed down.* She put action to her thoughts and rocked.

> Zanny,
>
> I'm glad you had an easy labor, but a redhead? Never been a redhead in my family (except for Dook), and I don't know any in yours. Not sure I'd claim it to be mine!

Susan knew that her grandma's heart hurt. She could hear Grandma say, "Delphy is his. I ain't ne'er even looked at another man, and I don't ne'er want one."

There was more to that letter, mostly what he was doing and that he felt better than he had for years by staying in warm climate over the winter.

Subsequent letters throughout January till Luther got home in April were pleasant, a little playful, but lacked the ardent romance that was in the early letters.

I wonder if she tried to light a new fire in his heart when he came home. I'm remembering some of what Grandma used to tell me about the family. They had their life here whether Grandpa was around or not.

Each of the older children still at home had special duties to perform. Luther was married and lived a few yards up the road; Roby was off working in the woods and cutting trees down to send to the sawmill. He stayed at Luther's house what times he was home.

Although Rancie, Harvey, and Coliah were in school, they were good workers. But Rancie was a big help at home. She could cook, clean, do the laundry, and mind the little ones. Harvey had charge of the firewood, keeping the house warm, and heating water. Coliah, not as healthy as the other children, was good at her job to watch Herbie, to keep him from getting too close to the fireplace or the cookstove. Ossie's job was to pick up things Herbie played with on the floor and to set the table for meals.

Susan could only imagine the heartrending her grandma endured, especially the letter suggesting that if the baby had red hair it wasn't his. She saw a paperweight on the table beside her and wanted to throw it at his picture on the wall. She read on through 1917 through 1920. Her eyes were tired from attempting to decipher his beautiful, but difficult to read, script. She put the letters aside for later and went back to the attic. She had no idea what she would find or even why it would be important. One thing she did know was Grandma had a horrible life, and she loved her for it.

Susan decided it was time to take a break.

Chapter 11

Mac Searches for Clues

Willson's Cove, North Carolina

Meanwhile Mac and Mike were having a great time in Grandpa's workshop. The tools were old, but with a little cleaning off dust and a spot of WD-40 here and there, they should work well.

"Mike, what would you take for all these tools? I can pay you what you think they are worth, within reason."

"Aw, Mac. I dearly hate to sell 'em. They didn't just belong to Grandpa, they are Grandpa. They're him. I used to come in here with him before he died, and he'd work while I played in the sawdust with scraps of stuff he'd throw on the floor. Tell you what, ye wanna come over here and work here in the shop, you kin do it ary time ye want. I don't have to be here, and I'll give ye a key."

"Deal!"

They looked through every little drawer and all the nooks and crannies in the shop, but there was one door that was locked. Mac tried it, but Mike shook his head.

"Never been in there. Grandpa wouldn't let no one go in there, and I don't e'en have a key that fits the lock. I've looked high and low in here and never found it. But I'm a-feared to go in there."

"How about getting a locksmith?"

"Don't know any. Maybe someone at the hardware o'er in Newland might know of someone."

A locked door was just the challenge Mac needed. He decided he would find a locksmith if he had to bring one from off the mountain. But since they had to go through Newland to go back home, he'd stop by the hardware store and ask; that was if Susan ever got done reading letters.

Meanwhile, being a surgeon, he knew how to probe small places, release body parts from the body, and get all the remaining tissues back in their proper place. What could be so hard about opening an old lock? It was rusty, for one thing, so back to the WD-40. He would bring a can next time. He also had some probes that he could work into the lock and try to jimmy it loose, if he couldn't find a local locksmith. He grinned at Mike, who had no earthly idea what his companion had in mind.

"Any place a man locks and doesn't want someone to see, is a place that will tell his tale. I imagine the real Luther Willson is hidden behind that door," he muttered as Mike left the shop.

Mike had gone to the house to use the phone. When he came back to the shop, he was beaming from ear to ear. "Found ye a locksmith. I called down to Newland to the hardware. He is sending a feller out here this afternoon. Works there in the store. Takes about twenty, thirty minutes to get here. He said if that feller cain't open it, the only way to get in is break down the door. Thing is, I allus been afeared Grandpa would come back and hant me, if'n I's to go in there. You ain't his kin, so maybe he won't hant you."

Mac looked askance.

"Ye don't believe in hants? They's real!"

"If you say so."

Mac set about to organize the confusion in the shop. He was aware of the purpose of most of the tools, and those he did not, he would find out. As predicted by Mike, the locksmith arrived in less than thirty minutes. Twenty-six to be exact.

Mac laughed at Mike. He didn't want to stay inside while the locksmith worked, in case he would open the door and Grandpa's ghost would appear. He really believed it. "I'm gonna go see what Susan's up to. See you fellers later." With that, Mike was gone.

Mac shook hands with the man. "My name is Mac McBride. Mike Willson is my wife's cousin. This is his place. Seems we got an old lock that hasn't been opened in the last sixty years. Think you can budge it? We are curious what we might find on the other side."

The locksmith was an older man who looked like he had seen many years of experience in the art of breaking and entering. He nodded at Mike and then answered, "Can't do nuthin' but try. My name is Jerry Johnson. Live down in Newland. Been a long while since I was up here. My daddy brought me up here to buy a fiddle from the old man when he was still livin'. Beautiful place. Let's see what you got."

Jerry saw right away that he would have to get rid of the rust before he could do anything to the lock. He had foreseen the event that it would be heavily rusted and had a spray can of WD-40 with an extension nozzle. He sprayed and then used a thin rasp to get the rust out of the keyhole. He worked at it for twenty minutes before it was cleared well enough that he could use his tools to open it. It was an old lock and of relatively simple construction. It popped open on his first try. The handle moved, but the door did not.

Jerry then worked on the hinges, which were also rusted. Once they were free, the next thing would be to open the door. Right? It still didn't budge.

"This'n air a booger!" Jerry shook his head in frustration.

"Maybe the booger is Grandpa's ghost. That's what Mike would tell you. But, Jerry, we might be able to pry it loose with this crowbar." Mack handed it to Jerry and picked up another smaller one.

The two men worked along the jamb of the door, the sill, and across the top. It was almost a surprise when it finally got loose enough to open. But even that was not easy. It creaked and resisted.

Mac laughed. "If Mike had stayed in here, he would have sworn it was his grandfather holding it so we couldn't open it."

Jerry shrugged. "Don't judge Mike and his belief in spooks. He might be right."

But it was open, and Mac was anxious to see what was there. He paid Johnson for his labors and looked for a light switch. *How did he see anything in here? Get a flashlight from the car.*

Mac went to the car to get his flashlight. It was missing. "Oh right. Susan took it."

Since Mike had gone into the house, he assumed he would easily find him with Susan. The two were sitting on the floor of the attic. It was a cute picture: his proper ladylike wife and the redneck cousin had their heads together reading a letter.

"What do you have there?"

"Ah, my husband! Letters from Uncle Herbie, Mike's daddy, from Germany in World War II."

"Aha! Just wanted to let you know, Mike, we got the door open. I need my flashlight so I can see what's in there. It is dark and dusty, so I have no idea what we'll find."

"No we about it. I ain't goin' in there!"

Mac decided to play him a bit. "Yeah, I understand. Grandpa did try to hold the door shut for Johnson and me, but we finally convinced him to let us in."

Mike shivered and gave Mac a dark look. Flashlight in hand, Mac laughed all the way back downstairs and back to the shop.

Back in the now-unlocked room, Mac shone the flashlight all about. "Aha!"

There was a banjo in the process of being crafted. Mac picked up an old cloth lying on the bench, shook the dust from it, and rubbed the dust from the banjo. He could see the beauty in the wood. It was curly maple, darkened with age, but still beautiful. There were plans drawn in faded pencil on several pieces of lined tablet paper. They looked fragile, so he did not pick them up. On the floor beneath the workbench was a crude wooden chest with a wood-hinged lid and a hasp closure. It had a padlock on it.

Mac pulled out the box and looked about for a key. As neat and well-ordered as the room was, in contrast to the outer shop, he knew the key must be well hidden.

Mac brought the box out into the shop, dusted it off well, and looked about for a hiding place for a key, or keys. He shone his flashlight on all the possible nooks and crannies for a hiding place. His pursuit paid off after about fifteen minutes. He was just about to give up when he spied a loose brick in the corner of the back wall. It was behind a crate, and he'd missed it the first time he had flashed the light around the room.

Mac had to get up on a stepladder to reach it, but since he was so sure this was what he wanted to find, he moved the crate, pulled the ladder over, and began to climb. Second step, the ladder broke, and he ended up on his backside. Nothing hurt, so he got up and checked the rest of the steps on the ladder. They were seemingly secure. He tried again, climbed onto the workbench, and began jiggling the loose brick. Like everything else in the old shop, it, too, resisted movement.

"Patience, my boy. You are a surgeon, and you know what it means to be persistent."

Finally, it started to budge. He continued to wiggle it back and forth, and alternately brushing away debris that fell as he wiggled. He sneezed from the dust, blew his nose, and got back to the task at hand. It took another fifteen minutes after it began to move for him to get it out, but get it out, he did.

"Aha! There you are! Something in there. Need the flashlight."

He got off the workbench, swinging his legs over and hopping down rather than using the ladder, retreated his flashlight, and climbed back using the ladder, avoiding the broken step. As he shone the flashlight in the hole made by the loose brick, he saw what appeared to be a small gift box, like something used for a piece of jewelry. It appeared to be intact, but knowing how long it had been there, he considered retrieving it with a pair of tongs, rather than his fingers.

"Maybe there would be tongs in the kitchen. Speaking of the kitchen, what time is it? I'm getting hungry!" He looked at his cell phone and saw that it was half past noon. "Ahhh. I wonder if my wife has meal plans or if she is going to keep devouring old letters."

Coming into the house by the kitchen door, he saw that Susan and her cousin were in the process of laying out a little lunch. Mike, although he lived in the old house, didn't stock his larder with company food. He ate like a bachelor: bread, hotdogs, beans, canned meats, cheese, eggs, and Co-Colas.

"Looks like good old bachelor fare to me, Mike. Ever think you might need a woman's touch here?"

"Tried that. Didn't work. She left after a couple of years. Never heard from her again. Well, at least not after she divorced me. Never had any young'uns, so the bachelor's life was good enough for me."

After enough lunch to stem off starvation, he asked to borrow the tongs. "I'll bring them right back. I have to retrieve something from a hole and don't want to destroy it in the process."

"Yeah. Help yourself," Mike said, as he washed the dishes for Susan to dry.

Tongs in hand, he went back to the shop. Mac climbed up again onto the workbench with tongs in one pocket and flashlight in the other, stepping carefully over the broken step of the ladder. Once standing on the bench, he looked for a place to secure the light. He was able to prop it on a shelf next to where he was working, applied the tongs to the little box, and gently removed it, like extracting an embedded appendix during surgery. "Aha! Gotcha."

Pocketing his tongs and light, he slid off the bench and took the box outside to see better. Opening it, he did find a key, but it was not a padlock key. Rather it looked like the one for the room. "Eureka! But we still don't have the key to the wooden box! Maybe there is another one up there."

He laid the box on the bench. Back up the ladder with his equipment. As he shone the light in the hole, he saw what might be another key, at least the shape of a key, lying in the dust. He blew into the hole to dislodge the dust. "Achoo! Ah, a key. This has to be it." He was able to retrieve it with the kitchen tongs.

He pocketed his tools and put the key in his shirt pocket, slid down, and went to where he had placed the box. He tried the key. It fit, but it was difficult to turn, given that it had set idly in a dusty room for sixty years or more. After jiggling it without results, his eye caught the can of WD-40, evidently left behind by Jerry Johnson. "Well, if there is anything left in it. Jerry had to use a lot to get that lock loose."

There was enough remaining in the can to lubricate the lock and the key well enough, that after a few more tries, it popped open. "Aha! Gotcha, you old dragon!"

"Are you St. George slaying the dragon? I've always wondered who you really are." It was Susan, tired of reading letters, coming to check on her husband and delivering a message from Mike.

"Hey, babe! Just in time to reveal the secrets of one Luther Willson, perhaps aka Luke Harvey. Uh, where is Mike? Not certain if we should divulge this if he's around. Might be a bit of a shock."

"Oh, that's what I came to tell you. He left to go get a haircut. We have time."

Together, they opened the box. Letters. Stacks of them. Some were from Zanny, but the majority of them were postmarked St. Petersburg, Florida. There were two distinct handwritings but no names on the return address, just an address.

"Mac, let's put this in the car and go through it at home. Mike doesn't need to know about this now. In time, we need to tell everyone about the double life of Grandpa."

"You're sure about his double life, aren't you?"

"Not a doubt. If you read her letters, you wouldn't either. I'll tell you about them later."

Mac put the box in the trunk of the car, closed up the inner room, locked it, and pocketed the key. Then he locked the shop with the extra key Mike had given him. They returned the tongs to the kitchen and wrote a note to Mike. It was midafternoon when they left for home in Blowing Rock.

Chapter 12

Luther (aka Luke)

St. Petersburg, Florida, May 1922

As soon as the McBrides arrived home, they unloaded the wooden box and delved into the contents. There were stacks of letters. The letters Susan and Mac found in the box, rather than in order of when they were posted, appeared that there were two piles: ones from Zanny and ones from St. Petersburg. The first one Susan picked up was from Zanny, April 1922. Luther had not received it until May.

*****

Luther had written to Zanny that he would not be able to come home for a while because he was ill. When he went to his post office box to check his mail, there was a letter from her. He dreaded opening it. He suspected that she was suspicious of him in the past, but she had never mentioned it. When he was home, she was the same loving woman she always had been. Even after eight children—nine now—she was still a passionate lover. He could not ask for better. Truth be told, Martha meant little to him beyond a means to relieve his own passions and a good home to live in when he was in Florida. Did he love her? His love for her was raw, a needy love. He pocketed the letter and headed for the bay. It would wait until he got there where he could read it without interruption.

>Dear Luther,
>
>I call you dear 'cause I've always and will always love you. I've learned so much from you and been with you for twenty-four years. You even taught me to read and write. You taught me to love. Have I always believed you? Most of the time, but I don't for a minute buy your story of being sick. It wouldn't surprise me if you have a woman there in St. Petersburg. This tale of yours now makes me certain of it. If you give her up now and come home, I'll take you back. It will be like nothing ever happened. Stay till July if you must, but when you come home, you will not return for the long stays if you want me. If you continue to need to sell your instruments in Florida, I have no heartache about that, but the woman can never be a part of our lives again.
>
>>Your true wife,
>>Zanny

Luther's heart sank. He loved Zanny. He really did. But he definitely liked Martha, too. And Maggie was part of that.

Pushing his guilt to the back of his mind, he wrote back to Zanny while he was still at the post office and posted the letter right away.

>My dearest Zanny,
>
>I have not meant to offend you, and I am sorry you can't believe me. You know how I always suffer more when I'm ill than many others do. I

guess I inherited that from my mother. I am sick at heart, too, for your distrust in me. Why would I ever be unfaithful? You are all that I need. I don't know how long I will need to stay, but the doctor thinks I should recover in a month if I get plenty of rest. I will surely let you know in my next letter how I am. The doctor doesn't believe my illness is serious, but he thinks it could turn that way if I do not rest. If I am not able to travel by June, I will send for you.

Please trust me and pray for me, as I know you do.

Love much,
Luther

That's what she will want to hear. I hate to tell her lies, but there is nothing to be done for it. I have to stay till Martha either dies or has the baby. I don't look for either one to survive. I just don't want to leave Maggie here to go through with this herself. That part about sending for her, I'll deal with that if I have to.

He took Zanny's letter back to the house to lock it in his suitcase with other letters she had written that winter. When he arrived at the house, a gentleman caller, obviously courting Maggie, had the girl in his arms. Luke had seen the fellow before and thought he was a bit too old for Maggie. Now, it seemed as if he was a little free with his attentions to her, and Luke attempted to set the young man straight.

"Young fellow, I don't know about your upbringing, but in this household, a gentleman is not to be overly familiar with our daughter. If you choose to court Maggie, you will refrain from the familiarity I witnessed when I came in. You may go, but don't return unless you are willing to act like a gentleman."

The man turned his head, more to hide the smirk than to act remorseful. "Sorry, sir. Ms. Maggie is so beautiful. I just couldn't restrain myself. Good day, sir." And he left, whistling, as though Luther had not lectured.

Luke wondered how a nice young man could see the beauty in an overweight teenager. *Who is to account for some men's tastes? I think he is after something else!*

"Papa! He didn't mean to insult me. He has been ever so nice. Please be nice to him if he doesn't get mad and not come back. He's from a good family, going to be a lawyer."

"Maggie, we have enough to worry with in Mama's illness and the baby coming. Be careful, honey. That's all I want."

That was the end of the conversation, but Maggie had an odd look that almost frightened Luther. *Is she aware that her mother's and my marriage is a sham?*

In two short months, Maggie had finished school, was home nursing her mother, and alleged that she had no time for gentlemen callers. Then when little Luke Junior was born, with the subsequent death of his mother, her hands were full. Luther was happy to see that she could fulfill the role of motherhood. His Zanny had not been as old as Maggie when they were married. It wasn't that he didn't want to see Maggie married, but he believed she was the best person to take care of Junior, along with Georgie.

He sent a telegram to his son Roby, who would relay the message home to Zanny: "Coming home. Stop. Arrive Johnson City. Stop. 4:10 p.m., Tuesday. Stop. Luther."

All the way north, he thought about what he would tell Zanny. Should he admit he was involved with a woman? *She's no longer alive, so it is over. No need to weep over spilled milk. But maybe I need to get it all out in the open. Tell her the truth. She's a good woman and deserves better than me. If she runs me off, so be it.*

He went back and forth to tell or not to tell, all the way to Jacksonville, to Atlanta, to Knoxville, to Johnson City. When he saw that Roby was there to meet him, he still had not made up his mind. Roby had a 1915 Ford Model T. So instead of taking the narrow gauge railroad[6] the next morning, as he usually did, they jostled and bumped off into North Carolina over Roan Mountain and up the hollers to Willson's Cove. It was a scary ride; so scary that he almost decided to tell Zanny everything.

It was after midnight till they got home, but Dook was there to greet him. He was always excited when Luther got home, but this time, since it had been an extra two months, he was wary at first. Luther petted him and gave him a piece of cheese he had in his pack. That satisfied him that Luther was okay.

Luther looked up to the front of the house. There was an oil lamp burning in the upstairs front window, and he could see Zanny sitting in her rocker. She was feeding baby Carolina. Luther's heart flipped, and he knew he couldn't tell Zanny. *Not now. I love her too much.*

He could smell the scents of home. Roses on the trellis by the porch, pines, loamy soil, and wood smoke. It was good. All good. He was both excited and dreading to face Zanny but patted his son on the back, thanked him for the ride, and went on into the house. Unlike his workshop, no key was needed because folks didn't have to lock their doors here like in St. Petersburg. He shuddered to think of Maggie living in that house with the doors unlocked. He shook his head, as though to dislodge all thoughts of St. Petersburg.

Setting down his suitcases, he walked up the stairs, head erect, in charge, and called softly, "Zanny? I'm here."

"Come on up. I'm in the front room, Luther. Ye need to meet yer youngest daughter. She woken up jes in time to meet her papa, didn' ya, Carrikins?"

Carrikins, her mama's nickname for Carolina, was as bright-eyed as her mama. What a lovely picture they made. Luther was stricken nearly immobile and speechless at the beauty of the Madonna and baby bathed in the flickering light from the oil lamp. The few strands of gray at her temples glowed like a halo. Tears came to his eyes; tears of deep emotion. Yes, his Zanny beat all other women to Hades and back.

"Zanny! You are so beautiful!" He rushed to her and fell to his knees by her side and kissed her cheek. Then he looked into Carolina's eyes and saw his own. Never would he doubt his wife. And never would he suggest her infidelity as he had when Delphy was born four years earlier.

"Glad yer home, Luther. Get yerself ta bed. Ye look plumb wore out. Tomorry's another day."

Luther loved everything about Zanny: her simple beauty, her hickish speech, and her practical mind. Yes, he would cut back his trips to one month from now on, January only.

He took off his shoes, hung his jacket over a chair, and fell into bed with the rest of his clothes on. He was asleep before he hit the pillow. He slept till he smelled coffee brewing and side meat frying. When he first awakened, he was addled at first, not remembering where he was. It didn't take long because three heads peeped around the door frame, giggling. It was Ossie, Herbie, and Delphy.

"What's the matter? Never seen ary man a-sleeping in his day clothes? Come hyar y'all. Give yer papa a big hug."

The three ran and jumped on top of him, ready for him to tickle them. Life was back to normal again. Luther Willson was home.

He settled into life on the mountain as if he had never been gone. The only thing different was their little congregation had no more use for the log church, and now the finished building of their brand-new church was ready for worship. The white clapboard with a bell on top stood out in the little community. The men of the community had worked to finish the building all winter, when they had nothing to do in the fields. Now they were seeing some newcomers every service, as they now had a preacher coming over from Banner Elk every other week.

The next time supplies were needed and a trip to Johnson City was in order, Roby offered to take him, but he opted for the train. "No, son. I 'preciate the offer, but that Ford Model T and me ain't on right friendly terms. I'll take the train."

Of course he checked his post office box there, paid for another year's rent on it, and checked to see if Maggie had written. It was now August, and he wondered if baby Junior had lived or gone to be with his mother. There was a letter from Maggie.

> Dear Papa:
>
> Wanted to know if you got back to Tennessee safely and to let you know we are fine. Luke Junior is growing. I know you are happy to be

with your children, and I hope all is well with them. I hope you will come back again this fall, even if Momma is no longer with us. I miss her so much, but Georgie has been like a mother to me. Let me know when you will be here. Miss you so much.

Your daughter,
Maggie

Reading the letter, Luther's eyes teared up. *Poor motherless girl. Glad she's got Georgie. Good that Junior's well. She's gonna be right weepy when I tell her I'm only gonna be there in January. I am determined to do the right thing as much as I can. Only, I can't let 'er know I'm really not Luke Harvey. Some bridges are too hard to be rebuilt.*

He wrote to Maggie, outlining his plans for the winter of 1923.

July 1922

Dear Maggie and Junior,

I made it back safe and sound. A fellow from back home picked me up in his 1915 Ford Model T, but it was not a good trip on these mountain roads. I will stick to train riding, I guess.

I hope Luke Junior is thriving despite the death of his mother. We will miss her, but I know he will be cared for well by you and see you as his true momma. It was so sad to leave you with the burden of a baby and arranging your mother's burial. I could not procrastinate any longer but needed to be back in the mountains to work with my children in planting and harvesting. Maggie, I will not be returning for the entire winter anymore. It takes too much time away from my children here. I plan to return in January and stay the month as I did before I married your mother. Please know that I do care for you, and my heart is broken at the loss of your mother. She was a good woman.

> Love,
> Papa

*****

Reading the letters in the stack before them, Mac and Susan shared little respect for the grandfather Susan thought she had known. Susan knew she would have to contact Harry Harvey. He had given her his cell phone number.

Chapter 13

Martha

St. Petersburg, Florida, 1921

Before Susan could talk to Harry, she wanted to delve into the letters to Grandpa from Martha. They went back to early 1916 and went through 1921. It appeared that she had died in 1922. The first letter was evidently soon after she had met Luther Willson.

*****

February 1916

Dear Mr. Luke,

I miss hearing you play at the club. No one else is nearly as good. I am looking forward to you coming back next year. I hope you will be able to stay more than the month of January. Maggie and I enjoyed having you here for dinner. She thinks you are very special. I do too.

Your friend,
Martha Lindsay

The next letter was in the summer. It appeared that the postal romance was ramping up.

> July 1916
>
> Dear Luke,
>
> I am so happy you have decided to spend the winter with us. We have a nice room you can call home while you are here. I love your letters and look forward to you being here. I'm embarrassed to admit this, but your letters make me feel like I haven't felt for a long time.
>
> Warm thoughts for you,
> Martha

There were weekly letters after that, and each more sensual that the previous. She was obviously expecting a full-fledged courtship when he arrived in October. The last phrase in the final letter of 1916 left no doubt to the imagination:

> I am yours, Luke. I need you, and you need me. I know a preacher who will marry us whenever you see fit. I love you.
>
> Martha

Martha thought about those early letters as she and Maggie waited at the train station for the train bringing him from Tennessee. *We were crazy in love. Who would have thought we'd a gotten married right off the bat when he got here? Can hardly wait to be in his arms again. I think Maggie is as excited as I am, but she can't know how I feel. We're still crazy in love!*

When Luke arrived, for Martha, everything was good. She was excited. Luke suggested a party for Maggie, and that would be right before Christmas. But first there was Thanksgiving. Then Christmas. The party was fun, but there was no romance resulting by Maggie's banjo picking. Georgie told stories about the old days when her folks were slaves. And Luke told mountain tales. Too soon it was time to break up the party and get to bed.

Then Christmastime came with more food and festive times. Christmas Eve was one of the few nights that Luke and Martha did not go out to speakeasies. It was a family night with lots of music and storytelling. Georgie and Jesse were included. Luke and Maggie played the banjos; Martha was on the fiddle; Jesse played the bones; and Georgie sang in her rich contralto voice. There was even a jug of hooch, as Jesse called it, but Luke never touched a drop. Then at quarter till midnight, they all walked over a couple of streets together to the church to hear the choir.

The next morning, there were presents. It was Christmas Day. Georgie made a big turkey with oyster stuffing, candied yams, scalloped corn, and all sorts of sweet relishes and pumpkin pies. Now that Maggie had gotten into making desserts, she made the pies.

Martha had a special present for Luke. She whispered in his ear, "Guess what? You and I are going to be parents. I am going to have us a baby!"

Luke grabbed her and pulled her out to the kitchen. "Are you certain? Could it be the change?"

Martha scowled at him. "Of course I am certain. I'm only thirty-five. I am not going through the change, and I know what it is like to be with child. It's yours, Luke. I hope you are as happy about it as I am."

"Of...of course, I am." He fumbled. "It was just a surprise. I'm a bit older than you, and I wasn't sure we would have any children."

Then after the first of the year, it came to light that she had the tumors in her breast. It was cancer. Luke was more than gracious with her, and she felt safe with him. She knew she would die, but she would give him a child. *It's good. It will be a happy event, if I can last until it's time for the baby to come, if I don't miscarry.*

The baby seemed to grow inside her and was healthy. On the other hand, the pregnancy sapped the strength she needed to remain healthy enough to maintain the pregnancy. It was doubtful, Dr. Morgan told her, that she would carry the baby to term. As fast as her body was failing, she might not even live until the baby was old enough to survive. He urged her to terminate the pregnancy. She refused. She put it in writing:

> Dr. Morgan:
>
> You have advised me to have my baby aborted. I will never let you take it from me. If I die before it is big enough to live, so be it. I am in God's hands.
>
> Martha Harvey

*****

This letter was tucked in with the ones that Susan had been reading. Tears streamed down her face as she read it. If she felt no respect for her grandfather in these moments, she did feel sorry for this woman who thought she was legally married to her grandfather.

Chapter 14

Harry

US 98 South, August 2009

Susan dialed the number, but it immediately went to voice mail. "Hi, you have reached Banjo Harry. Please leave a brief message and a callback number. I will return your call as soon as I can. Thanks."

"Hey, Banjo Harry, this is Susan. I have some very important information for you that might knock your socks off, if you wear any. We need to talk face-to-face. Please call me at your earliest convenience. Number is 828-291-3338. Looking to hear from you soon."

Meanwhile, Harry had packed up his paraphernalia, gotten his hair cut short, and took off for St. Petersburg. His father had signed over the old house on Eighth Avenue NE, to him when he knew maintaining the house would be more than the old fellow could handle. He and his daughter, Gwen, would take over, the fourth generation. When he was not off somewhere trying to make money playing his banjo, he stayed there, but now his daughter lived there and went to University of South Florida, St. Petersburg campus, only blocks from the house. She worked part-time as a nurses' aide at St. Anthony's Hospital, so she was in and out. Harry never knew when she would be there and when she wouldn't. He had called and left a message before he took off from Apalachicola. "On my way home.

Should be there late this afternoon." She might or might not be ready for him when he got there.

"Might as well expect to go to the grocery store as soon as I get home, if I know Gwen!"

He heard the phone ring while he was driving, but he ignored it. *Too much of a distraction.* He thought it could be Gwen. "Check you later, babes!" he said to the phone.

The purpose of this trip would be to search the house for any information about his grandfather. That Susan woman had put an eerie feeling in him that all was not what it seemed to be. *Could her grandfather have known my grandfather? Stranger things have happened. Bunches of old letters and papers up in the attic. If the silverfishes haven't destroyed them, I may find a clue or so.*

Harry thought about how long it would have taken his grandfather to ride from Johnson City, Tennessee, to St. Petersburg back in the day. *I'll bet it was a couple of days. Maybe Knoxville, Chattanooga, Atlanta, and lots of little places on down the line to St. Petersburg. I can drive from the Big Bend in Florida to the house in five or six hours. Maybe double that from Johnson City. I've been through there. All great roads. Interstate.*

It was already dark till he got home, and as expected, Gwen wasn't home. He checked the refrigerator and the cupboards. Coffee. Cereal. Bread. Bacon and eggs. "That'll get me through breakfast tomorrow." He went back out to the supermarket anyway and loaded up with those items and a few more. He took them home and crashed. He forgot to check his phone messages.

After a hot shower and a big breakfast the next morning, he was ready to hit the attic. Just as he crawled out of the shower, Gwen sleepily crept out of her room, looking like roadkill. He laughed and whispered, "Good morning," and pointed toward the kitchen.

"Uh."

Fifteen minutes later, she came in looking slightly more alive and joined him for his coffee. "Sorry I didn't get back to you, Dad. Classes all day yesterday, and I pulled the all-night shift at St. Anthony's. I'm working there now as a nursing assistant. Oh, did I tell you I changed majors? I'm in the nursing program instead of education. Really like working at St. Anthony's. Hope it's okay with you."

"Why wouldn't it be okay with me? I want you to be happy with whatever you do. You know that."

"Yeah, but Mom, you know. Dying there. Thought—"

"If your mother had a nurse anesthetist who cared as I know you will, she may not have died like that. Anyway, I'm here for another reason. I am going to go through things in the attic to see if I can learn something about my grandfather. He has always been a mystery. Dad is clueless."

"Oh, I went over to visit him the other day, Dad. He had just been giving a concert with some lady playing a banjo. I got in on the tail end of it. They were great. I don't know if she is a resident there or if she was visiting him. I didn't get to meet her because I had to go to the office and sign some papers for Grandpa. Glad you gave me the POA for him since you are gone so much. Glad to do it.

"When I got back, the lady was gone, and he was back in his room. He couldn't remember her name. Poor Grandpa. But you know, he's still pretty keen other than the name thing."

"I know. That could have been the woman I met in Apalachicola. She said she wanted to come and see him. She is sort of why I'm here, but I will tell you later all about it."

"Well, Dad, I'm off and running again today. Classes all morning, library this afternoon, work till midnight tonight."

Harry looked after his daughter as she left the room. She looked so much like her mother. It hurt sometimes to look at her. Death was never easy, but Gloria's hurt more because it was so senseless. *At least the hospital agreed to a settlement.*

After Gwen was gone for the day, Harry stripped to only a pair of gym shorts, grabbed a fan from the storage, and headed to the attic. *Where to start?*

There were old pieces of furniture that needed to be repaired, needed to be reupholstered, or needed to be pitched out, as far as Harry was concerned. *I remember that old chair. Terrible upholstery, but it was comfortable. Maybe recycle that. Where are Grandma's papers?*

He saw an old trunk. He pulled it out where he could get to it and dusted it off. He hoped there would be letters. Dad said she kept every letter she ever got.

The latch popped easily. Linens and blankets. Old clothes. Baby items. A baby book for his dad. He pulled it out and set it aside. *No letters here.*

He closed up the trunk and pushed it back where it had been. Then he saw an old desk. *Funny, I don't remember seeing that before. Beautiful.* The desk was an Edwardian period piece of furniture, a bit worse for wear, but definitely fine quality. There was a deep drawer on each side at chair level, pigeonholes and small drawers behind the writing surface, and a rolltop drawer on either side of the writing surface. The writing surface had an inlaid leather pad that had evidently seen a lot of writing. The desk was wobbly, but it looked salvageable.

He opened the larger drawer on the right side. *Bingo! Letters to Mom and her mother, too!* There were more in both the other large drawer and the rolltops. They dated back to the summer of 1916 and went through 1929.

Guess folks didn't write a lot of letters during the Depression. Well, let's read 'em.

He put them in order as to when they were received. The first was the spring of 1916 and written to Martha. Harry knew that was his great-grandmother. It surprised him that Martha, and not Maggie, was the object of his letter.

My Dear Martha,

Meeting you was the highlight of my stay in St. Petersburg this year. I do hope we can get together when I return again. I am planning to come back in October instead of waiting until after Christmas. I think our sales will benefit from a longer stay.

The writer continued with many complimentary comments about Martha and only a small reference to Maggie. *Who was he courting, anyway? I thought it was Grandma, although she was awfully young.*

> I do not know if your feelings are the same as mine, Ms. Martha, but I dearly love being in your company. You have been the highlight of my stay in St. Petersburg. Do give my warmest regards to Little Maggie. I look forward to seeing you again in October. You may write to me at the following address: Luke Harvey PO BOX 29, Johnson City, TN.
>
> Your friend,
> Luke Harvey

"Wow! This is new information. Dad never told me that his father was courting Maggie's mother. So who was his mother? Maggie, I always thought. Must have been Martha." *Got to read more.*

> May 1917 [addressed to Martha]
>
> My dearest wife,
>
> I am so glad I was able to spend the winter with you. You have been in my thoughts since I got back to the mountains. I look forward to coming back to you in October, so long as travel is still permitted on the trains, despite the war. I long for the war to be over, and then perhaps we can relax.

"Ah! He was married to Martha, not Maggie. I hope he did not treat Maggie as a wife, too. That would be a hard pill to swallow!" As he read through more letters, he learned little more, except in some letters he would give Martha advice on dealing with an adolescent daughter. One from 1919 was amusing:

> I understand how difficult it must be having to deal with the moods of a young lady. I don't suppose you were ever fourteen years old. Ho, ho. It is a difficult age. She feels grown-up, but she thinks as a child. She is still young enough for you to wallop her across her broadside if she gives you too much sass, to be blunt. Perhaps one day we will have children of our own, and Maggie will see that she is not the queen bee anymore.

Then when he got to the letters in the summer of 1922, he began to figure out what occurred that his dad always called Maggie, Mom.

July 1922

Dear Maggie and Junior,

> I made it back safe and sound. A fellow from back home picked me up in his 1915 Ford Model T, but it was not a good trip on these mountain roads. I will stick to train riding, I guess.
> I hope Luke Junior is thriving despite the death of his mother. We will miss her, but I know he will be cared for well by you and see you as his true momma. It was so sad to leave you with the burden of a baby and arranging your mother's burial. I could not procrastinate any longer but needed to be back in the mountains to work with my children in planting and harvesting. Maggie, I will not be returning for the entire winter anymore. It takes too much time away from my children here. I plan to return in January and stay

the month as I did before I married your mother. Please know that I do care for you, and my heart is broken at the loss of your mother. She was a good woman.

> Love,
> Papa

Had Martha died in childbirth? I may never know, but I intend to see if there are records in any of the old doctor offices or hospitals. Maybe I can learn something. I suppose the first place to look would be courthouse records of marriages, births, and deaths.

Finishing all letters, he put them back in the desk and got cleaned up. The attic was disgustingly hot and smelly. A nice shower and some clean clothes made him feel like a new guy.

He checked his cell phone and saw that he had forgotten about the missed call while he had been driving. *It's from that old gal from North Carolina who bought my fretted banjo. Wonder what she wants.* He punched in her number.

When she answered, he was his usual abrupt self. "What's up?"

"Glad you called back. We need to talk, but not on the phone. I visited your dad in Tampa last week, and then we came back to North Carolina and have been reading some letters to my grandfather. Seems he led two lives."

"And that has what to do with me?"

"Look, Harry. I can't begin to tell you about this on the phone. Just believe me. I'm afraid I've found more than we bargained for. Are you still in Apalachicola?"

"No. St. Pete. Be here at least a couple of weeks and then hope to be on the road again. Perhaps it is your bargain and not mine, but I'll hear you out."

"Good. Mac and I will come to St. Pete. I'll call when we get there."

"Do what floats your boat. What did you think of Junior? My daughter evidently saw you when you and Dad were playing at the retirement home. She said she didn't get to meet you."

"Junior's great. We had a lot of fun. See you soon. I didn't know you have a daughter."

"Call when you get to town. And, Susan, bring your banjo."

"Will do."

More than she bargained for, huh? I've already run into a dilemma of my own. Hope her mess won't complicate mine.

He pocketed his phone and left to go see Junior at Legacy at Highwoods in Tampa, an assisted living retirement facility.

Junior was in good health and enjoying the company of some other seniors around coffee and cookies. He grinned when he saw Harry. "Where you been keepin' yourself, boy? Did ya bring yer banjer?"

"Not today, Dad. I just got in town last evening. I've been rooting about in the attic and found out something interesting."

"Aha! Ya learned that Mom wasn't my real mother, didn't you?"

That surprised Harry as much as learning the information. His surprise was that Dad remembered it when sometimes he didn't even remember Harry's name. "That's right. Why did you keep on letting me believe Grandma was your real mother all these years?"

"Easier that way. I never knew Martha. She died a day or so after I was born. Mom told me she had cancer and that it was a miracle that she was even able to give birth. And Harry, she never told me about it until I was eighteen years old. If I had thought about it, I probably could have figured it out. But callow lad that I was, it never occurred to me that a man as old as Papa would not have married a teenager. I should have guessed it because when Papa came in January every year, he slept in his room, and Maggie slept in hers. It should have dawned on me that Maggie and Papa weren't together, especially since she was only twelve when he first started living there. But as far as I was concerned, Mom Maggie was my mother. Harry, leave things as they are."

Harry didn't reply to his father. His nod was noncommittal. *Not certain I can leave things as they are when that old banjo gal stirs them up.*

The two chatted easily for half an hour about nothing. Junior tended to repeat himself, though not necessarily confused. Harry hugged his dad and made his farewell.

Chapter 15

Luke Junior

Tampa, Florida

As Junior walked back to his room, his mind went back to his own foray in the attic many years before. Stella, his wife, was still living. They had buried Mom the day before, and he decided to go up into the attic and see what he could find. He located the Edwardian desk. *Wonder why she brought this up here. It's still a beautiful piece of furniture, just a bit wobbly. I could fix it good as new.*

Looking through the letters, he came upon one that struck him as odd. It had obviously been wrinkled up and then smoothed out again. It was to Maggie, not from Luke, but from someone named Luther.

The letter was a confession from his father that he was not the man he had pretended to be. Luther explained who he was, told about his family, and asked forgiveness for the deception. He ended the letter with a heartbreaking announcement:

> I can no longer come to be with you, as my life has to change for good.
>
> I remain your papa,
> Luther Willson

Junior felt faint as he read the letter. He would never tell anyone, not even Stella. It was too shameful to even talk about. He hid the letter in a secret compartment he had found in the desk, planning to destroy it someday.

Returning his mind to the present day, he got out his fiddle and played for a while, playing some of the old songs Mom had taught him. When his shoulders began to ache and his fingers grew tired, he put the fiddle away and thought about Stella.

Never forget the day when I told Stella that Maggie was my half sister and not my mother. Don't know if she was as much surprised as she was relieved. She said, "Junior, I hated to think you were a 'woods colt.' Maggie didn't seem like the type who'd seduce her step-father."

If she'd a-known that Luke Harvey wasn't his real name, that woulda really blown her away. Guess genealogically, I'm a Willson, but I'll never tell.

Stella was from quality. Her daddy was a highbrow lawyer, and her mama was Tampa society. They were not exactly thrilled that we got married, but with the Depression and then World War II, their money and status were not what they once had. I met her at the USO in 1942. Prettiest gal there. I'd just been drafted and was about to be shipped off to Germany. We had the world's fastest courtship and got married the week before I was sent across. She was waiting for me in New York when we got back to American soil four years later. No, I could never tell her about my ignominious beginnings. Stella deserved the best, and I planned to live it for her. We had a beautiful life together till she passed those twenty years ago. Never destroyed that letter. Bet Harry will find it.

He fell asleep on his chair to a confused dream, waking up when the dinner bell rang and wondering why Papa and Stella were playing cards over by the window. It took a minute or so to get his bearings. When he was fully awake, he had put aside all the reminiscing and took off down the hallway to the dining room. It was baked chicken tonight.

Chapter 16

Harry

St. Petersburg, Florida, August 2009

Harry thought about his dad, wondering why he had kept the secret about his real grandmother all these years. Since it was early afternoon, he figured it would only take him forty-five minutes to get to the Pinellas County Courthouse, beating the heavy traffic of evening rush hour. He wanted to see if he could locate some records. *They should go back to the 1920s at least.*

A youngish but plain-appearing lady behind the desk assured him the records went back to 1912 and could be assessed on microfilm. She pointed him in the right direction. For the next two hours, he scrolled through records. He did find his dad's birth record, June 1, 1922. But he did not find a record of a marriage between a Luke Harvey and Martha Lindsay. He went back as far as 1912, and there were no records to suggest there had ever been a marriage. *Hmmm.* Then he looked at death records and easily found Martha Lindsay, with Harvey in parenthesis. *Maybe they got married somewhere else and that is why it isn't here, but now I wonder if they were actually married. Interesting. Perhaps we are not who we think we are!*

Harry stewed about the seeming dilemma all the way home. Just as he pulled his car into the driveway, his cell phone rang. *That banjo lady again! Guess I'll have to see what her problem is.*

"Hey, Banjo Lady. Are you in St. Pete?"

"We are. We are checking into our lodging right now. We're staying at the Larelle House[7] on Sixth Avenue. How close is it to your place?"

"Close. I'm just pulling into my driveway. You want me to come over there? I could walk. Show you a great restaurant close to where you're staying."

"Sounds great. We will meet you in the lobby."

"See ya in fifteen minutes."

Since Harry had already gotten cleaned up well before he went to see his dad, he only needed to brush his teeth before he set out for the Larelle.

They must be pretty well-heeled to travel all over the place and stay there. Hope they pay for their own supper. And I'm gonna take them to Marchlands. Mediterranean food.

Chapter 17

Susan

St. Petersburg, Florida

As promised, he was there in fifteen minutes. Mac and Susan were in the lobby when he got there. Not expecting to see him without his signature T-shirt, jeans, and ponytail, they didn't recognize him at first.

"Oh! Harry! I didn't recognize you. You clean up well!"

"Ha. The ponytail and rags are my persona. Started the ponytail bit when I played several folk music festivals in the Adirondacks a couple of years ago. Lots of hippies. I've been doing some business here and need to look a bit more gentlemanly. Maybe I'll grow a beard before I set out on the road again. Huh?"

"Why not?" Mac agreed. "Thought about that for myself."

"Oh no, you don't!" Susan gave him the eye.

"Want to walk to the restaurant? It's a couple of blocks and right on the water. I'm a bit hungry, so maybe we can have our discussion after we eat, if that's okay with you."

"Suits us," Mac and Susan agreed.

Happily, Mac footed the bill for everyone without batting an eye. Harry felt only slightly guilty, but what the hey?

After the meal, they walked back to the bed-and-breakfast and sat on the porch where it was quiet and private.

Susan began. "Harry what do you know about your grandfather?"

"Humph! I am wondering who I am about this time. I went up into the attic at the house and found a pile of letters. Some from my grandfather to my grandmother and several to Maggie. I learned that Maggie was actually my aunt and not my grandmother. She raised Dad when his mother died. Dad had known this since he was eighteen, but for some unknown reason, he never told me. Today, he admitted it and said he didn't think it really mattered because Maggie was his mom as far as he was concerned. He said something odd before I left. He said, 'Harry, leave things as they are.' I'm not certain what he was talking about."

"I think we do, Harry. You may not like to hear this, but I think we have ample proof. Your grandfather was my grandfather. You and I are half first cousins. Our grandfather's real name was Luther Willson. The Luke Harvey was a pseudonym. Luke, perhaps short for Luther, and Harvey? Well, my father's name was Harvey. It may have been a family name, like, maybe his grandmother was a Harvey. Never done much in the way of genealogy. Grandpa was the luthier who crafted those wonderful banjos and fiddles. He had been traveling in Florida since 1911. He 'married'—a loose term—Martha in 1916, would spend half the year with her and half the year in North Carolina."

Harry shook his head, partly in disbelief. He felt a sinking sensation in the pit of his stomach. Her story at least partly confirmed what he had suspected after reading the letters in the attic.

Susan had brought several of the letters with her, ones that were obvious about the relationships, so she could share them with Harry. She handed them to him, and he began reading. He would read, shake his head, and sigh. He picked up the next one and went through the same read, shake head, and sigh, until he had read them all. The entire time, he said nothing. Meanwhile, Susan and Mac gave him privacy. They strolled about the premises, chatting with other people who were staying at the inn and keeping an eye on Harry.

After reading the final one, he beckoned to them to come back, and he handed the pile back. He said, "Sit."

Susan sat next to him, and Mac leaned against the porch railing. Harry looked dark, almost ready to explode.

The situation brought on by these discoveries seemed to loosen his tongue. The terse speech was set aside, and a different Harry emerged. "Guess that's why dad said to let it alone. I've been reading letters in my attic all morning. I haven't run into any like these, but there were some hints. You can come over tomorrow and read them if you want to. There may be more as well that might confirm your story. I still find it difficult to believe. You know, you believe something for nearly sixty years, and then your world gets turned upside down." He shook his head again.

"I went to the Pinellas County Courthouse this afternoon and found Dad's birth record and Grandmother's death record, but there was no marriage record. If Grandmother and Luke Harvey were married, it wasn't here. Grandmother's death record had her name as Martha Lindsay with Harvey in parenthesis.

"What would you say, Susan, about having DNA done? I don't want to believe this, but I know I should. I want to prove it one way or another."

"Good idea, and I'm all for it, and we can pick them up later this afternoon. I saw a CVS a few blocks from here. Harry, it wouldn't be a bad thing to know we are cousins. Our family are all good people, despite our grandfather. We'd like for you to be part of it. Do you have other family besides your dad? And you mentioned a daughter."

"I have a daughter. Mom and Dad didn't have any other kids, and Dad, at least as far as we knew, was an only other child, except for Mom, his half sister, Maggie. By the way, are any of your aunts or uncles still living that you could confirm any of this stuff with them?"

"Aunt Carrie, Carolina, is still living. She is eighty-seven. She has recently moved into a retirement village in Banner Elk, North Carolina. I don't think it would serve any purpose to stir the pot with her at this time.

"I can see your next family reunion, if you have them. I would come as a long-lost cousin! We might get thrown off your mountain!" Saying this pulled Harry away from his dark visage, and he began laughing hilariously.

Once he was able to stop laughing, he continued, "Okay. Here's the deal. Tomorrow after breakfast, come to my place." He gave them the address on Eighth Avenue NE, gave his home phone number, and suggested they should be quiet, since his daughter worked late at the hospital. "Wear something cool because the attic is like the third floor of hell. It's so hot. The fan is almost useless."

"Ah! Then your attic is the abode of gluttons," Mac joked.

Susan laughed. "Dante."

Harry shrugged. "Yeah, I only read CliffsNotes. See you around nine or so in the morning. Did you bring your banjo? Bring it along."

"Okay."

Susan and Mac enjoyed their restful night at the Larelle; they were up by six, garbed in lightweight clothing, and after a gourmet breakfast on the patio, drove to the address Harry gave them. The house was a lovely old Craftsman from the 1910s that was white framed and a three-story construction with an upstairs porch.

Harry's daughter, who was tall and slender with long dark hair and blue eyes, met them at the door. A cat wound about her feet. "Daddy said you are friends from North Carolina. I'm Gwen. Cat's name is Catastrophe. Oh, your banjo. You played with Grandpa. It was great. Daddy's out there." She pointed toward the kitchen.

Susan thanked her. "Hope we didn't waken you."

She shook her head. "No. Been up two hours. Studying. Gotta leave for school. Have a great day. Later." With that, she was out the door and headed toward the bus stop. Not a good day to walk the several blocks to the university. Too hot.

"Nice, polite young lady, even if she does have her father's brevity of words." Mac looked after her in appreciation.

Indeed, Harry was in the kitchen, looking as though he hadn't slept well. He confirmed it. "Nothing to be done about it, but after we wear ourselves out in the attic, maybe a nap."

Susan held out two boxes. "We stopped on the way over and picked up these at a drugstore. Shall we spit?"

"Yeah. I'm not certain what to tell Gwen, if anything. It's hard to tell what she will say. I haven't said anything to her about who you are. I told her I was having friends over this morning." He pointed to the coffee maker. "Help yourself."

Harry and Susan opened their boxes simultaneously, read the directions silently, and commenced to spitting.

"Sheesh! Why do they need so much?" Susan complained.

Harry kept spitting until his was full. He stood by until Susan had finished with her test tube. "Okay, I'll run these over to the post office and be back in a few minutes.

Susan got two coffee mugs from the counter and poured coffee in each. As she brought them to the table, she grinned. "I'll be chomping at the bit for the next six to eight weeks, until it's back. I put our Macon e-mail address on it, since we need to go there next month when Jack and his family take over the place. Does that make sense to send it there?"

"That's what I would have done."

They had barely finished their coffee before Harry was back.

"Deed done. Now the waiting game. Let's go to the attic. Hope you don't mind me stripped down to my gym shorts, Susan. You can do the same, Mac, if you want. You, too, Susan, although I wouldn't recommend it."

"Ha! Thank you, no," she said.

They followed their host up two flights of stairs to the attic. Opening the door confirmed that the Third Circle of hell might not be far-fetched. Harry turned the fan on, switched on a light, and led them first to the Edwardian desk.

"Whoa! Look at this." Mac rubbed his hands over the patina. "Fixed up, you have a valuable piece of furniture. These beauties always have secret compartments. Have you found one in it, Harry?"

"Never thought about it. Let's look."

Mac was familiar with the hidden treasuries of such desks, and it did not take him long to discover at least one secret compartment.

"Eureka, Archimedes!" Harry grinned as Mac gently retrieved an old envelope from the compartment. "Let's see what else someone wanted to hide. "It's addressed to Maggie, and the return address is Luther Willson! Guess what?"

Susan was excited. It was all she could do not to grab the envelope from Harry's hands. He opened it and read it aloud. This was the exact letter that Luke Junior had read that he thought was shameful; the letter he had hid in the desk, planning one day to destroy, but never did.

March 1934

Dear Maggie,

I apologize for not answering your letters for the last few years. I need to come clean with you. I have been living a double life since you were just a girl. I pretended I was a salesman of musical instruments, sent by the fellow who crafted them. I, myself, was the craftsman. At the time I already had a wife here in the mountains, and she is still living. We have nine children together, and many of them are grown, with families of their own. I have asked God to forgive me, and I hope you can find it in your heart to forgive me. I will always carry the guilt with me that I deceived your mother. I have loved visiting with you and Junior. I hope one day you will marry and have children of your own. I can no longer come to be with you, as my life has to change for good.

I remain your papa,
Luther Willson

The three treasure hunters looked at each other dumbfounded. Finally, Susan spoke softly, "Harry, I can't imagine the emotions flooding Maggie when she read that letter. It must have been horrible for her."

After mulling the letter over in her mind a bit, she told them about the grandfather she knew. "He was a godly man. Never missed going to church, was an elder, teacher, and good neighbor. I recall going on and on to my daddy about how great a Christian Grandpa was. He said, 'Yeah, after he quit going to Floridy every winter, he walked the aisle. Don't know what he confessed, but he was different after that. It was during the Depression, so yer uncles Luther and Roby told me it was 'cause times were tough.'"

She shook her head as though she was trying to dislodge this strange image of a man she loved dearly. "But even after the Depression, the grandfather I remembered was a wonderful man. I found all this so difficult to believe. I guess there is something to redemption."

The three family detectives continued to look for other things in the attic that would shed more light on the subject, but nothing else turned up.

"Well, I'm sure that desk has more secrets to give up. Harry, why don't we carry it down to where it's cool and probe a bit more."

"Yeah, we can take it down, but we kinda know what we wanted to find out. I will get the desk fixed up. It would be a great graduation present for Gwen, don't you think?"

Susan nodded in the affirmative. "Wish I had some of the old furniture from the homeplace, but I doubt if my cousin Mike will ever let it out of the family home. He thinks of the place as a museum."

She thought about the banjo she had brought along. "By the way, Harry, you need to come to our mountains to play your music. I'm going to work up a festival for old-time ballads and folk music. The mountain music scene has been hot for years, but we need new blood instead of the same old players. You would fit right in. Maybe we can fit a family reunion in at the same time and sneak you in."

Chapter 18

Maggie

St. Petersburg, Florida, March 1934

The music had gone out of Maggie's heart. She didn't know whether to be angry or sad. Instead of these, her first reaction to Luther, or whoever he was, was to exact vengeance. "I'll pack up my things, take Junior with me, and show up on his doorstep. He looks enough like Papa that not a soul will doubt it. That would be an interesting family reunion." She fixed an evil sneer on her face.

But after her anger simmered and fizzled, she wondered if maybe it was a bad dream. She'd wake up, and it wouldn't be true. Maybe he was sick, and someone else wrote this and sent it to her. Maybe, maybe, maybe. She went through several scenarios. Here she was, saddled with an eight-year-old boy and no husband, and the boy's father had abandoned her.

People will see me as an unfit mother. That's how people are. Georgie will know what to do.

But with the hard times the country was going through and no more income from Luke, would Georgie and Jesse even stay with her? *Mom left a good bit in the bank; but will it lose value? I'm scared.*

When she got the letter, Junior was at school. She would go out back to Georgie's cottage and have a talk with the woman who had been as much a mother to her as her own mother had been.

Georgie knew something was wrong by the way Maggie stomped up the steps to their cottage. "Georgie, I gotta talk."

"Whatsa matta wif my baby girl? G'orgie be all ears." The plump, old black woman grabbed her ears and wiggled them. Usually that made Maggie laugh, but she was in no laughing mood.

Georgie had never learned to read and write, but her promised ears heard every word as Maggie read the letter to her.

"Oh lawsy, chile! I'd a neber thought dat nice man would turn out to be nuthin' else but de devil! What you gonna do? He won't be a-sendin' you money for de boy no more. How you gonna make it in dis bad Depression dat goin' on in de country?"

"We'll have to pull our belts tighter, Georgie. You need to teach me how to cook cheap food, for one thing. I can make desserts, and that's about it. And for certain, I don't need desserts! You've been cooking for us since my grandmother's time. But Georgie, I can't afford to pay you and Jesse, let alone buy nice things for Junior. I don't want to let you go, but what can I do?"

"Don' you worry dat head o' yourn, sweet chile. Jesse and me don' mind livin' here and makin' do wif what we got. You don' hafta pay us."

Georgie puzzled for a few moments. Then continuing, she said, "'Nother thing. We kin go live wif our daughter Sadie. She been a-wantin' us to live wif her ebber since Mistress Martha done passed. You could rent dis li'l cottage out."

"No! You stay here. We can eat the same food that you do, but you need to teach me how to make it. Not only can we not live on cake, but we can't afford it."

"Yassum."

Maggie cried, weeping on Georgie's shoulder for a long time. Finally, Georgie lifted her away. "Chile, you gotta dry dem eyes and be pert fo' Junior. He be comin' in from school any minute. Don' you let on to him dey's any trouble. He be de sunshine 'round hyar. De sunshine!"

Maggie did as Georgie advised, dried her tears, and put on her good face for Junior.

Over the next few months, Maggie got through the day seeing the sunny disposition of her boy. At first she didn't want music. But as her heart settled down, she began teaching him the banjo and fiddle, began teaching him the old songs, and found him an apt student. By the time school was ready to begin in the fall, he was pretty good at the banjo, and he seemed to pick up the fiddle as naturally as breathing. In fact, at school, he tried out and made it into the orchestra. He wanted to take lessons from the music teacher at school in the fall.

But by the end of the summer, it became obvious that Georgie and Jesse would not be able to remain there. Jesse was failing in his health, and Georgie was concerned. "He gonna die workin' de garden. Chile, we gotta move to live wif Sadie. Onliest thing we kin do. You gettin' good at cookin' dis simple food, so you gonna be okay. An' chile, I neber gwine tell no one what I knows."

Maggie's face paled and then reddened. Georgie was the only one who knew about the letter from Luther Willson. Maggie wanted to keep it that way. Forever. She knew she would have to hide the letter. With Junior getting to the age where exploration was a big thing, the letter would either need to be destroyed or hidden where no one would ever find it.

She left Georgie and went right to her mother's room, the first-floor bedroom where Martha had died. She knew there was a secret compartment in the desk. She had found it when she was a little girl, surprising her mother. *Mama didn't even know it was there, and we found some old coins in it.* Hide the letter, forget about Papa, and make a good life for Junior and herself.

After Christmas and into January 1935, she really missed Papa. That was always the worst because he had always been there until the years after Martha died. On a whim, she sent a letter to her old boyfriend. She knew he had gotten married and had a family, but with Georgie gone, she didn't have anyone she could talk to.

Eddie used to always listen to me. I don't know why Papa didn't like him. He saw him twice and ran him off both times. Eddie was sweet. She thought back to the last time he had come to see her. *Eddie and Junior were having a great time playing tiddlywinks on the kitchen table. Papa came in from one of his sales or maybe playing at a club. When he saw Eddie, he became angry. "Young man, I believe you are the cad who took liberties with my daughter a year or so ago. I asked you to leave then. Now, you have no business in our kitchen, and you have no business with my son. I will thank you to mind your priorities." That was all he said, and Eddie never came back. What did Papa know? What did Eddie know, for that matter? Well, I'm going to write to Eddie and tell him about Papa. That's what.*

She wrote the letter, telling him who Papa really was, and that she would like to talk with him. She hand carried it to Eddie's office, where he worked as junior partner in his father's law firm. She saw the brass nameplate on the door: Edward Meister Jr., Esq. She gave the letter to his secretary. Eddie never responded. She knew he wouldn't, but he had to know about Papa. One day she saw him on the street, and he turned his head the other way. Maggie knew she had no one. No one but Junior and her memories.

I'm twenty-nine years old, and I don't look too bad. Yes, I've had a weight problem, but now that I can't afford to eat all those sweets, maybe I'll lose weight and look good enough for a fellow.

She brainstormed ways she could meet a fellow. *Go to the few clubs that were still open and play the banjo and sing. The woman across the street would love to keep Junior for me if I did that. She'd fuss that a nice girl like me ought to stay out of places like that. She'd have me going to church with her. Well, I might do that. Maybe there would be a fellow there.* Her mind went in that vein for several scenarios, but in the end, she didn't do anything. Junior was her life. Junior was her boy.

Every now and then, she would retrieve the letter from her mother's desk and read it again. But it always made her cry. Then she would keep it away for months at a time. She loved the old desk, but it was getting wobbly. Maybe she should take it up to the attic. She would need help, and Junior was still too small. She let it remain in Martha's room for another year.

Chapter 19

Luke

Willson's Cove Chapel, North Carolina, April 1, 1934

Luther knew he had to make things right. *There is no going back to what wrongs I have done, but if I want God to forgive me, I have to come clean.*

Earlier in March, knowing he needed to come clean, difficult as it was to do, he had written to Maggie. Now it was time to make it right with Zanny. He only hoped she would not turn him out.

On Good Friday, March 30, 1934, he asked Zanny to take a walk with him. It was a short walk to the church graveyard. He led her to the spot where he wanted to be buried. "Zanny, I know one day both you and I will be a-lying here, dead and gone. But I have somethin' worse than my ol' bones that need to be dead and planted here now."

Zanny took a deep breath and placed her hand on Luther's arm. He looked at her face. He saw no condemnation, but he could see that she knew.

"You were right, darlin', when you figgered I had another woman in Floridy. I did. I have a son by her. She died right after the boy was born. I hope you will forgive me, although I will never deserve it even if I could erase it like it ne'er happened."

Zanny had tears in her eyes. She did not berate him. Instead, she slid her hand down his sleeve and took his hands in hers and looked into his eyes. "Luther, I forgave you twelve years ago. Forgiving don't mean the sin goes away, but the sin ain't gonna make me better or worse. If God can put our sins behind his back, how can I do less? I love you, and that's all there is to it."

As they walked out through the graveyard gate, Luther picked up an almost-dried cow pie where a cow had been some days before and tossed it into the nearby creek. "Hit's gone downstream. Gone, Zanny."

Two days later at the little chapel, on Easter Sunday, Luther walked the aisle as soon as the choir began singing "Come Ye Sinners." He knelt at the altar rail and poured his heart out to God. His words to God were between him and his Maker. Luther Willson stood a new man.

Chapter 20

Susan

Harry's house, St. Petersburg, Florida, August 2009

Susan watched as Harry and Mac hauled the desk to the second floor. There was a nice spot for it in the front bedroom, the room where Maggie had always slept. Harry currently designated it as one of their two guest rooms, although he said he never had guests. He produced some tools, and Mac got to work on tightening up loose bolts and gluing a fracture in one of the front legs.

"Not bad work for a general surgeon, Mac." Susan teased him.

"Yeah, I didn't have too much help from Catastrophe, but she kept winding her legs around mine and one of the back legs of the desk. Once this beauty is stable and the glue set, you can get some lemon oil furniture polish to clean it up. Probably take half an hour."

They stopped and played music for an hour, and then Susan took the items Harry brought from the broom closet and got to work on the desk, while the men went to the kitchen to get a drink and talk.

"You are a beauty! If you could only tell the tales of everyone who has sat here writing, you would be able to write the great American story, and it would all be true."

As she descended the steps, the doorbell rang. It was a pizza delivery guy. Harry was going to treat them to pizza and whatever for lunch.

"How long are you two planning to stay in St. Pete? Not that I want to get rid of you."

Susan shrugged and grinned. She could think of a lot of things she'd like to do while they were in St. Petersburg. "Maybe a few more days. We need to get back to Blowing Rock and enjoy some cool weather before we leave for Macon next month."

"Then we need to help get Jack's family moved into my place and downsize our part of the house," Mac added.

The three sat down to enjoy their pizza and some soft drinks, each occupied with their own thoughts.

Susan was thinking, *What if the DNA proves that we are kin? Well, I have no doubt, but what are the consequences? Do I tell our family? I'm an only child, but I have a zillion cousins—well, twelve living—who would be shocked at the least and irate at the most. Who would I talk to first? What if someone told Aunt Carrie and really hurt her.*

Harry voiced what she was thinking. "Susan, what are you going to do about it when we prove what we already know? Will you tell your cousins? Your aunt? And I never asked: do you have children?"

"No children. My daddy's line stopped with me. I was just mulling the same thing over in my mind. I am uncertain whether to tell Aunt Carrie. She might be hurt too deeply. On the other hand, she isn't all that fragile, but she was Grandpa's pet. I just realized she is only six months older than Junior."

"That's wild. Sister and brother only six months apart."

"We are the dozen cozzin family. Used to be a lot more, but only twelve of us left. I do need to tell them, but tactfully. There will be a reunion next summer, so I will need to approach each of my cousins before reunion arrangements are made, and go from there. Oh boy!"

"Then there is dealing with my children." Mac grinned at his wife. "I have two sons and a daughter. My boys, Jack and Bob, are down to earth despite their successes in life, but my daughter, Jessica, tends to be a bit uppity when it comes to social proprieties. I can hear her now. 'Father, you have married into a common family. Blah, blah, blah.' Don't be surprised at a snub, honey."

"Snubs I can handle. Snobs? Well, I can be just as snobbish! But I don't see Jessica as a snob."

They chatted more about the implications of the newly discovered relationship. "Harry, what about your daughter? Will you tell her?"

"Of course. She will love this. Gwen is the best thing that ever happened to my wife and me. When you get to know her better, you'll see what I mean."

"What happened to your wife? Death? Divorce?"

"No, Gloria died five years ago when Gwen was sixteen. It was a botched anesthesia job during a simple colonoscopy procedure. I was bitter after that for a long time. In fact, this business with Papa Whoever has brought me out of my five-year funk to the world of the living. Thank you, Susan. You have given me a shot in the arm."

Susan looked on her probable cousin with compassion. She had lost a mate many years ago. Her first husband had died in Vietnam, and she never wanted to remarry until she met Mac. "It's hard to lose someone you love. I know Gwen is a comfort."

"Yeah. Humph. Wish she didn't look so much like her momma. You were married before, Mac?"

She briefly told him about Joe, but she didn't like to talk about him. "Short marriage, no kids. I hate any reference to Vietnam!"

"Yeah. I was there. Thank goodness I survived."

While Susan helped Harry clean up the lunch mess, Mac went back to reassess the desk in the guest room.

Harry winked at Susan as they joined Mac in the guest bedroom. "Okay! Let's see what the surgeon has extracted from his procedure."

Mac was under the desk, probing every little spot that even gave an inkling of some button or box to push. Gwen's cat was curled up sleeping on the rug next to him, and her tail was wrapped around one of the back desk legs. "I've expected something to jump out at me for the last hour, but nothing but the cat has jumped out of anything. I may well relinquish my search. Nothing."

"Well, we know what we want to know most likely. Mac, I think we need to go back to our lodging and take a rest. I'm plumb wore to a frazzle, as my grandma used to say."

"How about a bit of jammin' before you two go back to your bed-and-breakfast?"

They got out their instruments and played through three or four songs. But Susan was tired, and Harry, too, had not had much sleep.

"Fun, but maybe tomorrow, huh?"

"Gotcha. Harry, thank you for the enjoyable time together. We will hang around town and sightsee for a couple of days and then head back to North Carolina. Come with me, my bride."

"The pleasure has been mutual, Mac. I have some business to tend to tomorrow, but I should be free in the evening. Gwen has off tomorrow evening, so how about dinner here? I want you to get to know her, and we can tell her all about our family relationship. No sense waiting for DNA."

"I'd like that. Sixish?"

"Yeah. Sixish is good."

In the car going back to the Larelle, Susan was quiet.

"Did Catastrophe get your tongue?"

"No. Just trying to process all this. Mac, what if the DNA comes back that we actually aren't kin. I think I will be terribly disappointed. I think Harry will be, too. He doesn't have anyone but an aged father and a busy daughter. I want him to have us."

"Think of this, honey: even if it is negative for kinship, you have given him hope, and our friendship can serve as family."

"Yeah. Adopt him."

"I doubt if this will be an issue. He's family. I'm looking forward to getting to know his daughter, too."

Susan nodded and retreated into her silence.

When they got back to the inn, Mac grabbed some brochures from the lobby. Since they planned to stay a couple more days, it would be well spent enjoying some local tourist attractions. "How about this one, Susan? The Dolphin Racer Speedboat Adventure. It's a two-hour cruise around the gulf. One thirty tomorrow afternoon. I'll call them in the morning to see if they have room. What do you say?"

"I'd love it. Another thing we can do is go to the fine arts museum. There is plenty to keep us out of, or maybe I should say, in trouble!"

They went to bed talking about their plans for the next few days. Mac drifted off, while Susan was quiet for a few minutes. Then she touched his shoulder to awaken him. "Mac, do you think Harry should tell his dad? And should I tell Aunt Carrie? I want to do the right thing, and I think he does as well. If I had a sister or brother, I'd want to know."

Mac grunted and turned his back to her. Susan fretted for another half hour before she went to sleep.

Chapter 21

Susan

St. Petersburg, Florida, August 2009

After a delightful two-hour cruise on the Dolphin and a little nap, Susan and Mac cleaned up and walked to Harry's place. Gwen met them at the door; the ever-present Catastrophe was rubbing up against her leg.

"Just in time. I think between the two of us, Dad and I have managed to put together a suitable meal. We don't get to cook too often, but we enjoy it when we do. Follow me." She led them to the front room. "Want some drinks? Wine, cocktail, soda?"

Mac asked for a glass of wine, but Susan only wanted water. Harry brought in a ring of shrimp and dip, and they sat around chatting while a delicious aroma wafted in from the kitchen, despite the swinging door that separated it from the rest of the house.

"Dad tells me you are a retired surgeon, Mac. General surgery or a specialty?" Gwen showed her interest.

"General for the most part. I have done my share of, shall we say, more challenging surgeries, but these were when I got into the surgery and found more than we bargained for. It was good to have someone to consult when such things happened. No, I'm just an appendix and gallbladder guy."

Gwen laughed at his easy interaction. She wasn't used to the doctors treating her like a real person. "I like you. Most doctors at the hospital just look through me like I'm not there."

Mac laughed, lifting his eyebrows, but made no comment.

Gwen went on to tell him what she did. "I'm in nursing college right now and jockeying bedpans at St. Anthony's Hospital. Nursing assistant. Highfalutin name for a nurse's aide."

"What area?"

"General population, so I get all your appendectomies and gallbladders."

She turned to Susan. "I heard you playing with Grandpa at Legacy. You're good. I see you brought your banjo with you tonight."

Susan nodded. "Yes. I used to play a bluegrass banjo with a heavy resonator on the back. My arthritis compromised my ability to play. I had almost given up playing when your father sold me this little gem. I had the best time playing with your grandfather. Do you play?"

"No. Got my mom's genetic code. I enjoy listening, but don't ask me to even sing, unless it's 'Froggy Went A-Courtin'.'"

Harry laughed. "She claims she sounds like the frog."

"Hopefully not when he gets 'swallered by a water snake." Susan started humming it.

Harry put his hand on his daughter's arm. "Uh, Gwen, speaking of genetic code, we need to talk about that tonight. Susan and I think we are related and have sent off DNA to be tested. We will know in six to eight weeks."

"Say what? Thought you were just friends. Something more?"

Harry looked at her, indicating it could wait. "Let's get supper on the table and eat, then we can talk about it. Come, folks. *Un grande cuoco* Enrico's famous chicken cacciatore coming up. And Gwen, please put that cat out on the back porch. We don't need her underfoot at the table."

"And I made the salad and dessert," Gwen said, as she closed the porch door on the cat.

The mealtime was filled with nonconsequential chatter about everything from the weather, to politics, to advances in medical care;

things those at the table really cared little about at the moment. What Gwen really wanted to talk about, she didn't dare.

The meal did honor to *grande cuoco* Enrico and Gwen, and after Susan helped Gwen clear the table, they all went back to the living room. Gwen said they could load the dishwasher after they talked.

"Okay, Gwen, here it is." Harry began. "Susan heard me playing up in Apalachicola and recognized her grandfather's style of playing the fretless banjo and his versions of the old songs. She was certain the banjo was one her grandfather had built and asked to see it. Susan, go on and tell her."

"I could not only recognize the songs, but I pinpointed them to our hollow, Willson's Cove. It was uncanny. I had been searching for a banjo Grandpa had made back in his day for years, but they were as elusive as the fog on Grandfather Mountain, if you know about that."

Gwen shrugged. "I've never been to the mountains."

"I asked your dad if I could see his banjo, looked inside, and saw Grandpa's initials. Bingo! Then I asked about the banjo and the songs. He told me his grandfather had sold banjos, fiddles, and dulcimers. He sang the old songs and taught his daddy and grandmother to play and sing.

"I was suspicious right away that his grandfather, Luke Harvey, and mine, Luther Willson, may have been the same person. I went to the family home and rooted about in the attic, looking for something to confirm or dispute the fact. I found letters he wrote to my grandmother back in North Carolina. Meanwhile, Mac found stacks of letters from my grandmother and from your great-grandmother, Martha, to him and some from Maggie after Martha had died. He had obviously used a false name in St. Petersburg, courted and supposedly married Martha, and lived a double life."

Gwen's brow was furrowed, but she was silent. She looked at her dad.

"Gwen, here's the abbreviated story: I found bunches of letters here, too. Letters from a man named Luke Harvey, and then a final letter to Maggie in 1934. In that letter, he confessed who he really was, Luther Willson. He asked her to forgive him and told her he couldn't send any more money to her for Dad. They were in an old desk in the attic. Mac and I brought the desk down and put it in the guest room. He fixed it up."

"Geez-Loo-eeze, Dad! I'm confused here. You are talking about him being married to Martha? I thought Maggie was grandpa's mom. What was going on?"

"Oh, yeah. Dad knew that Martha was his mother since he was eighteen, but since Martha died a day or two after he was born, he considered Maggie to be his mother. And that's what he always told me. But Grandma Maggie was his mother as far as he was concerned, although she was really his half sister."

"Ha! Dad, wait till Mom's hoity-toity sister hears this. She always considered us white trash, and now she can gloat. Love it! Susan, you will make far better kinfolk that Aunt Elvina's set. You gonna crash the next Willson family reunion, Dad?"

"Thought about it."

Susan giggled at Gwen's magnanimous, almost devil-may-care attitude about the entire situation. "I have invited him. We are planning one next summer. You will need to come as well."

"So let me get this straight: Luke and Luther are one and the same. Luther was married to a wife in North Carolina. Luke was so-called married to Martha Lindsay, my great-grandmother. Maggie raised grandpa. So how many kids did my great-grandfather have in North Carolina?"

"Nine. Only one, Aunt Carrie, is still living. She is only six months older than Junior."

"Oh! They've gotta meet! Just gotta. This is so cool."

"Oh yeah, and more, Dad. It really doesn't have a lot to do with this situation, but I've found letters in Grandpa's room. I moved in there after he went to Legacy. I loved having that fireplace in there, not that I'd use it. I never noticed before when he was here that there were little cupboards on each side, facing ninety degrees to the room and the windows on each side. They are little and had been mostly concealed by the drapes he had at the windows. I was cleaning, having taken the drapes down for cleaning, when I noticed them. 'Letters, we've got letters. We've got lots and lots of letters.'"

"From Perry Como?" Mac asked.

"Huh? Who?" The reference to the 1950s crooner was missed on this millennial person. "No, they are back-and-forth letters from Grandpa and Nana, when he was in World War II, and a few from Grandma Maggie—guess it's still okay to call her that—from her to Grandpa. They look like an answer to ones he must have written to her. Okay, this is what I learned: Grandpa met Nana Stella at the USO right after he was drafted into the army. Her family, I gathered, wasn't too happy, but the lovers figured it would be wise to marry since she was pregnant. Dad, you had a sister. She died while Grandpa was in the army. He never got to see his daughter. Grandma Maggie was excited and was looking forward to having Nana and the baby here, but when the little one died, Nana went back to stay with her people in Tampa."

"Humph. Never knew it. Maybe that's why Mom doted on me. Used to drive me bonkers. Funny Dad never mentioned it."

"You gonna ask him about it?"

Harry shrugged. "In light of our present situation, it makes no difference. Gwen, we need to deal with the Harvey-Willson connection now."

Susan explained to Gwen her supposed origin of the Luke Harvey name. "I think that since Grandpa's real name was Luther, Luke was close but different, so he chose to be Luke. My father, Harvey, was Grandpa's third son. That may be a family name back a couple of generations. I do intend to look into it."

"That's interesting. Ha! The *Genealogy of a Mixed-up Family*. Might make for good tabloid reading. Oh, when do you find out the scientific confirmation of our kinship to this lovely lady, Dad?"

"Might be a couple of months. We both have pretty much accepted the reality of our kinship."

"Dad, what if it turns up to be negative? Will you be disappointed?"

"Of course. I never had cousins or siblings, despite the sister you sprang on me a few minutes ago. I want family, and I want it for you. I know you have cousins on your mother's side, but they are pretty much out of the picture. Your mother's sister has seen to that, especially after Gloria passed away. Yeah, I want to prove that I am a true Willson, legitimate or not."

"Yeah. The last time I saw my cousins, they completely isolated me and talked behind their hands, giggling in my direction. I can't say I hate them. Mom would take exception to that. But I don't particularly like them."

"Honest, aren't you? Mind your manners, lady. Company here."

Susan laughed. "We aren't company. We're family. And this part of the family needs to help cleaning up the dishes and getting back to our lodgings."

"Not without some music first. I need to hear you and Dad play together. 'Dueling Banjos!'"

"You're on!" Harry said. "You know that one, don't you, Susan?"

"I do."

They got out the banjos and dueled. Then they went into "Cripple Creek" and "Little Maggie."

While putting away her banjo, Susan outlined their plan for the next day. "We plan a day of tourist attractions tomorrow. By the way, this was the most delicious meal we have had since being in St. Petersburg, including the Marchlands. You two could go into restaurant business. And Gwen, I need your recipe for your chocolate mousse."

Gwen grinned at her dad, and they both bowed dramatically. "And Susan, you may help me in the kitchen and give Dad and Dr. Mac a chance to sit outside and lie to each other. And we can get a chance to have some girl talk."

"No lies, daughter. I intend to get into those letters from Mom and Dad. And Mac wants to do further surgery on the old desk. We moved it down to the guest room."

"No more 'surgery'. Just 'physical examination'. I am convinced there is more to find," Mac said.

Gwen let Catastrophe back in the house and then delved right into what was on her mind. "Susan, I think we need to tell Grandpa about this. I know him. He would want to know the truth. He has always been reticent to talk about the family. I'll bet he knows more than we think he does. His mind isn't as bad most of the time as Dad thinks it is. He uses his forgetfulness as a convenience sometimes. We have had long talks about things since he went to Legacy. He's sharper than he lets on. They changed his medications, and I think that has made a huge difference in his memory issues."

"You may be right, Gwen. Do you think you have the rapport with him to tell him?"

"Dad may not agree, but I think I would be better at it than he is. After Mom died, most of the time it was just Grandpa and me. Dad couldn't stand to stay around long. That's when he started touring with his banjo. He's good, and he can make money at it, not that he needs to. He has a pretty healthy retirement nest egg, and then there is a settlement we got for negligence from Mom's death."

"We've never discussed his career prior to retirement. What did he do?"

"He was a financial advisor with Raymond James Investments here in St. Pete. Did well in the organization. He took early retirement. Got into investments after Vietnam."

Susan nodded. "Ah! Now I have a new appreciation for the man whose first impression suggested more of a hippie or beachcomber than a financier."

"Dad wants it that way. So do you agree that I should tell Grandpa?"

"Gwen, only you and Harry can make that determination. If you get an argument from him, though, I will be happy to encourage him to consider it. That said, don't push it too hard. It may be that your dad needs to do this as a part of resolution to what has been a real crisis for him. I'm speaking from the feelings I've had related to this."

"I see what you mean. I'll tread gently."

"Let me tell you why I am reluctant to tell Aunt Carrie. My aunt is a strong person and could probably take it without emotional collapse. However, she adored my grandfather. She was the youngest of the nine children, and until she went to school, she shadowed him continuously. He even took her along on his train trips to Johnson City when she was just a little girl, the only one of the children he ever took with him. She told me once that her best memories were before the Great Depression when they took the train over the mountain. She said that the trips stopped during after the Crash in 1929, and it was a great disappointment to her. Did she know about the secret post office box in Johnson City, Tennessee? Did she know about the secret cache of letters in his workroom? I don't know. If she did know about it, she has purposely kept it to herself for more than eighty years. Honestly, I am afraid to tell her. Yet like you feel about telling Junior, I think I should tell her."

Gwen hesitated before saying anything else. Susan noticed that she raised her face, eyes closed toward the ceiling, like she was praying.

"Susan, I act tough and irreverent. I'm not really that way. I believe in God, and I believe he has opened up this situation for his purposes. Dad is not religious and might pooh-pooh that statement. I truly believe this situation has come to light so a wrong can be made right. By that I mean, I think your, or our, Aunt Carrie and my grandfather are meant to know each other. What I would like to see happen, if they both live until your family reunion next summer, is that they should both be there and unite our family."

"I tend to agree with you. I never thought about what we call providence. But you may be right. If you believe that way, I suppose you could pray for the right decisions."

The dishes were done, and Gwen handed her a recipe card for Frangelico chocolate mousse. The two women went in search of Harry and Mac.

When they found Harry, he was seated on Gwen's bed, surround by letters. He looked up at his daughter with tears edging his eyes. "Her name was Gwen. When you were born, Dad had asked if we could name you Gwen. Now I know why."

Gwen gave her dad a hug and pulled Susan away from the door. They went to the guest room to find Mac prodding and poking about the desk. Catastrophe was settled at his feet.

"Looks like Catastrophe thinks you are special," Gwen said.

"She's no bother. I don't have pets, but she's okay."

"Any luck?" his wife asked.

"Nope. Maybe we have found everything we need to find. I was just rereading some of the letters. Harry put them back in the desk.

The one he had been reading was the infamous confession letter to Maggie in 1934. He handed it to Gwen. She cried when she read it.

Chapter 22

Luke Junior

Legacy at Highwoods Assisted Living, Tampa, Florida, August 2009

The next day, Junior thought about that letter his granddaughter had cried over the night before. *I remember when Mom got a letter from Papa that made her cry. I was at school when the mail boy came, but when I got home, I could see she had been crying. Mom was such a bright and cherry person; it frightened me to see her eyes red and her face so sad. She wouldn't tell me why but just sent me outside. Didn't even make me do my arithmetic like she usually did. What was I? About twelve? Yeah.*

That's the letter I found in her old desk. When I read that, after Stella died, I hated Papa. I can't hate anymore. Luther Willson: a name I'll never forget. I don't know who I am. I'm not a Harvey because that name didn't really exist for me. I'm not truly a Willson because my mother was not really married to him, no matter who he was. Guess I'm really a Lindsay. But I've got nine Willson brothers and sisters. Wonder if any of them are still living.

Junior's mind wandered off into what he termed as *neverland* for a long time, until the attendant brought his evening medicine for him. The girl's name was Jasmine Jones, but he called all the girls good-lookin'.

"Hey, good-lookin', whatcha got cookin'?" he sang.

"Let's see, a red one for my eyes, white one for my cholesterol, tan one to help me sleep, two orange ones for my arthritis, and that vile stuff to keep my bowels working. Why don't you just bring me a bottle of beer? It oughta do the same thing."

"Now, Mister Junior! Why do we have to have this same conversation every night. You'd think you could think of something more exciting to talk about than your pills and vile stuff."

"Okay, how about this. My real name isn't Junior Harvey. It's Luke Lindsay. I'm really not a junior at all because my father's name was Luther. Yes, I'm the last of the Mohicans."

"Oh? Can we take that to the bank?"

"Not on my bank account. I am legally Luke Harvey Jr., but if the truth were told, there was never a Luke Harvey Sr. Guess I'm stuck with what I got. Just Luke."

Jasmine giggled and shook her head. She would report Mister Junior's delusions to the head nurse.

When she left, he went back to his reminiscing.

I went out back to find Jesse. He was huffin' and puffin' with the hoe in the garden, almost too short of breath to do the most minimal gardening. I grabbed the hoe and began cultivating. The corn and the beans were up, and the cabbage and cucumber seedlings needed to be set in the ground. I needed to learn this stuff, if we were to survive the Depression. I would rather be inside playing the fiddle, but Mom needed me to get away. I guess I understood more than I wanted to.

Later that evening, at the supper table, she seemed to be her old self again. She told me that Papa would not be coming back anymore, that I was never to ask about it again.

I used to ask all the time "When is Papa coming home?" That was the end of that.

When she told me that, I didn't want to play my fiddle. I didn't want to sing the songs he taught me. I was hurt? Angry? Confused? Yeah, I guess all three. I would just stick to the violin music I was playing at school.

Then one day, Mom got out her banjer—that's what Papa always called the banjo. I don't know that I realized till now, that when I wasn't sawing on my fiddle, neither was she plinking her banjer. When I heard her pickin', I went and got the fiddle, and we started playing. I think we sounded lots better for the vacation from the music.

One day she said, "You know, Junior, Papa made these instruments himself. It wasn't anyone else but him. Don't you tell it, but don't you forget neither."

He crawled into bed and was soon asleep, but he dreamed of the lady who came and played banjo with him several weeks before. But in the dream, it was Mom, not the white-haired lady. It wasn't until the next evening that he thought about the banjo lady, and the dream filtered back into his head. He was a little confused at first but then recalled that it had happened here at Legacy.

That woman. Can't recall her name. Good-lookin' is good enough for a name. She was, too. And she played the way Mom played. The way Papa played. Odd. Wonder if she knew any of Papa's people. Hope she comes back someday.

He got out his fiddle and played for the next half hour, ignoring his stiff hands. The music took him back to the last time he played with Mom before he left for World War II.

It was the second time I had seen her cry. I didn't want her to cry, but I had to leave. We played and sang all the old songs till our fingers were sore and our throats were hoarse. I told her about Stella. She was mad at first till I told her a baby was on the way. My, how that woman loved babies, so it was good. She said, "Marry the girl."

He dozed off and dreamed again, but the dreams were mixed up with people he saw every day and those from when he was a boy. When he woke up, he was addled and wandered out to the common area. There was a nice-looking white-haired lady seated by a window, doing a crossword. He approached her.

"Aren't you the lady who came and played banjo with me?"

She jerked her head back and scowled, and then she laughed. "Me? Play the banjo? No, I only play piano. It's been a long time since I have even heard a banjo."

"I am sorry, my dear. I mistook you for someone else. May I introduce myself? I'm Juni—I mean, Luke Harvey. Why don't you join me for a doughnut and a cup of coffee or tea, and then you can tickle the ivories on that grand piano over there?"

She frowned. "Could I?"

She took a deep breath and smiled. "Good to meet a friendly person. I'm new here."

He must have hit her soft spot. She got up, and they walked together to the coffee bar. That was where Harry found him half an hour later.

Chapter 23

Harry

Legacy at Highwoods Assisted Living, Tampa, Florida, August 2009

Harry knew after reading the letters from his parents to each other, he needed to see Junior. He and Gwen had the discussion about telling Junior, but Harry insisted that he should be the one to tell him. Gwen had read only one of those letters. She conceded.

Harry was surprised to see his father chatting away with an elegant lady. *I've seen her before.* He scratched his head and watched them for a few minutes, hating to interrupt. *Dad hasn't really socialized since he came here, according to the staff. I'm glad to see him interact with someone.*

About that time, they got up from their refreshments and headed to the piano. *This should be interesting. I never knew Dad to be much for piano. He was a string band fellow from the get-go.*

But when the woman began to play, Harry saw his father was fascinated. The woman was an accomplished artist. *Ah, I've seen her picture in the entertainment section of the* Tampa Bay Times. She was playing Chopin, Beethoven, and Rubenstein like she belonged in a concert hall. It took him back to the records Gloria would play for hours on end. His heart gave a lurch.

It wasn't long before an audience had gathered, and when she was done, the applause and bravos filled the room. She stood and curtsied. Junior was beaming, obviously enjoying the fact that she was his friend.

Harry joined them.

"Hey there, son. How did you like that? Isn't she a wonder? It's been awhile since I heard music like that. Meet my new friend, Miss... I didn't get your name."

"Hello. I am Lynelle Van Sant. You can call me Lynnie, if you wish. I just moved in here. This is the first I played the piano as a resident. I have played it before when I came here to entertain." She nodded to Harry. "You are Luke's son?"

Luke, is it? "I know Dad will enjoy having a musical friend. He is very good on the fiddle. He surprises me all the time. My name is Harry, Harry Harvey. Do you mind if I steal him for a while?"

"Not at all." She turned to Junior and thanked him for encouraging her to play. "I wanted to play that beautiful piano again, but I needed your encouragement, Luke. Maybe you would like to join me for dinner? I like to eat at six."

"I would like that. I may have to be reminded. Seem to have some short-term memory issues. Though they aren't as bad as they used to be before the doc changed my medicine."

"I understand. Me too." She turned and went toward her suite.

Junior's room was called a regency suite, with a bedroom and living room, a large bathroom, and a microwave and tiny refrigerator. It was all Junior needed. When they got to the room, Junior looked quizzically at his son and laughed. "I'm surprised to see you. Weren't you here not too long ago? I'm not used to that, you know."

"It is always my intention to see you as often as possible when I'm in town. I have been doing some research, so I need to hang around for a while before I head out for more lucrative gigs."

"You got something on your mind. I can see that look in your eyes."

"Yeah." He sighed, dreading to broach the subject. "Yeah, I know you told me the last time I was here to let things alone, but I have had something come up. Well, someone came along who has really stirred the pot. Dad, I have learned that we are not who we think we are."

Junior grinned like a monkey.

"I imagine you know what I have learned, but up to now, you have kept it to yourself. I know that your father was really Luther Willson, not Luke Harvey. Dad, we have bunches of family in North Carolina!"

"Aha. You found Mom's letter from my father. Yes, I've known about it since the day your mother was buried. You had gone, so I wandered up to the attic and was messing around with an old desk of Mom's. I found the letter hidden in a secret compartment. I was shocked and angry, but I decided it would serve no purpose to delve into it. Why did you get interested, Harry?"

Harry wasn't sure his father would remember the conversation. If he did, could he keep it straight? But he charged ahead, telling about his initial encounter with Susan and the subsequent research both of them had done.

"Dad, this Susan was the woman who came and played banjo with you a few weeks ago. You remember that?"

"Oh yes, I was a bit mixed up about it today, thinking that pretty piano player was her. What did you think of her?"

"She is great, but let's get back to the situation at hand. Susan is your niece, and you still have a living sister. Her name is Carrie, or Carolina, and she is only six months older than you. She lives in a retirement home in the mountains of North Carolina, but her mind is good."

Junior looked out the window as though he was trying to take in what his son was telling him. Then he turned back to Harry with tears running down his cheeks. "Will you take me to see her? I can't drive anymore. I wish I had pursued it when I learned about it."

"It's okay, Dad. There is to be a family reunion next year. How about if we go then? The weather up there will be getting a bit too wintery soon, but next summer would be ideal."

"I hate to wait. After all, I'm eighty-seven, be eighty-eight by then, if I am still alive. I guess my sister would need to learn that I exist before I show up on her doorstep. This Susan: would she talk to her and let her know she has a brother who wants to meet her?"

"I'm sure she will. One thing, though. We are accepting that it's true based on piles of letters. Susan and I have considered that it may not be true, so we sent off DNA tests. It will be awhile for the results. On the outside chance that Susan and I do not match, would you be able to confirm that the letters are authentic?"

"I have no doubt, Harry. My mind isn't nearly as fragile as you think it is. This I know: it will be true. I've known it for twenty years, and now I'm ashamed that I never did anything about it. It is sad. I need to meet my sister. What's her name again?"

"Carrie, short for Carolina."

"I like that. Carolina."

"Sister. Uh, Dad, I learned from some other letters we found that I had a sister, too. Why didn't you and Mom tell me?"

Junior looked out the window again and was quiet for an uncomfortable minute. Finally, he turned back to his son. "Your mother refused to talk about it. She doted on you, of course, but she never got over the baby she lost. Her name was Gwen. That is why we wanted you to name your baby Gwen. That way she would be our girl, too. Guess it was silly on our part. I'm sorry I never told you."

"It's okay, Dad. Like Gwen said, we have a mixed-up family."

"Nah. All families are mixed up. Ours is unique."

"I will work with Susan to see if we can get you to North Carolina before the bad weather sets in. Might be nice up there in October with the bright-colored leaves. Maybe the DNA results will be back before then."

Chapter 24

Susan

Macon, Georgia, October 2009

After three of days of sightseeing, Susan and Mac headed back to Blowing Rock. They were only staying a few days to take care of some business and run over to see Aunt Carrie in her new surroundings at the Life Care Center in Banner Elk.[8] *Not sure if I should tell her what I know just yet. Maybe the DNA will be back soon, and I can prove what we already know.*

Susan was pleased to see her aunt in a fresh, clean, and safe place, but she wished she could have the amenities Junior had in Tampa.

"La, honey, where have you been? How was the honeymoon? Y'ain't gonna have a baby yet, are ya?" Aunt Carrie laughed at her own joke.

"I guess age seventy is a bit old for that, unless I am a reincarnated mother of John the Baptist!"

They visited half an hour, and then Susan had to leave. Visiting Aunt Carrie was always a pleasant event. It was like being with Mama and Daddy.

On her way out, she saw many residents in various stages of debilitation. She shuddered to think she would end up here in the future. *Maybe Mac and I can go live somewhere like where Junior lives.*

She and Mac left for Macon the next day, hoping to get their business done there and back to the High Country before cold weather. October would be great with changing leaves.

It was hot in Macon.

Mac wiped his brow. "Now I know why I bought a place in Blowing Rock. I didn't mind St. Petersburg as much as this."

"The bay breeze. I enjoyed it there, especially early morning and late evening. But I don't want to move there anytime soon."

Part of the perspiration induced was a result of moving furniture from various parts of the house into the three rooms they would claim as their quarters anytime they were in Macon. And they were getting rid of a lot of furniture, books, and other household goods. Jack's wife, Judy, was there every day to help and to determine what she would like to retain as the new lady of the house. She and Susan got along famously.

Susan smiled at her step-daughter-in-law. "Judy, I'm so glad you will keep some of these treasured things. I'm sure they will mean a lot to the family. A lot more than they would mean to me if I took them. Mac and I have all we need."

Later that evening, when Susan checked her e-mail on Mac's big computer, the DNA website popped up on the screen. *Results? I hope so. Might just be a letter acknowledging that they are working on it.*

Actually, it was two separate e-mails. One was several days old, but since they hadn't been at the Macon house, the computer had not been on. The first was the acknowledgment letter. The second was a link to the actual report.

"Yippee! Hope Harry got his, too."

She went through all the sections and finally came to lists of family names. There were Vance relatives, Frampton relatives, and fifty other names. *Where is Willson? Where is Gentry? I don't see any until way down the line!*

She scanned every name listed on down to potential fourth and fifth cousins before she found even one Gentry and still no Willson.

"What's going on here? Mac, come here," she called him from the next room, where he was putting books in a bookshelf.

"Yes, my love? You have a frown on your pretty face. What's wrong?"

"I have no evidence that I am a Willson! It was a waste of effort to do a DNA! Worse, I'm probably adopted! Oddly enough, I have a connection to my first cousin, Will, Aunt Carrie's son, as first cousin, a Vance. I don't understand. Could they have gotten my spit mixed up with someone else's?"

"Honey, there may be a perfectly logical reason for no Willsons listed. Maybe no one with that spelling has ever been tested. As for your cousin, Will, I wouldn't say it is wrong. What about your mother's family name?"

"I had some Gentrys listed like potential fourth cousins. And Grandma's name was Gregg. I had one Gregg potential fifth cousin. That's just wrong. Who am I?"

Susan's cell phone rang. It was Harry. "Hey, coz! It's real. I have Willson relatives, at least two first cousins listed, and some second and thirds, too."

"No, we aren't cousins. I just got mine back, and I'm not a Willson! Oh, Harry! How can this be?"

"No! Of course you are. What do you mean?"

She repeated what she had just told Mac. "Harry, I don't know who I am. Mac suggested that maybe there have not been anyone with the name Willson who have ever been tested."

"Not true. Do we have a first cousin named Clyde?"

"Yes! He's Uncle Luther's boy. I'm not too surprised that he would have had his DNA tested. He's pretty savvy and the most well-off of all my cousins. He left, spent four years in the Navy during World War II, went to college on the GI bill, and eventually became a successful businessman in Raleigh. It would be like him to think about ancestry DNA. Do you have a Lily May Sturgill? I don't know if she had hers done, but she is big into genealogy."

"There is a LMS, Banner Elk, North Carolina, listed as first cousin."

"That's her. Then how about William Vance, Aunt Carrie's son? He is the only one listed for me. It doesn't make sense. If he's my cousin, why aren't Clyde and Lily May listed as mine?"

"Oh, Susan. Could you have been a child of one of Aunt Carrie's in-laws? That's weird!"

"Well, I'm headed up to North Carolina as soon as I can get there. Aunt Carrie has some explaining to do!"

"I'm happy with my results. Kind of gave me a settled feeling. But now you are unsettled."

"Well, to change the subject, if not reality, did you go visit your daddy?"

"Yeah. I need to coordinate something with you. He wants to meet his sister. What do you think? He said he needs to meet her, but he doesn't want to wait till next summer. He is afraid one of them will die before then. I thought maybe now would be a great time to be in the mountains, with all the turning leaves in a couple of weeks. Since you plan to go see our aunt, will you tell her what we learned and see if she is amenable to meet her half brother?"

"I will. We will get it arranged as soon as we can. You know, Harry, Aunt Carrie's husband was a Vance, so I would guess she would have been in on the ground floor of where I came from. I'm hurt that no one ever considered telling me the truth, and I'm angry that I had to find out from a sterile DNA lab! I think I have to tell her now, since I just found out I'm probably adopted."

After her pouting, in a brighter tone, she agreed. "It will be beautiful by the second week of October. I'll consult with Aunt Carrie's oldest daughter, Gladdie, and test the waters with her before I see Aunt Carrie. I don't think Auntie is so fragile that her health would suffer. Yes, it will be emotional, but she has been through enough in her life to withstand a tsunami."

"I told Dad about the DNAs we are doing. He indicated that even if the DNA proved otherwise, what we found out is true."

"I'm glad for your sake and for his, but for mine, well, you get the picture!"

"Ticked."

"Yeah!"

After Susan hung up the phone, she printed out several pages of the DNA results, shut down the computer, and went directly to the bathroom and plugged in her hot brush. As soon as it was ready, she straightened her hair and put on platform sandals.

When Mac saw her hair, he scowled. "What the? Where are your curls?"

"Well, since I'm the only one with the last name of Willson with curly hair, I decided to straighten it. I'm adopted. Now I know why my hair was different and why I'm the runt of the litter."

"You really think so? Adopted, huh? What about Harry?"

"He's a Willson and a Lindsay, of course. He's more Willson than I will ever be."

"I doubt that. If you are adopted, it is because they wanted you. By the way: I like curls / I like short girls. / They caught my eye, / When I did spy!"

"My, aren't we poetic!"

Mac handed her his pocketknife. "Here, you can scrape off the sarcasm."

Chapter 25

Susan

Life Care Center, Banner Elk, North Carolina, three days later

Susan, with her straight hair, and Mac left Macon. They had all their changes made in the house, and it was ready for Jack and his family to move in. It was two days after she received the readout on the DNA. The platform shoes had lasted on her feet for about two hours, and by the end of the day, her hair was curly again. She straightened it again before they left for North Carolina. She was still angry, but her fury had abated enough that she was calm enough to drive. She alternately fumed and speculated, with Mac enduring the brunt of her diatribe. He was patient with her, allowing her to be the first driver. Despite the fact that they were newlyweds, he knew that if she concentrated on driving, her fire would soon fizzle out. When it did, he took over the wheel. They drove straight through, stopping for food and fuel and arriving in Blowing Rock at midnight. When she looked in the mirror before going to bed, her hair was curly again. She just sighed.

Driving home, Susan called her cousin Gladdie. "Hey, young'un. I'm on my way back to the mountains, and I need to see your mama tomorrow. Something has come up in the family that I think she is the only one who can set it straight. I would like to see you first and tell you what it's all about, but I can't talk about it over the phone."

"She's doing fine, and yeah, I'll be home tomorrow all day. Do I need to go to the home with you?"

"Not sure. After I talk to you, we can decide that together."

Now twenty-four hours later, she and Gladdie were driving down the little driveway in front of Life Care Center. Gladdie had voiced her shock with the news about Grandpa. Susan had only given her a summarized version, but it was enough to confirm the truth of the matter.

Gladdie was wearing a wrinkled brow. "I never knew anything about this, Susan. And I sure never heard that you're adopted. Could the test have been wrong?"

"That is why I have to talk to your mother. I am going to point-blank ask her if I was adopted, but should I go ahead and drop the real bombshell?"

"Not so sure. Did you consider that if her brother knew about it, she may have known, too? Let's just take one step at a time, honey."

By that time, they were at Carrie's room. She wasn't there. Her roommate said she had gone to the common area where she was putting a jigsaw puzzle together. When they found her, she was in the room with several others in various stages of frailties and need for assisted living. A TV was on with several oldsters looking at a game show.

Carrie was pretty deaf, but her eyes were good. "Why, looka here, if it's not little Susan! Where'd ye scrape her up, Gladdie?"

Susan cringed at being referred to as little. Suddenly she had become sensitive about her short stature.

Gladdie talked close to her mother's ear in an even but low voice. "She scraped me up, Mama. She's got some big questions to ask you. Are you up to a Willson's Cove interrogation?"

"La! I invented them! What's on yer mind, honey? Let's go back to my room so I can hear you better."

Susan copied her cousin's way of speaking, close to Carrie's ear, so she could hear, but hopefully not so everyone in the entire home would. "Great idea."

Carrie used her walker to manipulate the hallways, but in her room, she didn't need it. It was a slow walk back to her room, but she chatted the entire time about the food, some of her old friends who had died, and how nice the attendants were. She stopped once to introduce one of the nursing assistants. Once they got settled in her little room, she looked at Susan. "Okay, what's on your mind, young'un? Don't mind Sary"—referring to her roommate—"she'll not gossip."

Sary's bland expression denied the statement.

"Aunt Carrie, in the process of some research I was doing, I had my DNA done. I learned that I am not really a Willson. Who am I? It's pretty bad to find out at age seventy that I'm not who I thought I was. I can only assume I was adopted or found under a rock!"

"I have always dreaded this day. You are every bit as much a Willson as the rest of us, but yes, your birth parents were not Harvey and Bea. Bea couldn't have babies, so when a baby was born in, well, some unfortunate circumstances, as they say, Harvey and Bea took you when you were born. You mightn't have a drop of Willson blood in ye, but yer a Willson from the get-go."

"Well." That was all Susan could say at first.

Then she asked, "Aunt Carrie, the two names that had the greatest percentage in my DNA were Vance and Frampton. Evidently, Will had his DNA done, and he's listed as a first cousin. Might I assume my mother and my father may have been close kin to Uncle Vance?"

Sary might not have been a gossip, but she was all ears.

Carrie ignored Sary. "Sweet girl, I could never tell you anything more than I've done told you. You were adopted. Just leave it there. I will tell you no more." She got that look on her face that this was the end of the conversation.

But it wasn't. "I was there when they brought you home before I got married. My sister Delphy had just had your cousin Lily May, and I was with her, then I helped your mama learn how to take care of you. The entire family chose you to be a part of the Willson clan. You were chosen. It was what Mama always called Willson love."

Gladdie nodded to Susan, suggesting that it would be okay to tell her mama about Grandpa and her half brother. But she excused herself and left them, allowing Susan and her mother to talk alone. She would visit some of the other residents.

"Susan, living in this world, there are lots of wrong things that happen, but I truly believe there are no accidents in the lives of God's people. There are incidents. The incident of your birth was tragic for one person, but it was the best thing that could have happened for your mama and daddy. And it was certainly the best thing that could have happened for you."

"Was it the best thing that happened to my poor, unfortunate mother?"

Aunt Carrie ignored the question. She went on. "You know God adopts us? Think about that. You are what the preacher calls an object lesson about that" (Galatians 4:5).

"I'm not very religious, Aunt Carrie, but I remember enough Sunday school to understand what you are saying. I'll think about it."

Susan took a deep breath as if to dispel an uncomfortable bit of preaching and get to the other half of her purpose in talking with her aunt. "While I'm here, I want to know what you can tell me about Grandpa's trips to St. Petersburg to sell his musical instruments."

Carrie didn't tell her much that she hadn't already known before her Apalachicola trip. So Susan barreled on ahead. "Aunt Carrie, were you aware of any affair that Grandpa may have had?"

"Ha, ha! What are you getting at? I know more. Well, Delphy and I knew more than we were supposed to know. One day we were just little girls, Delphy had learned to read, but I only knew my ABCs. We were playing with some scraps of wood in Papa's shop while he was working on a fiddle, I think. Suddenly he took off runnin' for the outhouse, leavin' the door of his small workroom ajar. He never did that. We took advantage of the time. There was a letter open on his workbench, so Delphy read it. It was from a womern in Floridy. She called him Papa and was tellin' him about a little boy named Junior. We both stuck that in our heads and never told anyone about it. After Papa died, we talked about it and drew the conclusion that our sweet and godly papa had another family in Floridy. Delphy is gone, but neither of us ever told it. I s'pose you found out about it."

Susan nodded. "Yes. Aunt Carrie, you have a half brother living in a retirement home in Tampa. He knows about you, and he would like to come and see you. How do you feel about it?"

Carrie screwed up her brow. "Say that again. I didn't quite get that."

Susan repeated it more distinctly and in her good ear.

"La, yes! Is that the boy named Junior?"

"Yes, his real name is Luke Harvey, but they call him Junior. He is eighty-seven, just six months younger than you are. He still plays the fiddle, and his son, Harry, plays a fretless banjo that Grandpa made and sings just like Grandpa."

"Susan, I may not live another day, but each day I live from now till God takes me home, I will count it a blessing. An added blessing will be to meet my brother. Bring him here. I'll love him like he was your papa or any of your uncles. Oh, what joy you have given me!" Tears streamed down her soft, wrinkled cheeks and onto her dress.

Susan went on and gave Aunt Carrie a detailed but not exhaustive rundown of how she and Harry had found the letters and what they had learned.

Carrie was almost stoic while Susan told her. Sometimes she would ask for her to repeat something she didn't quite hear. When Susan was finished, Carrie gave a big sigh. "Thank you, sweetheart, for telling me. It relieves a big burden I always had. I remember when Papa walked the aisle at church and fell to his knees at the altar one Easter Sunday. He was a stalwart in the church and the community after that. You couldn't have known a better man. It just goes to show that God can work in the heart of anybody."

Susan hugged her aunt. When Gladdie returned from her rounds with the other residents, she found them both with glistening eyes and holding a box of tissues between them.

"You told her everything?"

Susan nodded. "Yes. I'm going to call Harry and ask him to bring Junior up to visit her as soon as he can. Both your mom and Junior have voiced their concerns that they may not live long enough to see one another if we wait till the reunion next summer."

"Guess we need to have a family meeting, huh. I'll get hold of Mike about meeting at the old homeplace. No need to tell them until we are together. Hah! Lily May will jump on this like a chigger on

Mike's dog, ol' Dook. She's big into family genealogy. I'm glad we have this out in the open, aren't you?"

Carrie giggled. "Genealogy or gossipology!"

Susan nodded. She was crying and laughing at the same time.

Carrie got up from her chair and stood at the door to her room. She hugged Susan again and kissed Gladdie. "Let me know when to get all gussied up to entertain my brother. I want to look my best."

Susan and Gladdie left her laughing after them.

As they walked down the hallway toward the car, they passed some of the residents sitting in their wheelchairs. Some were asleep, but Susan stopped and spoke to those who were alert. One old lady standing in a doorway drew her attention. She stopped and spoke to her but didn't really engage in conversation. The lady grasped her hand and said in a soft melodic voice, "You are so beautiful. Thank you for stopping by. Come and see us again soon."

This made Susan cry some more. "Gladdie, I don't know why I don't take time to visit here. I'll bet some of these old souls don't get any visitors, do they?"

"No. I always try to make my rounds and visit them whenever I come to visit Mom. That cutie is one of my kinfolk. I don't know her very well."

Susan turned around and looked back toward Aunt Carrie's room. Her aunt was standing in the hallway outside her door, looking after them. Susan waved, and she waved back.

Carrie looked after them until they disappeared into the lobby. What she was thinking might have been written on her face. She said, "Ay la," and turned back to her room.

Chapter 26

Susan

Blowing Rock, North Carolina, later the same day

Susan could hardly wait to get home and tell Mac all the news. *I'm so glad Aunt Carrie now knows a little bit about Grandpa's philandering. But it would serve no purpose in letting her read all those letters. I'll take a general sample of them to the family meeting, and the family can decide what Aunt Carrie needs to see. Huh.*

The leaves were starting to show their glory, and as she saw them, she put aside all the family drama, including her adoption, and simply enjoyed nature. It seemed that, although Aunt Carrie refused to tell her who her birth mother was, it didn't matter so much because she was wanted. She was chosen. A fragment of a verse she had learned in Sunday school came to mind: "I am fearfully and wonderfully made" (Psalm 139:14). *Must have been all that preacher talk Aunt Carrie was doing, but I understand it. Might be something to think about.*

Rather than going the regular route home, since the leaves and the weather were so pretty, she took the Blue Ridge Parkway back to Blowing Rock instead of going by Grandfather Mountain on Highway 105. By the time she met Mac at the front door of their house, she felt calmer and more content than she had felt since learning that she had no Willson blood in her veins.

Mac held her in his arms for a long moment and then led her to the kitchen where he had just finished brewing a pot of coffee. They sat at the kitchen table and drank coffee, and she told him all about her interview with Aunt Carrie.

"She was already aware that there was some philandering before she was born, and she seems actually relieved that I was able to share the details. She, like Junior, wants to meet as soon as possible. I'll call Harry in a few minutes and see what arrangements can be made."

"What about the adoption?"

"Yep. I'm adopted. All Aunt Carrie would tell me was that Mama couldn't have babies, so when 'some unfortunate circumstances,' as she termed it, produced a baby, Daddy and Mama adopted me when I was born. I couldn't get her to tell me more. I suggested the last names Vance and Frampton, but she said she couldn't tell me more. I'm sure she knows who my birth mother or father was, but since she won't tell me, I will have to be satisfied that I am a Willson by the choice of my parents. I do wonder if Uncle Jeb's brother, Tommy, mightn't be my father. Vance or Frampton."

"I'll take you, whoever you are, sweetheart."

After grabbing a brownie from the cookie jar to eat as she finished her coffee, she picked up her cell phone and dialed Harry. He answered on the first ring.

"Hey! I assume you got to North Carolina without any mishaps. Gwen and I have been on pins and needles, on the edge of our chairs, biting our fingernails, and any other cliché you might come up with. How did it go with Aunt Carrie?"

"Beautifully! First of all, in relation to our DNA testing, yes, I was adopted, but I'm okay with it. She wouldn't tell me who my birth mother or father is or was, but she confirmed it. I liked what she said: 'You were chosen.' As for the Grandpa story, she was not surprised at all. In fact, she and Aunt Delphy had known there was a child in Florida. They were six and ten years old when they read a letter from Maggie about Junior. They came to the right conclusion that he had a family in Florida, but they kept the secret to themselves. I remember the letter. I'm going to look for it and take it to her."

"Great idea. When we come, I'll bring letters, too."

"Good. She is anxious to meet your dad. She said sort of the same thing he did: at eighty-seven, she might die any day. She wants to meet him before it's too late."

"I can go over tomorrow and get him ready to go. I don't think he has any doctor appointments until November, so it shouldn't be a problem. He is on no special diet, and he is a great traveler. I think I can have him there by, say, Sunday."

"Wonderful! I need to get the family together and bring everyone on board. I'll attempt to get them together Saturday night to tell them what we know. We don't want any of them to make a scene they will regret and jeopardize the anticipated meeting."

"Any recommendations for a hotel?"

"There is a Holiday Inn here in Blowing Rock, and that would be close to Mac and me, and you will have a fantastic view of the valley. Here, let me give you the number." She got it from the phone book and told him. "You can call me when you get here."

"Thank you. How about if we bring our musical instruments along? Would that be appropriate?"

"Definitely! We can give a concert at Aunt Carrie's retirement home, and if you stay long enough, we can have a family gathering at the homeplace with music and lots of food, a mini family reunion."

"You are already a great cousin. Hope to see you Sunday, if all goes as planned. I will call you after I make arrangements with Dad. Oh, what should we bring to wear? He isn't used to cold weather."

"The temperature will likely range between midforties to midsixties and, at night, could get down to freezing. Warm clothes, layering is good. If he doesn't have what you need, we'll go shopping. I'd like to share a welcome-to-the-Willson-family for him anyway."

"You are too good! See you Sunday. Lord willin' and the crick don't rise."

Chapter 27

Gladdie

Willson's Cove, North Carolina, same day

Gladdie stopped by the homeplace, hoping that Mike was not off somewhere. But if he was, she'd leave him a note to call her. If he was outside, he wouldn't hear the phone. So the old-fashioned way would have to work. Thankfully, he was home. Dook met her with his friendly tail-wagging. She was family, so he didn't bark.

Mike yelled at her from the garden, where he was burying cabbages for the winter. "Hey, Gladdie! What did I do to deserve you to come to see po' folks?"

Without divulging anything, she asked, "Can we have a family meeting here, say Saturday afternoon? We have some important business to discuss."

"Well, sure, but ain't it a mite soon to work on the reunion?"

"Thinkin' like we need a minireunion. But there is some important information we need to discuss now. I can't tell you about it until we are all together."

"Yeah, go ahead and get 'em here. Want me to fix a pot of chili?"

"Not for Saturday, but maybe later. We'll talk about it Saturday."

"You bein' mighty mysterious, womern. This have anything to do with Susan findin' old letters up in the attic? I ain't as dumb as I look."

"Just wait and see." Gladdie just laughed and crawled back in her four-wheel-drive jeep. "See you Saturday, and hopefully we'll get at least half of the locals here."

Mike would be easy compared to some of the other cousins. Lily May will want to know everything. I'll just tell her to bring her genealogy stuff. Clyde and Reatha probably won't be able to make it. Both of them are a bit feeble. In fact, Mama said Reatha has her name in the Life Care Center. Ray and Francine live too far away to come on such short notice, and I'll probably have to twist Will's arm to get him away from Saturday afternoon college football, especially if Carolina or Tennessee are playing. Susan and I will have to talk one-on-one with anyone who doesn't show up. Whew!

Before she went to the retirement home with Susan, she had put a Crock-Pot of chili on to simmer. Chili was something Dan Johnson could eat every night if she'd make it. *He oughta consider himself lucky to get it as often as he does! Slaw, cornbread, and I'll be ready when he walks in the door. While the cornbread's baking, I'll start my calls.*

Gladdie began with her brothers; Will first.

"Hey, old man! Whatcha doin' Saturday afternoon?"

"Whaddya think, girl? Football. Why for?"

"We need a family meeting with as many of the cousins as possible. We'll be meeting at Mike's at two. I imagine he has a TV you can check for the scores, but we really need you."

"We who?"

"Susan has learned some significant information that will impact us all, particularly Mama. I'm not bringing Mama over to the meeting at this time, but we all need to be on the same page. That's why I need you here. You can be a stable influence when Pansy or Ozzie get on their high and mighty horses."

"That important, huh. It's nice to be needed. Yeah, I'll do my best. Does Sherry need to come? I think she has a hairdo customer Saturday afternoon."

"Not especially. See you Saturday."

Yeah! One down, ten to go. She called Jerry next.

"Glad-yass! What can your little brother do to make your day?"

"Don't call me that or I'll tell Mama, and she'll whup ya! And be at the homeplace at two, Saturday afternoon. Family business, and we need you."

"We who?"

She went into the same spiel with him. He consented and said he'd call Oscar. They were good friends as well as cousins. "Ozzie will cut a fuss, be he'll do whatever I tell him."

By that time, Dan had come in for supper, and she told him what was going on.

"Day-um, you don't say. That's a kag o' fireworks, ain't it? I'll be there for you, sugar, and run interference between Pansy and y'all."

She hugged him, feeling grateful for her big bear of a husband. "You just keep what I told you under your hat, mister!"

After dinner, she called Lily May and Pansy. She suggested to Lily May that she might bring her genealogy stuff. She asked her, too, if she'd call her sister, Leanne.

"She'll be there if I have to hog-tie her. I know she doesn't have anything important for Saturday 'cause she asked me to come over and help her make a Halloween costume for her grandson. We will be there."

Pansy, true to form, needled her to find out what it was all about. Gladdie didn't tell her, despite the prodding. Since Pansy threatened to not show up, Gladdie knew she would be there.

It was now eight o'clock. "Danny Boy, guess I've called all the ones who can actually come, but I'll call Clyde, Reatha, Ray, and Francine tomorrow. What do you think?"

"I think." He nodded his agreement.

Gladdie called Susan to report her good work. "I reckon all of them will be there. I'm saving the other four till tomorrow. And Susan, thank you for doing this for Mama."

"Thank you for all you did, Gladdie. How about if I call the other four tomorrow, and I will arrange to run by to see Clyde and Reatha after our meeting Saturday."

"Sounds good. Now, time for dinner and relaxation!"

Chapter 28

Susan

Blowing Rock, North Carolina, the next morning

Susan was anything but relaxed. She would need to focus the remainder of the week on how she would approach the family meeting. It was typically Pansy who took control, so she would need to give Pansy something to do to divert her nosiness.

"Mac, you are an enterprising person."

"Glad you think so." He gave her a suspicious look. "What is it, my dear organizer, that you want from your enterprising person?"

"I need for you to help me figure out something for my cousin Pansy to do to derail her getting her nosy nose into what this is all about. I can only assume she will call me sooner than later. I need to be prepared. Once she finds out what this is all about, she will likely be offended that I didn't tell her twenty seconds after I found out or ask her to come and help me snoop in the attic."

"That bad, huh? Hmmm. Does she cook or organize food?"

"Oh yeah. Really good at that."

"There's your answer. First, call her before she calls you. That will give you the upper hand. Ask her to organize getting a few snacks and drinks, and tell her that the spouses will be able to help her Saturday. What do you think?"

"That may work. I am going to give the final four cousins a call now. I doubt if any of them will be able to come Saturday. I told

Gladdie that after our meeting I'd run over to Clyde's. Reatha's, too, if she can't come after the meeting. Hope the family confab doesn't last all afternoon and into the evening."

"You should call Pansy even before you make those other calls."

"You are right. Thank you."

Susan dialed Pansy's number. Of course, she answered on the first ring.

"What in thee world is goin' on, Suze? Gladdie wouldn't tell me even a tidbit? Seems a bit hokey to me. I told her I wouldn't even come if she didn't tell me."

"I'm sure. Pansy, I think it would be inappropriate for us to tell what this is all about. News bounces off the mountains and boomerangs into places that it shouldn't. We need to all be on the same page as a family at the same time. That way we won't jeopardize a sensitive situation for Aunt Carrie. That's all I can tell you. We do want you there, and I wondered if you would call all the women to ask if they can bring snacks. You are really good at that. Once we are all gathered, our spouses can make certain everyone has refreshments. Will that work for you?"

"Well, I guess so. I'll bring Jake along, too. He can have charge of the ice and sody pop. Sorry, Suze, that I got on my high horse. Must be something big or you wouldn't be so secretive about it. I'd never want to hurt Aunt Carrie. Ever."

"Thanks, Pansy, for understanding."

Firecracker diffused.

Susan looked at Mac. He was grinning at her. "I can't wait to meet this nosy-nose cousin of yours. I take it she was not at the wedding."

"No. She was on vacation in 'Noo' York City, and she had her nose out of joint that we had the wedding when she was on vacation."

Susan picked up her cell phone and began the rest of her calls. First was Uncle Clyde.

"No, I'm not so good these days. The sins of my youth catching up with me, I guess. Just hoping to get well enough for the reunion next summer."

Susan told him she'd try to get out and see him late Saturday afternoon to give him the lowdown. She hung up and called Reatha.

"La, sugar. Good to hear your voice. I'd love to come if Joyce can bring me. If I can't make it, why don't you come over for Sunday dinner?"

"I have other obligations Sunday, Reatha, but I'll be stopping by to visit Clyde Saturday evening. I'll drop in on you on the way back, if you don't make it. Will that work for you?"

"Yes, indeedy. See you one way or the other."

The next call was to Francine, or Fran, as she preferred to be called. Fran lived west of Johnson City, Tennessee, and a last-minute trip to the High Country might be out of the question on such short notice.

"Saturday afternoon? Whoo. I think my grandson has a youth meeting 'do', and I may need to take him. Not sure I could get back in time if I come. What's this all about anyway?"

"Fran, I can't tell you over the phone now, but Gladdie and I both think it's important enough that we need to involve the entire family. Nothing bad, of course, but maybe seeing the family from a different perspective. If you can come, that will be great. If not, I will call you, and we can figure out when to get together so I can bring you up to speed. Hope to see you Saturday."

Ten down, one to go.

Cousin Ray was Pansy's little brother. He lived in St. Louis, Missouri, and there was no doubt that he would not make the last-minute trip. He would probably be there in the summer for the family reunion. *But he needs to know. I could go ahead and tell him what's going on, if it wasn't for the fact that he's Pansy's brother. I'll bet she's already called him!*

Pansy had called Ray, and he was expecting Susan's call. "What the deuce is this all about? You know I can't come. In the first place, I work for a living, unlike you rich retired teachers! Heard you got married. Congratulations!"

"Thank you. Ray, I'd love to tell you all that has happened, but I can't until after the meeting. We need to have the family together. We are a close clan, Ray, and what affects one of us has an impact on all of us. Something sensitive has come up, but it is a good thing. Look, I am certain Pansy will call you immediately, but I want you to call me Saturday evening. I'll be on my cell phone wherever I am." She gave him her number. "I'm headed over to Clyde's after the meeting."

"Okay, but this all seems like a lot of drama to me. If Panz calls me, I won't answer. I know how she gets all wound up and figures she's the only one who knows how to handle anything. Love her, but I know her! I'll be around Saturday evening, so I'll call you, say, around six our time, seven yours. Good luck with whatever this is."

Susan breathed. Relaxed breathing. She didn't realize that she had been holding her breath with each of her phone calls. Mac held out his arms again, and she melted into them. Yes, she needed a good hug, and she was so happy she had married a fellow who had welcoming arms.

Chapter 29

Susan Talks to the Willson Clan

Homeplace, Willson's Cove, North Carolina, Saturday

Anytime the Willson clan assembled, there were lots of hugs all around. Everyone converged on the hollow within fifteen minutes of each other, and one would think they had not seen one another for twenty-five years. His Dookness was in his glory, getting to bark at everyone and get lots of petting. Probably the smell of the food gave him something to look forward to. Those who lived within hollerin' distance were there early and helped Mike.

Mike had cleaned up what Grandma always referred to as the parlor and brought enough chairs in so the cousins could sit comfortably. Blue jeans, overalls, and plaid shirts for the men and knit slacks or jeans and pullover sweaters for the women were the uniform of the day. Once everyone had what snacks and drink they wanted and found a seat, Gladdie began.

"This may seem a bit odd to gather without really knowing why, but Susan has learned something that will impact us all, especially Mama. Susan, why don't you tell us what you have learned."

Susan stood by the fireplace. She noted that Lily May had her notebook on the family and nodded an acknowledgment. Lily May took the cue and prepared to take some notes.

"As you know, Mac and I got married last month. Most of you couldn't be here, and I hope you will make my husband welcome.

We went to Apalachicola, Florida, for our honeymoon. While we were there, I got a wonderful surprise. I found something I've been hunting down for at least twenty years: a banjo made by Grandpa. More than that, the man playing it, a man named Harry Harvey, was playing the Willson's Cove way and singing the exact songs just the way Grandpa did."

There were several undisguised sounds of surprise and approval.

She continued, "When he stopped playing and I got over my initial shock, I asked if I could see his banjo. I looked inside and saw Grandpa's initials. Then I spoke to him to find out where he got the banjo and learned Grandpa's music.

"He said the banjo came from his grandmother, who, along with his daddy, taught him to sing and play. And his grandfather had been the one who brought the banjo and a fiddle to them, having come from the mountains to sell them. He had told them he was a 'salesman'"—she held up her hands, giving air quotes—"for a musical instrument craftsman in North Carolina."

"Say what? That don't make sense," Gladdie's brother, Will, said. "It was Grandpa who did the sellin'."

"Right. I thought that way, too. So I decided to dig deeper, without telling the fellow what it was all about. When Mac and I got home, we came over here and looked around to see if we could find out what Grandpa may have been doing during that time. Mike, I'm sorry I couldn't tell you what was going on. Thank you for kind of staying out of our way."

Mike nodded. "I figured you was up to some kind o' investigation. Knew enough to not meddle. I was afeared o' ghosts anyway."

The less superstitious of the cousins tittered about Mike's overt admission that he believed the place was haunted.

Susan continued, "I took on the attic. There were ghosts aplenty, but not the Halloween type. I found bunches of letters from Grandpa to Grandma. Meanwhile, Mac tackled Grandpa's shop and was able to get into what we used to refer to as his 'inner sanctum.'"

Nods and grins around the room showed that everyone was aware of the forbidden room.

"It took a locksmith from down in Newland to get the door open, and when they did, Mac found a wooden box with another lock and no key. Being a surgeon, he knows how to probe stuff. He located a key to the box, and inside there were stacks of letters not only from Grandma, but from people in St. Petersburg, Florida."

"Yeah. I remember he used to go there to sell his banjos back in the late twenties, when I was just a tiny girl," Reatha said.

"Glad you could come, Reatha. I thought you might remember."

Heads turned to Reatha, but she didn't elaborate.

"This next is the shocker, and the reason why I refused to tell any of you why we needed this meeting. Grandpa had totally another life in St. Petersburg. He had another 'wife' of sorts. At least the woman thought they were legally married. Grandpa used an assumed name, Luke Harvey. They had a son, Luke Harvey Jr. He goes by the name Junior. The banjo man, Harry Harvey, is his grandson, just as much as we are his grandchildren."

At that, eight protests arose from around the room.

"No! I'll never believe it!"

"Prove it, Susan!"

"You mean he's our cousin?"

And a few mild expletives to punctuate the outrage.

"Now you see why I wouldn't tell any of you about this. After our discovery, I told Harry what I had found out, and at first, he denied it as much as you are doing now.

"He decided to look through his own attic. Sure enough there were more letters. These from so-called Luke Harvey to Martha, the woman who assumed they were married. There were other letters to her daughter, Maggie Lindsay. Harry had always thought Maggie was his grandmother, until we found a letter that her mother, Martha Lindsay Harvey, had been the woman Grandpa was with. Martha had died of cancer right after Harry's father was born, and this, Maggie raised him as her own. She never married."

Susan's cousins shook their heads, still in disbelief. Pansy asked her to repeat what she had just said. Susan summarized and then continued, "Harry's father, Luke Jr., was born in 1922. He is still living. He is in a retirement home in Tampa."

"You sure of that?" Pansy wanted to know.

"I am. Before I told Harry what I had found, I went to Tampa and met Junior, played banjo to his fiddle, also one that Grandpa had made. Then after I read all the letters, I called and told Harry what we had found. Mac and I went back to St. Petersburg to meet Harry at his home. We stayed for several days."

"La, honey, you got more money than common sense. I'd say let this all remain in the past. Forgotten, like our sins in God's sight," Pansy said.

Susan ignored her. "Now, as we speak, Harry is bringing his father here. Aunt Carrie knows he is coming and is looking forward to meet her half brother tomorrow."

"What? Mama knows?" Gerald asked. "Whew!"

"Yes. And the funny thing is, this was not really news to her. She told me about a time when she was six years old and Aunt Delphy was ten. They had snooped in Grandpa's secret room when he took off flying to the outhouse. They learned there was a child. You'll have to ask Aunt Carrie to tell you that entire story. She was hilarious describing the incident. I won't tell you anymore now, but we hope that maybe next Sunday we can have a gathering here with Aunt Carrie and our half uncle and his son, where we welcome them into the family. Can we all get on the same page here?"

It was quiet for a bit as everyone tried to digest this sensational information. It was no surprise that Pansy was the first to speak again, actually changing her tune from her former statement.

"Y'all, this is a shocking bit of information, and if you're like me, you can't get your head around it. But no, I see no reason why we can't be big and welcome our half uncle and half cousin. We need one of our big spreads, and Susan, how about a lot of music."

Susan nodded. "Good! Harry will be bringing his banjo, the one Grandpa made, and Junior will bring his fiddle. He is an excellent fiddler for a man his age. I played with him in Tampa. But there is more."

"What?" Pansy snipped out the question.

"Harry and I had our DNAs just to prove it."

Reatha opened her eyes wide and grimaced.

"Harry came up with the Willson and his mother's family name, Lindsay, as his highest percentage. Guess what? I did not. I found out that I'm adopted."

Mike shook his head. "Not you. Why, you look just like the rest of us. Are you sure?"

"Yes. Mike, everyone in this corner of North Carolina looks like you and me. The only difference is that I'm the only one with curly hair, even if it is white, and I'm short. There was a good reason why you boys always called me the runt of the litter. I have no doubts. Aunt Carrie confirmed it, but she wouldn't tell me who my birth parents were. I'm not certain I need to know, if I can be assured that this doesn't change how y'all feel about me. And…and I hope you will accept Harry as a cousin as much as you accept me. And I hope you will see Junior as an uncle, just as much. We were all part of circumstances beyond our control."

By this time, the clan spouses had come into the parlor to hear what was going on. There were a few whispers and lots of nodding and headshaking, but no interruptions as the cousins asked questions.

"Harry told me he was happy to finally have family. He has no siblings or cousins. He has a daughter, Gwen, who is just as excited as her dad to finally find roots."

"Will she be coming, too?" Gladdie asked.

"I doubt it. She is a nursing student at the University of South Florida in St. Petersburg and works at a hospital there. I doubt if she'd be able to come at this time. She was excited about our family reunion next year, so I hope she would be welcome."

Lily May had been quiet all this time. She had a troubled look as she stood, waving her big notebook. "Sure makes a big change in our genealogy. I'm not too sure if we can trust all this. I want to see each and every one of those letters. There's got to be something missing here. How come this Junior's name is Luke Harvey, and how can he be a junior to Luther Willson? It doesn't make sense."

"No, Lily May, it doesn't make sense that our grandfather, the man we knew, would have done such a thing. But Harry's DNA doesn't lie, and the letters document the entire story. You are welcome to archive all Grandpa's and Grandma's letters, and if Harry and Junior agree, archive the ones they have. Harry plans to bring them along. They will be staying at least for a week, so you and Harry can get your heads together on this if you choose to do so."

Ozzie started laughing. It was almost a hysterical laugh. When he got control of himself, he said what was on his mind. "Ya know, I always thought Grandpa was the most saintly feller in the world. Describe a Christian, and that was him. He knew more Bible than any preacher. He was loving, full of happiness, never ruffled or anxious, and man, I never knew a more patient feller. Why, you know he'd die before he'd touch a drop o' likker, and he was more than generous to anyone, whether he knew the feller or not. Pansy, you said you have a hard time getting your head around this. Neither can I. Okay, I'll meet these fellers, but don't ask me to just up and make 'em family. I gotta see how they are. There have fancier hoaxes that proved false with deeper investigation."

Reatha spoke quietly. "I know this is quite a shock to all of us and especially Susan, finding out she is adopted on top of the big revelation about our grandfather. But Grandpa and Grandma set a pattern for our family: we welcome folks. That's just what we do. Oscar, Pansy, y'all: I am the oldest one here. Clyde and me, we're pretty much the patriarch and matriarch of our generation, after Aunt Carrie. Clyde couldn't come this afternoon, so I'm speaking for him. We will treat our 'Uncle' Junior with welcoming ways and our 'cousin' Harry with respect. If any of you cannot do that, I trust you will stay home. When Susan came along, I knew she was adopted. Mama told me that, yes, she was adopted, but we were to treat her like she was born to Aunt Bea. We will do the same with them.

"I do remember Grandpa going to Florida every January. I was four years old the last trip he made, and I was with Grandma when he got off the train at Cranberry in 1929. He took Grandma in his arms and said, 'It's over, Zanny. I won't go back again.' Looking back at it these eighty years later, I think I know what he was saying to Grandma. She must have known what he had done in Florida. She only said, 'I love you, always have, always will.' If she could forgive him, so can we."

After Reatha's quiet speech, the feeling in the room smoothed out. One could almost feel the tension lifting and what Grandma used to say was Willson love flowing in the room.

Everyone looked at Reatha, and no one said a word. It looked as though her word would be law.

Susan added one other thought. "I would suggest that our meeting with Aunt Carrie and Uncle Junior next Sunday should be low-key. That means leaving children and grandchildren at home. If you need one of your children to bring you, no problem, like Joyce bringing Reatha. Do y'all agree?"

The only thing left was to organize the gathering for Sunday in a week. The women got their heads together for a menu, and Mike offered to make his huge kettle of what he called Willson's Cove chili.

And with that, the meeting had no reason to continue. Food was put away; hugs and farewells until the next week.

Chapter 30

Susan

Willson's Cove, North Carolina, Saturday

Mac was full. "Does your family always fix a spread like that when you get together? There was so much food there in the kitchen, and I felt obligated to try as much as I could, with those three wives, Wilda, Jennie, and Barb, breathing down my neck."

"If you think this was food, wait till next Sunday. We will be able to feed the entire US Navy! I'm glad you're full because I'm too tired to eat, and we still have to go over and see Clyde before we go home and call Fran. I'll be getting a call as well from Ray. Whew!"

Susan was driving because Mac was not familiar with all the back roads of the High Country, let alone the ones up Willson's Cove. "Clyde lives above Willson's Bluff, the place he built above the old house Grandpa built before Clyde was born. He's got the best view of anyone around. I don't even think Banner Elk has any better view."

"I think Blowing Rock has a pretty awesome view."

"You'll see. Well, Clyde moved back here and built this place when he retired. He lives well, to be honest. Better than the rest of us po' folks. He left here as an old country boy in 1943 when he was only seventeen and came back a gentleman."

"I hope it isn't dark till we get there. Good grief! These back roads are interminable!"

Susan pulled into a lane that climbed up the mountain, winding about for a couple of miles. In the hollow, there were a few scattered houses. Susan pointed out where some of the extended family lived. Then suddenly they were at the top, and a gorgeous log house crowned the side of the mountain. Sun was reflecting off the wall of windows in the front elevation of the house.

"Wow! I love it. If I had a place like this one, I wouldn't mind this country life. You are right about the view. Look! I see forever from here." Mac was totally enthralled.

There was a light on in the front room and smoke rising up the chimney. When Susan parked, a man came to open the car door. "Hey, Eddie. How's Clyde today?"

"Doin' better, Ms. Susan. He's been up most all day. Come on in. He's sittin' by the fire reading his *Bloomberg* magazine."

"Of course, he is. Eddie, this is my husband, Mac McBride. Mac, meet Eddie Jones, Clyde's right-hand man. Eddie and his wife, Millie, have been with Clyde since he lived in Raleigh. They are almost part of the family, too. Right, Eddie?"

"Yes, ma'am. We feel like family."

They went on into the house and found Clyde with his feet propped up on a hassock, a tumbler of Scotch, his glasses halfway down his nose, and said magazine draped across his lap. "Well, come on in. Want a little nip to take the chill off?"

Clyde looked the part of a distinguished college professor: slender, white hair trimmed neatly, and a neat white beard. He wore corduroy slacks with a smoking jacket and did not look nearly his eighty-two years.

"Hey there, cousin! I think I better pass that up since I'm driving. You haven't met my husband yet. Clyde Willson. Mac McBride."

The men shook hands, and then Clyde got right to the question, while Mac sat in a corner chair out of the way.

"How come it's so important for the clan to assemble? And what's all this hush-hush stuff?" Clyde asked.

Susan laughed at her cousin's straightforward introduction to the subject. "Nothing like getting to the point." She began with her meeting Harry and seeing the banjo. She explained about meeting

Harry's dad in Tampa, coming back and finding the letters, and then the subsequent trip, events, and DNA testing.

Clyde interjected with similar question the rest of the family had, but he was delighted with the turn of events. When she was done telling everything, he gave a hearty laugh. "Susan, Claude told me before I went off to World War II that he thought Grandpa had been with a woman in Florida. He said he remembered him going to Johnson City and always carried a letter with him and then would have one when he came back. We were, what, just wee young'uns, but you know how kids imagine stuff. Only when we grew up we talked about it, and when we arrived at that age when hormones are raging, our imagination turned to suspicion in evil-minded young men. So we were right."

When Susan told him about being adopted, neither was this a surprise to him. "I remember when you were born. I was, I guess, sixteen. Don't know who your birth parents were, but it was someone from around here. But, Suze, our family always has seen you as blood. Daddy told us you were adopted but to keep our mouths shut and only think of you as our cousin. Back in those days, there wasn't any birth control for women, and in a way, that was good. It was one deterrent from being loose with affections. But there were always girls who either didn't know any better or they were what we called 'fast.' Then there were a smattering of evil men tanked up on moonshine or some fellow not right in the head, who would hurt a girl. Every now and then, we fellows would hear the gossip that some girl went to a granny woman to get rid of a baby. Most of them would have the baby and raise it either single or marry in haste. Some of these girls would go away off the mountain. The grapevine never revealed who your birth mother might be, and no fellow would tell."

"Thanks, Clyde. I really don't care at my age whether I'm blood or not. I'm satisfied that I had the best family in the world to adopt me. My birth mother, whoever she was, is probably dead and long gone."

"Well, my point in telling you this, Suze, is that our half uncle and half cousin are blood. If we treat you like blood, we dare not treat them any less. I am delighted that you found out. And what's more, you found a couple of Grandpa's musical instruments: the banjo and the fiddle. What a treasure."

"I knew the music would please you. Do you still play guitar?"

"Doesn't sound too good anymore, but I get it out every few days and pick a few tunes."

"Wonderful! If you are able to come over to the homeplace next Sunday, bring it along. Harry will have Grandpa's banjo, and Junior plans to bring the fiddle. I'll bring my new banjo, too. I've given up my bluegrass banjo for a fretted mountain banjo."

"Wonderful! I'm not much for bluegrass, but I love our mountain music, especially Willson's Cove variety. I'll try my best to be there. I'm looking forward to meeting my uncle and cousin. Now thanks for coming over to tell me. That was very gracious of you."

"I always enjoy a visit with you. See you, hopefully, next week."

As soon as they got back on the main road, Susan pulled off and called Fran, since she was a no-show. "We had a great meeting, and now I need to pass on to you what it was about." She explained, mostly in summary, what it was about. She told her about the upcoming gathering on Sunday, in a week, and urged her to come.

Fran, since her marriage and subsequent divorce, was never fully into the family dynamic. She didn't live close by as the others. She had little to say but agreed to come. "I'll be there. My calendar is clear for next Sunday. I already heard a lot of this from Ozzie. He called as soon as he got home. I'm good with this and looking forward to meeting these kinfolk."

No sooner had Susan cut off her phone than it rang. It was Ray. "Okay, what's this all about. I did what I threatened. Pansy called and left a message, but I didn't call her back."

Susan went through the entire spiel again. Ray was polite enough not to interrupt. When she had finished, he laughed. "Well, isn't that something? Who'd a-thought that. Dolly told me that she bet it had to do with Grandpa. She said when she was a little girl there had been gossip in her family about him going to Florida every winter. But the grandpa we knew was a great guy. I think it's good to have it out in the open. Of course there will be mean-spirited folks who will try to make something of it. My suggestion is to keep it in the clan."

"That might be easier said than done, but I agree. I don't suppose you would come for next Sunday?"

"Why not. Dolly said we need to come and enjoy the leaves before they fall off."

"Oh? What about your job, you old workaholic?"

"I'm my own boss, so I say when I leave. We'll stay with Pansy and Jake. I'll give her a call when we hang up. Thanks for letting me know as though I was there. Did my sister try to run things?"

"She was good."

They said their goodbyes and punched off just as the sun began to set over the hills.

Chapter 31

Harry

*Holiday Inn, Blowing Rock, North Carolina,
later that same evening*

As Susan and Mac were pulling into their driveway in Blowing Rock just before sunset that Saturday evening, Harry, with an excited Junior aboard, was pulling up in front of Holiday Inn a few blocks away.

"I thought we'd never get up that mountain, but already, I like these mountains. I'm looking forward to every minute. These colorful leaves are worth the climb. To think I've never thought about coming to North Carolina or Tennessee, even if I did know Papa was a mountain man. But now that I know about my sister—"

Tears flowed down Junior's craggy cheeks. Harry looked over at him seated in the passenger seat, loving the blessing of having a father who could cry. On the trip north, he was surprised at Junior's positivity and purpose. In fact, he had very few memory issues. *Have these new events revitalized him to the point that his short-term memory problem has gone into some sort of remission? Wow!*

"Dad, you can wait here in the car while I sign in and find out where we are going to stay. Looks like a nice hotel. Be back in a few minutes."

"I'll just look at the setting sun, Harry." He adjusted his sunglasses.

The room had a view, two queen beds, and all the amenities they could wish for. Since they had eaten before heading up the mountain, there was little they needed to do once they were settled. No surprise that Junior went right to bed and slept through the night, only getting up to the bathroom a couple of night. Harry, on the other hand, had a lot going through his mind.

Wonder how the big meeting went today. Will these people accept me as a cousin? Will they treat Dad with respect? Yeah, I brought my banjo and Dad brought his fiddle, both made by Grandpa, but will they see that as an intrusion? They might demand that we give them to some sort of family or, as Susan terms it, clan museum. What about the letters? Will they accept them as authentic?

His mind went on and on in that frame for about half an hour, when he decided he should call Susan and let her know that they had arrived.

"Hey! Glad you got here safely. I hope you have a room that is to your satisfaction. We live a few blocks from where you are, so if you want to come here for breakfast, I'd love to have you. We can come and get you."

"The room's great. Dad is exhausted from the trip and already sound asleep. My mind is working overtime, so I can only hope to get to sleep. Yeah, breakfast would be great. So how did the meeting go today?"

"Wonderful that you will come for breakfast and that the meeting was great."

"Tell me."

"Everyone is excited about meeting you and your Dad. Aunt Carrie wasn't there, but Gladdie, her daughter, says she is so excited she didn't sleep all night the day we told her. Tomorrow will be going to the retirement home where she lives. Then next Sunday, after all the clan get in from wherever they go to church, we will meet at the homeplace for a big clan gathering with tons of food. I went to see Cousin Clyde. He wasn't feeling well enough to come to the meeting, and he said he and his brother thought Grandpa had a girlfriend in Florida, but evidently their suspicion rested on the letters he would post in Johnson City and the ones he would bring back. They never saw the letters. Flimsy evidence, but they were right. Reatha and Clyde are the oldest of the cousins, so they have opened our clan up for you. I guess you're in."

"Sounds good. Any opposition or skepticism voiced?"

"Of course. But Reatha set everyone straight. You'll love this." Susan attempted to use Reatha's soft mountain voice: "'We will treat our Uncle Junior with welcoming ways and our cousin Harry with respect. If any of you cannot do that, I trust you will stay home. When Susan came along, I knew she was adopted. Mama told me that, yes, she was adopted, but we were to treat her like she was born to Aunt Bea. We will do the same with them.'"

"Wow! I like her already. How old is this matriarch?"

"Eighty-three. We are all a bunch of oldsters. The youngest in the family is Aunt Carrie's youngest, Gerald. He is sixty. But we have a habit in our clan of living to ripe old ages. I think it's our music that makes us young."

"Yeah, I'm the youngest at fifty-nine! Thank you, Susan, for all you have done and are doing. To give Dad this opportunity is so beautiful. When we got here this evening, he was so overcome with emotion he cried. I love that about him. I think tomorrow will be a very emotional time, probably for both him and Aunt Carrie. I hope they will have privacy and maybe no one but you and me with them."

"Gladdie has set it up for you and your dad to visit in Aunt Carrie's room. She may be there if y'all want her to be, but no one else. I'll be there to introduce you and Junior, but I plan to leave and let it just be immediate family. Gladdie's brothers wanted to be there, but Aunt Carrie said she just wanted you and your dad. Harry, I have never been so excited about anything in my life, well, unless getting married."

"I know what you mean. Well, listen, I've left Dad alone in the room. Better get back in case he wakes up and gets confused. Funny thing, his mind has been so clear all the way here, that I wonder about his short-term memory problems."

"Thanks for calling. We will pick y'all up in the morning about eight. Okay?"

"Gotcha."

Chapter 32

Junior or Luke Jr.

Blowing Rock, North Carolina, Sunday

Harry? What's he saying? Where's my stuff? I'm befuddled. Again.
"Dad, time to get up and meet the day. We are in the North Carolina Mountains. You will be meeting your sister this afternoon, but we need to get up and get ready."

"Oh! Yes, my sister, Carolina. I must have died. Couldn't figure out what was going on. I am resurrected now." Junior got up and opened the curtains. The mountains were bathed in sunlight, reflecting a rainbow of colors from the fall leaves. "Beautiful! Look at that, Harry. Thank you for bringing me here."

"Dad, I talked with Susan last evening, and she and Mac will pick us up at eight this morning to go to their house for breakfast. You won't be meeting your sister till after lunch today."

"Splendid. I am hungry."

"Me too. Probably this brisk mountain air. Wear whatever is comfortable, but be sure to layer. The brisk air might prove cool in the morning and hot in the afternoon. You know as much as I do about it. I did look on a local weather site, Ray's Weather[9] and see it's supposed to be sunny all day. It got down to thirty-six degrees overnight, but it is supposed to be in the high fifties or low sixties this afternoon."

"Brrr. Reminds me of being stationed in Fort Monmouth, New Jersey, 1942, before I was shipped overseas, except there, it was cold in the day and colder at night. Well, these corduroys and a sweater with my jacket to take off if I need to. Glad I brought my hat."

"That beret? Not very mountain looking from what I have seen so far. Everyone around here wears a baseball cap! Wear the beret and be individual."

"Always have been. Where are we going for breakfast? I'm a little befuddled. A good cup of coffee might help."

"No sooner said than done." Harry handed his dad a cup of coffee from the pot in the room. "Susan is fixing breakfast for us."

Within a few minutes, Junior's mind had cleared, and he was raring to go.

Mac came to their hotel room door to get them. Junior had not met Mac previously; however, the two of them clicked immediately. It was a short ride to Mac's place, and Susan had a good old country breakfast ready for them: eggs, sausage, grits, biscuits and gravy, fried apples, and lots of coffee.

Junior, having issues recalling names, called most men brother and most women good-lookin'. "Well, brother," he said to Mac, "I love this view up here. Makes me feel like I'm on top of the world. And when I meet my sister, I'll be higher than the moon. My heart is full."

Susan laughed. "Uncle Junior, we don't go see her until after lunch. What we plan is to take you and Harry on a sightseeing trip, stop for lunch, and then get to the Life Care Center, where Aunt Carrie lives, about two this afternoon. It will just be you, Aunt Carrie, and her daughter, Gladdie, if you want her to stay."

"What kind of name is Gladdie?"

"Gladys. That's a nicer nickname than her brothers used to call her."

Both Harry and Junior snickered. Junior nodded. "I can imagine. I had a teacher named Gladys."

The sightseeing trip took in the Blue Ridge Parkway, the little village of Linville Falls, Crossnore, Newland, and a side trip to show them the family home in Willson's Cove.

Dook met them as they pulled into the lane at the homeplace. He recognized the car and cocked his head quizzically when they did not get out. Harry reminded his dad that this was where his Papa lived. Junior shook his head, trying to visualize the man he knew as Papa living in this beautiful setting. Indeed the house was framed by the woodlands on either side and up the mountain behind the house with golds and reds and sunshine. He said nothing, but his emotions were written on his face. A few tears coursed down his cheeks.

Harry snapped a photo of the house with his cell phone.

Although Mike's truck was in the yard, they didn't stop in. Susan guessed that he had walked to the chapel instead of driving.

They had just enough time to get to the restaurant for their lunch. Susan suggested Stonewalls because the restaurant would be open for lunch until two, and the variety would address all culinary tastes. She was up for shrimp scampi, but Junior asked, "Do they have steak?"

Mac affirmed it. "Real good steak. Good choice, Junior."

They were finished by half past one and had a few minutes to wash up and get to the Life Care Center by two o'clock.

"Dad, I know you are excited to meet Aunt Carrie. Are you okay? How about ten deep breaths before you get out of the car?"

"Good idea. How'd you get so smart, boy?"

"I'm your kid."

Junior took his ten deep breaths and stood tall and confident as he got out of the car. He looked around at the outside the facility and mentally compared it to Legacy in Tampa. *Smaller, but nice setting. Clean.*

Gladdie was right inside the door to greet them. She hugged Susan, and said, "Mama is waiting in her room. Her roommate is gone, healed up from her hip replacement well enough to make it at home. Mama will probably have a new roomie by tomorrow, but for today, we couldn't have asked for anything better."

Susan introduced Gladdie to their uncle and cousin. Junior said, "Well, good-lookin', you look like family, so I guess I'll follow you."

Mac sat in the lobby with his cell phone, using the opportunity to call his three children and tell them the happenings, while Junior, Harry, and Susan followed Gladdie down the hall to Carrie's room.

Carrie looked beautiful. Gladdie had fixed her long, white hair in a french roll, touched up her pale cheeks with a bit of blush, and donned her in her Sunday best. When Junior saw her, he saw a reflection of his own self in her face.

Carrie stood to greet him. They stared at one another for a brief moment and then, both talking at the same time, said, "Oh my!"

Junior stepped forward and took her hand, and she wrapped her arms about him. "My baby brother! My baby brother! Welcome to the family."

Tears eroded the blush on Carrie's cheeks, and Junior's eyes spilled over, running onto his sweater. Carrie led Junior to sit on the chair next to her better ear. "I'm a bit deaf, but I can hear better out of my left ear."

She looked up and saw Harry. "Ah! This is my nephew. Harry, is it?"

"Yes, ma'am. It's a pleasure to finally meet you, Aunt Carrie."

Junior nodded to Harry. "Why don't you and your cousins make a tour of the place and come back after a while? I want to get to know my sister, if that is all right with her."

"You bet." Carrie agreed. "Y'all get lost."

The three looked at each other, laughed at the siblings, and eased out the door.

"Do you want me to call you Junior or Luke?"

"If I can remember—and name recognition is a persistent problem with me—if I can remember, I'd like to be Luke. I am not a true junior, since our papa was Luther. I guess you know he went by Luke, and that's why I was called Junior."

"Luke it is. I'll try to remember for both of us."

Luke shared his life history with his sister, beginning with the early days in St. Petersburg. When he made no mention of religious affiliation, she asked, "Didn't you ever go to church? I been in church all my life since I was a week old."

"Well, we lived a few blocks from a church, and Mom would send me to Bible school every summer. When I was real little, well, when Papa was there every January, he would take me to church. I don't remember much about it. Mom always talked about going, but then she never did. I just never got in the routine of going since she didn't. But Carrie, I do believe."

I wonder where this is going. I hope she isn't going to preach at me! "I believe, but I'm not religious. I see the beauty of nature, and that tells me that there is a God who cares, and I read the Bible, and it tells me who this God is and about Jesus dying for us."

Carrie shook her head but did not pursue the religious discussion. Changing the subject, she asked about his wife.

Luke loved to talk about Stella. It was like she was still with him when he talked about her. "You would love her, Carrie. Beautiful, smart, talented, and the kindest woman I ever met. I met her at the USO a couple of months before I shipped out in World War II. We fell in love immediately. Against her parents and Mom's objections, we married a week before I left for Europe. To my shame, I got her in a family way before we got married. But the baby, a little girl, died. I never saw the baby. Harry came along, then, after I got out, and we were settled at home in St. Petersburg. Her family never accepted me, and when she died twenty years ago, there was no one from her family at the funeral."

"La, mercy. How sad for you. I know you miss her even after twenty years. I sure miss my Jeb. We knew each other from when we were young'uns, went to school together. We got married when I was eighteen and he was nineteen. He had been orphaned when he was young, he and his siblings. The Crossnore School[10] was a good place for children to go to live and go to school if they couldn't stay by themselves. Jeb and Tommy didn't like it and came back home. I told Jeb I'd marry him so he wouldn't have to eat his brother's cooking."

Luke got a good laugh from that.

She told Luke all about life in the mountains in the forties and fifties when she was a young wife, amazing him with the backward but harmonious community life of the mountain people.

"Wish I had grown-up here," he said with a bit of wistfulness for something he had never experienced.

They had talked on and on, enjoying each other for more than an hour, when Gladdie and Harry returned.

Chapter 33

Susan

Life Care Center, Banner Elk, North Carolina, Sunday

While Luke and Carrie were getting acquainted and Gladdie took Harry on the tour, Mac and Susan decided to visit with the residents sitting in the common room. A few of the people had visitors, some of the dementia patients were little more than forms tied in their wheelchairs, but there were two who were obviously alone. A man was sitting by the window, seemingly in his own little world. Mac gravitated to him.

The little lady who had drawn Susan's attention when she had come to visit Aunt Carrie last week had her cotton candy—white head bent over the same jigsaw puzzle Aunt Carrie was doing earlier in the week. Susan thought, *My hair will probably look like that in ten years.*

"Hi there. I remember you from the other day. How is the puzzle going?"

"Aw, it's lots of fun. Miss Carrie had it all together, but one of the other people came by and messed it all up. I've been reworking it for a couple of days. I think I'll have it back together soon. Why don't you sit here with me and help me finish it?"

Susan looked over at Mac, settling into a chair beside the old man. He shrugged. "Go ahead. I'm going to chat with this nice young fellow."

Susan, not much for puzzle patience, saw this as an opportunity to make the lady's day. "That's my husband, Mac. I'm Susan McBride. What is your name?"

"I'm Junie Lee Vance. And I know you. You are Carrie's niece, Susan Willson. She has told me all about you."

The name Vance perked up her ears. Was Vance her family name? "Are you kin to Aunt Carrie's husband, Jeb?"

"Oh yes. Didn't you know he was my brother? I never married. An unclaimed blessing, they say about old maids!"

"Oh. I never knew much about his family. Uncle Vance was a super fellow. Do you have any other family?"

"She shrugged. I've got Carrie, I guess. I was sort of like you. I taught school in West Jefferson for most of my life. Since I never married, I decided to come here. I'm eighty-two, and living alone isn't too smart anymore. I try to cheer my fellow residents up. I look at it as a calling beyond my teaching years." She had a little tinkly laugh that matched her personality.

Susan fitted a piece into the puzzle, but it looked like a long way to completion. She thought the lady was the cutest thing, but she knew she needed to get back to Mac.

"Ms. Junie Lee, it's been so nice to visit with you, but I need to get back to my husband." As she walked away, she thought, *Wish I could put the pieces of my life puzzle in place as easily as a jigsaw puzzle. I pretend I don't care where I came from, but I can't help but wonder.*

Mac was still chatting with the old guy by the window. The man was pointing out different places visible from the window. When Mac saw her, he introduced the man. "Susan, this young man was in World War II in Germany. He was among those who released the concentration camp victims at Buchenwald in April of 1945. He's got a lot of stories. Meet Sergeant Johnny Davis, US army, retired."

Susan reached for the old fellow's hand. He extended his left one. "Sorry, miss, right one's bum. They say I've had a stroke."

Tears rimmed Susan's eyes. *I gotta get out of here!* "Nice to meet a hero, Sarge." She gave the man a bleary smile.

"Uh, Mac, maybe we'd better go and meet up with the others."

Susan and Mac met up with Harry and Gladdie just before they were ready to go back to Aunt Carrie's room. They waited out in the hallway, chatting about the people they had met, while the cousins went into Aunt Carrie's room.

Gladdie came to the door. "Y'all come on in here. There's room with that other bed empty. We're havin' a party!"

Susan saw two beaming faces when she went in. "Looks like you two have made a happy acquaintance. Uncle Junior, you think you want to keep this sister?"

"I most certainly do, and I believe the feelings are mutual." Carrie nodded in agreement. "But from now on, I'm Uncle Luke, if that will be all right with you. Carrie and I both think I'm not really a junior, since Luke was a fabricated name. I am the only Luke in the family, or if you so desire, Luke would work."

"Uncle Luke it is, then," Gladdie said. Susan nodded in agreement.

Susan was a bit puzzled, though, not about Uncle Luke, his name, or the relationship. Helping the old lady with the puzzle stirred up her questions about her adoption—missing puzzle pieces. What were other secrets Aunt Carrie knew? *I have no doubt that Aunt Carrie knows exactly who my birth mother was, but she'll probably go to her grave with that secret. Better think of something else.*

That something-else thought led to question her aunt about Junie Lee. "Aunt Carrie, I met a delightful lady working on the jigsaw puzzle: Junie Lee Vance. I was surprised when she told me she was your sister-in-law. I thought the only family Uncle Vance had was his brother, Tommy."

"Oh, Junie Lee? She was gone from the time she was a girl. When their parents died—now, that is a story all in itself, getting ptomaine poisoning from eating bad pie in Asheville. When Ma and Pa Vance died, the family broke up. I was telling Luke earlier that I told Jeb the only reason I'd marry him is so he wouldn't have to eat Tommy's cooking."

Everyone laughed at that.

"But Junie Lee went to the Crossnore School and after graduation, went to Appalachian State Teachers College.[11] She got a teaching job in West Jefferson and taught there the rest of her life. I was surprised when I came here that she was living here. Guess I'm her only kin, and I'm just an in-law. I hadn't seen Junie Lee, I guess, in years. Didn't even recognize her at first. Last time I saw her was Jeb's funeral. She never married and was simply out of the picture. I don't hardly know her."

"I like her," Susan said.

Mac asked about Johnny Davis. Carrie said she only knew who the man was. "I don't think he's been here long. I've seen him in the dining room, but he isn't at my table."

Mac told her that he was one of the American soldiers who liberated Buchenwald. "I was really impressed by him. Neat fellow."

Harry talked about a couple of residents he had met, but the conversation began to lag. It was obvious that Uncle Luke and Aunt Carrie were getting tired. Susan stood from the chair where she had been sitting and got the ball rolling to make their exit.

"I don't know about you folks, but this has already been a long day. How about we take off to Blowing Rock?"

Luke grinned. "I'll likely sleep all the way back there." He stood and held his hands out to his sister. She grasped them firmly. "Carrie, if it is okay with you, and Susan will bring me back, I'd like to visit with you more this week. I know there are plans. Is it next Sunday? I'd like to get to know you even better. A couple of hours is a drop in the bucket to the lifetime that we've missed."

Carrie stood, still grasping his hands. "Oh, please do. Maybe we can have dinner together some this week. We have our big meal at noon. Just let the desk know when you will be here, and let me know, too. The meals are not gourmet, but they are elderly friendly."

"So be it, then." He hugged her and followed the others out.

Mac had driven all day up to this point. Susan offered to drive back. She knew the roads like the character lines on her face. "No side trips. The roads are mountain roads, fifteen miles as the crow flies, fifty minutes in the car. We don't measure miles here anyway."

Uncle Luke crawled into the back seat and promptly fell asleep. Mac and Harry talked softly of nothing of consequence, while Susan drove, engrossed in her own thoughts. Again, the sun was setting when she pulled into the Holiday Inn to discharge her passengers.

"Wake up, Dad. We're back at the hotel."

Luke looked slightly addled at first, but he laughed. "I was dreaming that that cute lady who played the piano at my place in Tampa last week and Carrie were playing gin rummy and smoking cigars."

"Sounds normal to me!" Harry said.

Chapter 34

Gwen

St. Petersburg, Florida, same day

While her dad and grandfather were enjoying the newfound family in Carolina's High Country, Gwen was seated on the guest room bed going through the letters her dad had not taken with him to North Carolina. She fell asleep and woke up as the clock struck six in the downstairs hallway. It was her rare day off on a weekend, so she took the opportunity to read the letters. She had been to church in the morning, stopped at a deli, and picked up some food for lunch. She had spent the greater part of the afternoon reading letters. *I love these people! My great-grandmother had no idea what she had gotten into, I guess. I wonder if she ever figured it out. I've read them all, and I can't see that she did. I wonder if that desk has any other secrets.*

She rolled off the bed and switched the overhead light on, examining the desk from every angle. Tilting it so she could see the bottom better, her hand hit the edge of the left back leg. She jumped when the side of the leg opened to reveal another hiding place. Catastrophe squalled and ran, too. A tiny rolled-up booklet fell out with pages yellowed with age but undamaged, it appeared.

She gingerly pressed it flat. It was a small notebook. Opening it, she saw that the handwriting was definitely Great-Grandma's handwriting. The pages were not dated, and it appeared that they were prayers and not meant to be shared with anyone. Gwen asked God to forgive her own intrusion into the soul of her great-grandmother. The first page told about her official diagnosis of cancer and that she feared she would lose the baby.

> Dear Lord:
>
> I knew, even before the doctor told me, that it was bad. I know I should have had it tended to back last summer, but I didn't want to lose my breast. Now it is beyond help. I feel bad for Maggie. She is so young to have to deal with this. If I carry the baby long enough that it will live, she will have to raise it as her own. Help her to be the mother I cannot be. Amen.

Gwen turned to the second page and through the little booklet. Most of the entries were short and asked God to bless Luke, help Maggie, and give strength to Georgie and Jesse. When she came to the final two entries, she saw that the handwriting, still in Martha's script, was shaky.

> Dear Lord:
>
> I am going to die. I keep wondering why all this has happened to me. Was I wrong to marry Luke, knowing that he would only be here half the time? That nagging thought that our marriage was a sham keeps haunting me. Maybe it would be better if you would take my baby now than if it should be born. I know that Georgie could give me something so I could miscarry. Would that be murder? I feel like I am murdering myself since I let the cancer go and didn't have it taken care of. I'll probably go to hell for my thoughts! Please forgive me.

Gwen had tears in her eyes. *Good grief! What a burden she must have had. If she was that ill, how did she have the strength to hide these?* She turned to the final page. It was not a prayer to God but an unsent note to Luke.

> Luke,
>
> You will never see this note, but I need to write it before I die to get it off my conscience. I wish you could know that I am glad that we have been together. You have given me joy I didn't think was possible after Paul was lost at sea. But Luke, I think I am right that we have never really been married. It has been a sham marriage, and I guess I knew it from the first. I knew that so-called preacher was not official when we brought him here. I have asked God to forgive me for what we have done. I pray that you will do the same. I have turned away from my upbringing in the church and lived for pleasure. My final prayers will be for you to turn back to God. Know that I have loved you.
>
> Martha

How sad. Gwen cried for her great-grandmother, for Maggie, for Grandpa, and for all of them. It was a comfort to her that Martha had seen her need to pray, but she wondered, too, if, as she said in the last prayer, "I'll probably go to hell for my thoughts!" She put the desk back in the position her dad had placed it, took the little prayer book to her room and put it with Grandpa's letters in the cubby cabinet, as she had dubbed it, and called her dad.

Harry picked up on the fourth ring. "Hey, Gwen, how's it going?"

"Hot, Dad. Hot enough that I would rather be where you and Grandpa are. I just wanted to let you know I found another secret compartment in the desk. Believe it or not, it was in one of the back legs. I found a small booklet with prayers written by Great-Grandmother."

"Ha! Catastrophe kept winding around that leg. Maybe she knew something was in there."

"Okay? Anyway, I sort of felt like I was intruding on her by reading them, but I did it anyway. She knew she wasn't truly married, and the final entry was an unsent note to Luke, telling him that she knew. She told him she had asked God to forgive her, and she hoped he would do the same. Oh, Dad. It was so sad."

"Honey, it's okay that you read it. I don't think it was wrong after eighty-seven years. Save it for me to read. Did you check the other legs?"

"I looked, but I don't think so. You can check it when you get home. So how did the meeting of the siblings go? Was Grandpa on his best behavior?"

"Absolutely!" He went on to tell her about the meeting and the plans for the week ahead. "The clan is planning a gathering of the first cousins and spouses next Sunday so they can meet us. I love this family, Gwen. Our family. I'm anxious for you to be part of it, too."

"Me, too, Dad. Give Grandpa a big hug for me."

She punched off the phone and gave her image in the mirror a big grin.

I don't imagine the hospital will take too kindly for what I plan to do, but I am going to take off next weekend. I will get out of classes Friday at noon and not need to return until Tuesday. So I'm going to fly to Charlotte, rent a car, and crash the party! So there!

Taking the time off was not a problem for St. Anthony's. She had worked enough overtime that they were willing to give her hours back. She made her reservations for the flight, looked up available hotels in the area, and booked a room at a different one from where Harry and Luke were staying. Her excitement built, and it would be a difficult week to get through waiting to leave.

Chapter 35

Susan

Blowing Rock, North Carolina, 2009

Gwen wasn't the only one with building excitement. Luke was wound tighter than a pocket watch, Harry was wary of something going wrong or his dad becoming ill, and Susan was as busy as she had been her entire teaching career. She had a week to organize the gathering: find out who would be there, make certain there would be the right kinds of foods for seniors who might have a restricted diet for health reasons, and get music organized. She was going to attempt to get Mac to play his bagpipes, take Uncle Luke to see Aunt Carrie for several days, and fix meals at home. *Oh, and I haven't worked out since before I got married! So run by the fitness center in Banner Elk. I can do that while Uncle Luke and Aunt Carrie visit. Whew!*

By Monday lunchtime, she thought she had her schedule of things to do in order. Harry had told her last evening when they got home that he was going to take his dad sightseeing in the morning, and then whenever she could manage it, they would like to go back to see Aunt Carrie. She called Harry midafternoon.

"How was the sightseeing?"

"We enjoyed a ride to Crossnore to see the fresco there at the school. I read about the Long Frescos[12] some years ago and thought we might view one of them. This is called *Suffer the Little Children.*

Dad was enthralled by the fresco. He told me that the eyes of Jesus reminded him of his papa's eyes. But the entire village is fascinating. While we were there, we stopped in the little sandwich shop run by the kids at the school and had lunch and then checked out the weaving room. I bought a handwoven purse for Gwen. Then we went to a little church that is built inside and out with native stone, even the pulpit. Dad's tired and sleeping. Guess he's done for the day."

"Want to come here for dinner tonight? I made a pot of spaghetti. Mac can come and get you if you want."

"Spaghetti? Yes, ma'am. Dad and I both love it. I think I can find my way. How about if we bring our instruments with us?"

"Absolutely. I'm trying to talk Mac into joining us with his pipes. Should make an interesting combo. By the way, I called the retirement home, and I'll take Uncle Luke to have lunch with Aunt Carrie tomorrow. While they are visiting, I'm going to Peak Fitness up the road from the home to work out. They are going to think I died. It's been so long since I worked out. And I'll need to work off my spaghetti."

"Tell me about it!"

Harry and Uncle Luke found their way to the house without any wrong turns. The spaghetti dinner, with some good Italian wine, mushrooms as a side dish, and a nice side salad was a hit.

Uncle Luke rubbed his tummy. "You expect me to play the fiddle now after filling me to my ears with spaghetti? My, that was good."

If Susan was overstressed by all she had to do before the big gathering on Sunday, she didn't show it. "Well, Uncle, you won't be any rustier than the rest of us. Let's leave the dishes and get our jammin' on."

"Are you certain you want me to play the pipes?" Mac asked. "I'm not nearly as proficient as you all are."

Harry looked up at him from where he was leaning over to get his banjo. "Hey, Mac, we just want to jam. This isn't a talent show. Anyway, aren't we family?"

Mac grinned and began a drone on his bagpipes, hoping each of the different parts would not only be in tune with one another, but would also be in tune with the banjos and fiddle. Somehow, despite his amateur status as a piper, it sounded right.

Soon the mountainside house was plunking, swirling, and soaring with some good old-time music. Mac knew enough of the mountain tunes that he was able to join in with the pipes, and actually, to his surprise, it sounded good.

The quartet played for maybe half an hour. Susan's hands were hurting; Mac was breathless; Uncle Luke was tired; and Harry was ready for another two hours.

"Good," Susan said. "You can entertain us while I clean up the kitchen and get y'all some ice cream."

After all was cleaned up, she returned to the living room. Harry had stopped playing, and she walked in on the conversation about her adoption.

"Here she is. Susan, we were talking about the possibilities of who your birth mother might be," Mac said. "I know you have said it doesn't matter, but I'm wondering if that is really how you feel."

Uh-oh, not something I'm comfortable with. She didn't answer immediately but shrugged. "Well, you know it is like that jigsaw puzzle Ms. Junie Lee and I were working on yesterday. It is a missing puzzle piece. I'm okay with that because I know what the picture is, even with a missing piece. I'm seventy. The woman who birthed me, if she is even alive now, would be well up in her eighties or older. I doubt that I would ever be able to find her. I'm willing to allow it be simply unfortunate circumstances that turned out well for my parents."

Uncle Luke, not knowing, or perhaps not remembering if he had been told that Susan had been adopted, had a quizzical look. "You are adopted? Hmmm. You adopted me, and I'm not who I thought I was. Sounds like a good recipe for a wonderful family."

It had been a beautiful evening together, and Susan, despite all the pressure she felt to get everything in order for the clan gathering on Sunday, was relaxed and content. Knowing her uncle was happy and felt like part of the family superseded any worries. If Uncle Luke was happy and Aunt Carrie was happy, why shouldn't she be happy?

When Harry left, taking Uncle Luke with him, she and Mac snuggled. She was almost content with all her life.

Yet there was this haunting thing about her adoption. *What was it Aunt Carrie said?* "You know, God adopts us? Think about that." *What if my mother is still living? Maybe she would want to know that I am okay. Would she want to connect?* As Susan fell asleep that night, she thought about all these things. *I think after all the hullabaloo from the family meeting Uncle Luke is over, I'll do a search, even if Aunt Carrie won't tell me.*

Chapter 36

Carrie

Life Care Center, Banner Elk, North Carolina, 2009

When Carrie woke up on Tuesday morning, anticipating Luke Jr. and his visit, she thought about Susan's adoption. *Maybe, with all this about honesty in our clan with Luke, I should tell her, but I promised I never would. I wouldn't be sad if she did learn, but it can't come from me.*

Carrie dressed carefully, but not seeing as well as Gladdie and not as dexterous as her sixty-one-year-old child, she decided to forego the fancy hairdo and opted for her usual granny knot and no blush. *Afterall, this is the way I am. No frills!* She thought to herself, as she looked in her mirror.

She went to breakfast and decided to sit at a different table. Junie Lee was by herself, so Carrie joined her.

"Good morning, Carrie. I know you must have enjoyed meeting your half brother. Was he a surprise?"

"Yes and no, I guess. I wasn't expecting him to look so much like Papa and even had some of Papa's mannerisms. We had a wonderful time together. He's coming back for dinner today."

She looked at her sister-in-law strangely. "How did you know about him being my half brother? I didn't really talk about it."

"The grapevine around here travels far. Sary told me about it before she left. She also told me that Susan found out she was adopted. Are you going to tell her the truth?"

"Junie Lee, I promised I never would, and I have to keep that promise."

Junie Lee shook her head. "I don't see where it would hurt, but she was given to your family."

"That's right. So let's leave it there. Please don't stir the pot, Junie Lee."

This bore on Carrie's mind the rest of breakfast, and she said little more to Junie Lee. By the time she got back to her room, waiting for Susan to bring Luke to visit, she thought of more pleasant things. *Susan said Luke was going to bring his fiddle and play for me. A fiddle Papa made. Oh, that is going to be so good. Think about that instead of Susan.*

Susan brought Uncle Luke to the Life Care Center just as Carrie was headed to the dining room with her walker. She saw them, and her heart skipped a beat, excited to have this opportunity with her brother. *Every day is a gift, and I feel like it's Christmas and birthday all rolled into one.*

They hugged briefly, and she sent Susan to her room with the fiddle, while she led the way to the table where they would sit. Usually she sat with two other ladies, but since she had a guest, the staff had set them up at a table by themselves. While at dinner, their chatter was mostly inconsequential but touched on some of their early memories of Papa. Although the meal was nothing spectacular, it was nourishing and senior friendly, as Carrie suggested: meat loaf, creamed new potatoes, carrots, a side salad, and applesauce.

When they were done eating, they started back toward her room. Junie Lee stopped them and wanted an introduction.

"Luke, this is my sister-in-law, Junie Lee Vance, my husband's little sister. Junie Lee, my brother, Luke Harvey. He lives in Tampa, Florida. We won't have a lot of opportunity to visit, so we need to make the most out of this one. Please excuse us if we don't stop and chat a bit."

Luke gave her a gentlemanly bow but said nothing.

"Tampa! Oh, yes. Enjoy your visit, Luke Harvey." With that said, she turned and went the other direction.

Once settled in Carrie's room, they talked some more. Carrie described their papa as she knew him in the years before she and Jeb were married. This was a different man from the one Luke had known as a boy.

"I'm amazed, Carrie. I think I would have liked the real Luther Willson even more than the man I knew as Papa. Those short one-month stays were almost as though they did not happen. Our lives were disrupted for a month, and then he was gone. I remember him teaching me to fiddle before I could really hold it well. I remember him taking me to church on Sundays. I remember him playing the banjo every night before we went to bed. He would be gone most of the day. Mom said he was trying to sell his musical instruments. He was good to us, but I can't say I really knew him. I knew him better when he didn't come anymore, after I read the letters. I found them in the attic after my wife died. I know him better now, with what you have told me."

Carrie shook her head back and forth. *Poor Luke. To have never known the good in him. Poor Luke.*

"Speaking of fiddles, how about playing for me? I only learned to play the dulcimer and put it up several years ago. But I know all the old tunes and the words to all the old songs. Maybe I'll sing along."

Luke got his fiddle out, tuned it up as well as his ears could tell, and played songs Carrie loved and carried in her heart from her childhood. Time flew by as they enjoyed a step back to a former time.

Too soon, Susan appeared to take her uncle home.

As they walked down the hallway, Junie Lee met them. Susan stopped and spoke to her. "Hey, Ms. Junie Lee. Have you met my uncle?"

"I did. Luke, I can see Luther Willson in you. I heard your fiddling, too, and it sounds like Mr. Luther."

"That's quite a compliment. I can't play the banjo, though, like he did. My boy, Harry, does. I can't remember names, but I can remember how to play the fiddle."

"Nice to see you again, Ms. Junie Lee. We have to get back to Blowing Rock. Maybe I'll see you again sometime this week when I bring him back to see Aunt Carrie. You and I can work on another jigsaw puzzle."

"I'd like that, Susan. I'd like that."

Carrie stood in the doorway of her room, looking at Luke and Susan leaving. *I hope Junie Lee keeps her big mouth shut.*

Chapter 37

Susan

North Carolina High Country, October 2009

There were two more trips for Uncle Luke to visit Carrie for lunch and an afternoon together. Susan enjoyed being busy getting things ready for the gathering on Sunday. She was able to take her uncle to Banner Elk on Thursday, but Mac took both Luke and Harry on Saturday, so they could play fiddle and banjo both for Aunt Carrie. In fact, Carrie set them up to go into the common room so all the residents could enjoy the music.

On Saturday, Susan was busy putting together her mama's squash casserole recipe for Sunday afternoon, which she would bake in the morning. She needed to clean the house a bit, but the big thing for the day was organizing all the letters in sequence. Harry had brought all the pertinent letters along with him, so Susan had them spread out on a bed in one of the guest rooms, attempting to get the back-and-forth communications organized. Rereading them was even more emotional now that she was able to connect the dots.

When the three men got back on Saturday afternoon and walked in the door, Harry's cell phone rang. It was Gwen.

"You're where? What did you do with Catastrophe?"

"I'm in Boone at Green's Motel. Catastrophe is being well cared for by one of my coworkers. I don't have to be back until Tuesday. Surprise!"

"You could have warned me."

"Well, by the end of classes Friday, I was pumped up and ready. My suitcase was packed, standing beside the front door, and all I needed was a taxi to take me to the airport. Since my flight didn't get into Charlotte until after nine last night, and I'd already booked my room in Boone, I crashed without even a face wash. Decided to wait to call you today. Hope the shock won't be too much for you."

"So what's this Green's Hotel?"

"Hey, it's a bed and a bath. What else do I need? It's clean and convenient. Can I come and join y'all?"

Susan got on the phone and gave her directions.

Gwen arrived about twenty minutes after they hung up. She raved about the leaves. "I'm so glad I came now instead of waiting till next summer, which I hope to do as well. The mountains are just gorgeous! How come you've been hiding them up here all my life?"

Susan laughed at her youthful exuberance.

Her grandpa gave her a big hug. "Glad you came, sugar. We need a shot of youth around here this afternoon. Say, how about we all go to the little church that Papa helped build. Tomorrow's Sunday, isn't it?"

Susan and Harry looked at each other wide-eyed.

"I haven't been to church except for funerals since I was a boy. I think I would like to be in Papa's church and get a good dose of religion as a grown-up. Would that be too much trouble?" Uncle Luke continued.

Susan's mind raced. *When will I bake the casserole? I haven't been there except for our wedding and a bunch of funerals for years. When will I bake the casserole? What will Harry and Mac think about our backwoods preacher? And Gwen? When will I bake the casserole?*

"Why not?" Her eyes implored Mac. Would he say, "Yes, he'd go," or would he say, "Yeah, help yourself!"

"Sure, let's do it," Mac agreed. "You will love the quaintness of the building, and I guess we could all stand a good dose of grown-up religion, huh?"

"I'm in," Gwen said.

Harry shrugged. "Why not?"

"Guess I can bake the casserole early and reheat it at Mike's, huh?" *Men just don't understand.*

On Sunday morning, dressed in their nicest Sunday clothes, casserole baked, and letters organized and packed in the wooden chest (incidentally refinished by Mac during the week while Susan was running around the High Country), Susan and Mac picked up Harry and Uncle Luke. They would stop in Boone as well to pick up Gwen.

They arrived at the church just as men were filing in, having spit out their wads of tobacco or snuffed out their cigarettes; women were already seated in their usual places.

This would be the week when Preacher Combs was preaching, instead of one of the deacons, although the preacher had to divide his time between Willson's Cove and another small church. Susan was glad he was preaching. Who knew which of her kinfolk would have preached? She knew they were all a lot better at providing music than preaching.

The music was typical of a little mountain church, with a group of men and woman off to one side of the front leading the singing. Anyone who wanted to sing was invited to sit in the choir. As soon as the song leader, Cousin Oscar "Ozzie" Boone, saw Susan, he grabbed her by the arm and pulled her into the choir. Susan, in turn, encouraged Harry, Gwen, and Uncle Luke to sit in the choir with her. She knew Mac wouldn't sing. "You can sit here and enjoy us."

Uncle Luke shook his head. "I'd just as soon sit and listen, good-lookin'. You and Harry, go ahead." Gwen sat with her grandpa and Mac.

Other cousins at the church were Mike Willson, Leanne and Jimmy Sturgill, and Gerald and Barb Vance. All of them came up to Uncle Luke and introduced themselves to their uncle and cousin. After Ozzie greeted them, it took him a few chords on the guitar to get everyone's eyes set toward Preacher Combs.

Ozzie used a guitar to lead the choir for some of the music, and Wilda, his wife, played the piano for other ones. Her piano playing was more of the Southern gospel quartet style than what Harry was used to. Harry, despite his unfamiliarity with the songs, still did a good job of singing. He had studied the shape note singing years before and got into the spirit of the singing. His tenor voice added a brighter note than usual.

In between songs, the man seated next to him, a distant cousin of an ancient age, leaned over and said, "'Hits like ol' Luther himself war a-singin'!"

The singing lasted twenty minutes or so, and the preacher got up to preach. Susan had not heard Preacher Combs other than at their wedding, which wasn't a preaching. She was surprised that he did not rant and rave like the old-time preacher would do, trying to preach sinners out of hell. He had not been to seminary, not uncommon for the mountain preachers, but he had gone to a preaching school over in Tennessee for a year. The local churches had gotten together and ordained him only a year before. Although he was a bit older than some of the preacher boys in the area, having been married with a wife and several children already, he was young in the ministry. Young, but he seemed to have a good grasp on how to get his message across without hollering. He took his text from Galatians 4:5, the very verse Aunt Carrie had loosely quoted to Susan only last week:

Galatians 4:4–5 said, "But when the fullness of the time was come, God sent forth his Son, made of a woman, made under the law, To redeem them that were under the law, that we might receive the adoption of sons."

In Combs' logical three-point sermon, he talked about how adopted children are chosen, wanted by their parents. He said it is the same when God chose us. It was because he wanted us, loved us, and paid for us with his own blood on Calvary. He put it so simply that even the children could understand it but not so simply that it would be irrelevant to more mature minds.

Tears rimmed Susan's eyes, but after she thought about it for a few minutes, she thought maybe one of her cousins put the preacher up to this sermon, and she was ready to be mad at everyone. She looked about her at her cousins, and no one was looking at her as though they were thinking, *Listen up, Susan.*

Then she thought, *Yes, listen up, Susan. It is time, as Uncle Luke said, for a dose of grown-up religion.* More than that, she understood that the faith she had been taught to believe was not about her but about a God who loved her enough to adopt her through Jesus. She silently prayed the first real prayer of her life. *Thank you, Jesus, for making a way for me to be adopted in your family.*

The song following the sermon was not the expected "Just as I Am," as typically sung in many mountain churches, but rather an old song, sung without the musical instruments.

Preacher Combs had resurrected from bygone days "Come Ye Sinners, Poor and Needy." It not only touched Susan's heart, but it also pulled a few latent heartstrings for Uncle Luke. As the two left the church arm in arm, they seemed to share the spirit of the meeting.

Chapter 38

The Willson Clan

Homeplace, Willson's Cove, North Carolina, October 2009

Mike, knowing that family would be arriving even before churches were let out from services, had left the kitchen door unlocked. He hurried home, but Will and Jennie were already there with Aunt Carrie. Reatha's grandson, Justin, had brought her and Clyde.

Francine had left home, truant from church for the day, and was there by ten thirty and greeted the others when they showed up. Although she was not usually involved with family, the business with a newly found uncle and cousin spurred her to resume being part of the clan.

Mike had set up the table in the big dining room for all of them, putting two tables together. There would be twenty-five of them all together if everyone showed up.

And then Gwen Harvey, coming up from St. Petersburg, would make twenty-six. It would be crowded, but everyone would have a seat. Grandpa had seen this in the future, if this was to be the family home, home for the clan. Back in his day, there were his brothers and sisters, too, with all their families. This would not have been the first time such a gathering had eaten together in this dining room.

Mike had set up two chairs at the head of the table, just like Grandpa used to do for Grandma Zanny and himself. These were for Aunt Carrie and Uncle Luke.

Francine got out Grandma's old linens from the sideboard, two big tablecloths, and spread them. She didn't use the linen napkins, but she had brought good disposable dinner napkins, plates, cutlery, and cups to use.

The short distance from the church to the house was barely enough time for conversation. As Mac drove to the family home after church, the car was quiet; each one with their own thoughts. Uncle Luke broke the silence. "I feel like I have truly come home. Thank you, Susan, for stirring the pot."

Susan responded with a gentle hug with her uncle. But in diffusing any emotional talk, she asked Gwen, "I imagine the service was a bit different than what you have encountered before, Gwen."

"Yes, well, I really enjoyed it though. The pastor's sermon was very good, kinda right down the alley of what is going on in our family. I know the concept, but his sermon clarified it to me. Is he typical of the ministers in these little churches?"

"Not exactly. Like many others, Preacher Combs has not been to college or seminary, just a little preacher boy school over in Tennessee. But his delivery doesn't have the typical animation that some of the old-timers used to do. I think he's a new breed of mountain preachers, and the churches are better for it in our current society."

When Luke emerged from the car, Dook sniffed at his feet, and the old man reached down and scratched behind his ears. Dook licked his hand. Luke was accepted, then, as a member of the clan.

By one o'clock in the afternoon, everyone had arrived and gone into the house, so Dook settled under the porch. *Food. Lots for me after they leave.* Soon he was in ham and casserole heaven in his dreams.

Since most of the family had not met Uncle Luke, they were a bit more subdued than the usual exuberant, talkative family. Aunt Carrie was already seated in her chair at the head of the dining room tables, and Susan led Uncle Luke to the seat beside her. Excitement could be seen in both of their eyes. Each of the family who had not met him at the church came and introduced themselves.

They began with Clyde, who came and seated himself next to him. He handed Uncle Luke a six-by-eight file card. "I am Clyde

Willson. My daddy was Luther, Papa's oldest. If you are like me, Uncle, you won't recall anyone's names, so I have taken the liberty of listing each of us with our family connections: parents, children, and spouses. I hope it will help, at least a little."

"Thank you, Clyde." Luke laughed, understanding the name thing. "You are correct that I won't remember names. I sometimes don't even recall my son's name, and that can be embarrassing. I try the trick of repeating names, but, Clyde, that doesn't work too well anymore."

Reatha was using a cane, and it was not a good day for her. She had been determined to come, so she sat down across from Clyde and next to Aunt Carrie. "Uncle Luke, I'm Reatha Cook. I hope you can hear me. I apologize for plopping down and talking across you, Aunt Carrie. And thank you, Clyde, for being so thoughtful about listing us on that card. That was smart. Uncle Luke, my daddy was Roby. Daddy was the first one of the family to have a car, but Papa hated it. He never wanted to ride in it. I think he rode in it three times."

"I remember Papa referring to a 1915 Model T in some of his letters. I can't imagine how awful it would have been to ride in such a beast even on these roads today, let alone those roads back in the 1920s. Whew!"

Reatha grabbed her grandson, Justin, by the hand. "This is my daughter Joyce's boy, Justin. He brought me here today, and he has learned to play the fiddle the way Papa did. In fact, he plays one of Papa's fiddles."

"Looking forward to hearing you, young fellow. You might want to hang out with my granddaughter, Gwen. She's probably in the kitchen."

"Thank you, sir. I've already met her." The young man, a junior at Appalachian State University in Boone, had liked what he saw in Gwen, and headed back to the kitchen.

Ozzie, Leanne, Gerald, with their spouses, and Mike had already met him at the church. They allowed the others to talk with Uncle in their own time.

Raymond and Dolly had flown into Charlotte from Kansas City on Saturday and drove up from Charlotte last evening. They were staying at the homeplace with Mike. They introduced themselves. Uncle Luke, this is my wife, Dolly, and I'm Ray Davis. Rancie was my mama. We live in Kansas City, Missouri, but we didn't want the rest of the family to keep you all to themselves. Welcome to the family. It's been a long time coming."

"Kansas City. I've heard that things are lookin' up in Kansas City. They've gone about as far as they can go! I played that song on my fiddle for my wife when she was living. She loved the musical *Oklahoma!* I'm honored that you have come." Luke shook his head. "It is a wonder to me how magnanimous our family is, considering the circumstances."

Ray's sister, Pansy, led her husband, Jake Burleson, to meet Uncle Luke. "Uncle, I've been telling Jake here that you look just like Grandpa, and he wouldn't believe me. See Jake. I'm telling the truth." Jake shook the old fellow's hand and stepped back. Pansy went on and introduced herself. "I'm your sister Rancie's daughter and Ray's sister. We had another brother, but he was killed in Korea, barely eighteen years old."

Pansy would have monopolized Uncle Luke's time, but Francine tapped her on her shoulder. "My turn, cousin!" Francine was the only of the cousins who was divorced, and she was very sensitive and guilt-ridden about it. She apologized even before she told him who she was. "Uncle, I suppose I was a bad wife. I have no husband to introduce. He left me when my daughter was a teenager. I am Francine Carlin. You met my brother at church this morning. He leads the choir. Our mama was your sister Ossie, Ossie Boone."

"Now, sweet lady, I know you weren't a bad wife. Papa didn't have any bad young'uns, and I know your mama didn't raise any bad young'uns. These things happen. You just stand up tall and be the best Willson you can be. Will you do that for your uncle?"

She nodded tearfully and squeezed his hand.

Lily May came from behind him and patted his shoulder. "Uncle Luke, you met my sister, Leanne, at church this morning. Our mama was Delphy, the first redhead in the family. I was a redhead before it turned white. Grandma used to say she got her red hair from petting old Dook. Was it Dook number two? Anyway, when she was carrying

Mama, she'd pet the dog, one of Dook's ancestors, all the time while Papa was in Florida. I'm glad that Clyde gave you the card with all our names on it. I do the genealogy for the family, so when I get it all caught up for the reunion next summer, I'll see that you get a copy. Hope you can come, though."

"If I'm alive and kicking, I'll be here. Look forward to the genealogy information."

"No doubt about it, Uncle Luke." Will stepped into Lily May's place. "You already know Mama. I'm her oldest, but not her meanest. You met him at church this morning, and you already know Gladdie. I'm Will Vance, and this little gal is Jennie." He led his less-than-little wife forward.

"Now I just want you to know that we think you are mighty important because there's a Panthers and Bucs game on this afternoon. I never miss watching it on TV. If the Panthers lose, I'll blame it on Susan, not you!"

"Oh, that's right. I forgot the Bucs were playing the Panthers today? Maybe we can sneak off and watch it together. Good to know I'm not the only one in the family who enjoys watching football. But since you came, I'll even promise not to get mad if the Bucs lose."

"Come on, Will." Mike grabbed his sleeve. "We're gettin' hungry! You can watch the game back in my bedroom while the rest of us eat! Now, folks, before we get in line for the food, Ozzie, will you bless it for us?"

Ozzie prayed a short prayer, and Susan led Uncle Luke to the kitchen to fill up his plate. Gladdie filled a plate for her mother and took it to the table, and Lily May took a plate to Reatha and one to Clyde. No one else had trouble finding their food and getting back to the table.

Lots of inconsequential chatter, banter, and laughter joined the clatter of utensils. Both Luke and Carrie ate and listened, periodically looking at each other and smiling or shaking their heads at the joyfulness of the gathering.

"Carrie, I never dreamed I could be a part of a family, not even after I learned I had one. I am full and not with food. Full of love and happiness."

"We got a lotta love, Luke. A lotta love. And it's yours, too."

After the main meal was consumed, there was dessert, but Susan suggested waiting. "Folks, listen up. We'd like to have a bit of music. I asked any of you who played instruments and would bring them today to join us for a jam in the living room. I even talked my husband into playing his bagpipes. I think he can start us off with a march, while we gather in the room. Let's wait and have our dessert after we have music. Once Aunt Carrie, Uncle Luke, Clyde, and Reatha get settled, then Mac can play the rest of us in. Let's burn up the hillsides with mountain music!"

"Hear, hear!" several people said.

As the family filtered into the living room, Dolly, Wilda, Jennie, and Barb cleaned up the table, tossed the trash, and covered the little bit of leftovers. Barb fixed a big plate of scraps for Dook. "He'll be a-roarin' when the music starts if we don't feed him. I know that pup!"

About that time, the drone on the bagpipes began and Dook roared anyway, joining the bagpipes. Instead of a march, Mac played the familiar "Amazing Grace." Once everyone was seated and the musicians gathered in front of the big bay window, they tuned together to the bagpipes. Susan and Harry were on banjo, Luke and Justin on their Luther Willson fiddles, Ozzie and Clyde with guitar, Jake brought his harmonica, and Lily May had her dulcimer. It was a good mix, and they began with "Cripple Creek," went through the familiar family repertoire, and then Luke had a request.

"My mom, well, actually my sister, was named Maggie. Papa always called her Little Maggie, and sang the song for her. Can we play that one?"

"We can and we will," Lily May said. "And Leanne will sing it, won't you? Mama used to sing it all the time, and Leanne sounds just like her."

So "Little Maggie" it was.

When the song ended, Aunt Carrie said a strange thing. "'Little Maggie' is the glue that will bond our two half families into one."

By this time, the aging fingers had done their best and needed rest. Justin fiddled some old fiddle tunes as they headed back to their dessert and some coffee and sweet tea.

Will came up to Uncle Luke, looking a bit sheepish. He had skipped out on the music and went to watch the game. "Sorry, Uncle Luke, but the Panthers won 28 to 21."

"Aw shoot! But we had a better game here, young fellow!"

Aunt Carrie looked exhausted, and Gladdie brought her walker to her and helped her to the car. Harry had told his dad that they would plan to leave Tuesday for Florida, so he would bring him to see his sister one more time the next day. Luke stood and hugged Carrie. "Wish the afternoon could go on forever, Carrie, but I'll be over to say so long tomorrow."

"Love you, little brother." Carrie had tears in her eyes.

Susan and her carload were the last to leave. Mike carried her banjo and Uncle Luke's fiddle to the car. "Suze, I thought you gave up the banjer because of your arthritis. You done pretty good this afternoon. La, you tore it up!"

"This mountain banjo is a lot lighter than my old bluegrass banjo." She winked at Mac and added, "Oh well, it helps to be married to a doctor, too. I had a great time, even if my hands might hurt all night."

As they walked to the car, Dook followed closely between Susan and Uncle Luke. Luke reached down and patted the hound on his head. "See you next summer, old boy."

After all the hullabaloo of the afternoon, everyone was tired, but Luke commented that it was a good tired. He had been on the go from the time he got up until now; it was four in the afternoon. "I plan to sleep all the way back to the hotel, but Susan, there is one last thing I need to do before the day is over. We have a little more sunshine, so I'd like to see where Papa is buried."

Susan gasped. Although it used to be a short walking distance by a path through the meadow from the homeplace, the only way to get there now was by the road, as the meadow was now all woodland. The cemetery was on the hill behind the church, and it was a steep hill. Mac could drive his SUV partway there, but there would still be another two hundred feet up the hill pathway to the entrance.

"Uncle Luke, I'm not certain I have the energy to walk up that hill after that big meal, let alone for you to walk up there. We can drive up to the gate, but it's still another couple hundred feet to the graves."

"I'd like to try, even if I'm just where I can see the tombstones from the gate."

"Okay. Let's do it."

Uncle Luke was persistent. He got out of the car and followed Susan through the gate and up the path, with Harry and Gwen tagging behind him. He stopped a couple of times to catch his breath, but he walked all the way to the place Luther Willson was buried beside Susanna. Carved on the left half of the stone was this:

Luther Willson
January 5, 1879 to September 4, 1950

Luke stood beside the grave quietly for about two minutes, sighed deeply, and turned to Susan. "Where are my brothers and sisters buried? Are they all here?"

Susan pointed toward both sides of the row and along the pathway. "Yes, all of them are here. They were buried in order away from Grandpa's and Grandma's plot. Girls on Grandma's side and boys on Grandpa's side." She showed him, as they walked along.

"I just realized something. He was not Luther Sr. and my brother Luther Jr. My brother was Martin Luther Willson. Hmmm." He walked on, looking at each tombstone and then looking at the card Clyde had given him. He said nothing more, and no one disturbed his thoughts.

When it appeared that he had been satisfied he had seen them all, he stopped and looked at Harry. "Son, I probably have no right to ask the Willsons if I could be buried here, but I want my ashes scattered here with my brothers and sisters. Can you do that for me?"

"Yes, Dad. If the family agrees, I will do that."

"Not Stella's. Just mine. We will scatter hers in Tampa Bay. That was what she had wanted anyway. I had planned to have you scatter our ashes at the same time. I need…need to have mine brought here. Shall we go now?"

No more had they left the cove than Uncle Luke was sound asleep. The others chatted quietly, reviewing the afternoon.

Chapter 39

Carrie

Banner Elk, North Carolina, October 2009

Luke had no trouble sleeping the night through except for his usual bathroom trips. The next morning, Harry got him up early, and they had their breakfast at the hotel. Rather than depending on Susan or Mac to take them to Banner Elk, Harry would drive there today. They both needed to say their goodbyes to Carrie.

Gwen joined them for breakfast before heading back to the Charlotte airport to make her late-afternoon flight back to PIE, St. Petersburg-Clearwater airport.

"So, good-lookin' granddaughter, what did you think of your North Carolina family?"

"Grandpa, I am so glad I came. I don't know about you and Dad, but I feel like I belong. I had a great time with Justin. But I loved the banter and chatter around the dinner table, but the family stories were wonderful. I'm really looking forward to the reunion next summer. I will be off school the week they have it, and I'm going to get my name in for vacation from the hospital for then, as well. You guys can stay in St. Petersburg if you want to, but I'm coming, God willing."

It was foggy outside, making the possibility of a slow trip for Gwen's trip down the mountain. She said her farewells to her dad and grandpa, and left as soon as she had eaten.

Hoping the fog would lift before they left for Banner Elk, Harry took his time with breakfast. Yesterday had been such a long and full day, too, that he didn't want to overtax his dad. It was about ten o'clock when they left, arriving at the retirement home just before lunch. Carrie was expecting them and had told the desk they would be coming.

I wish I could keep him here. He has given me a lift I never expected. I only wish Delphy had lived to know him. She was waiting for them at the entrance when they arrived.

But while she was waiting, Junie Lee saw her and came to sit with her. "Carrie, I know you and I haven't been very close for being sisters-in-law, but I want you to know that I'm real happy that your brother came and you got to know each other. I only wish you'd tell Susan what you know. You and I may be the only ones who could tell her."

Carrie, not wanting to get into a spat with Junie Lee, considered how she could diffuse her. She looked at the little lady, and said, "Junie Lee, I don't want to tell her because I promised Jeb I wouldn't. I promised Harvey and Bea that I wouldn't. They never wanted her to know she was wasn't theirs. Please don't tell her. Please drop it. She won't be here today with Luke, and I don't know when she'll be back. They will be going to Macon for the winter, I guess. What happened was unfortunate, and we all knew it, but it was the best thing that ever happened for Harvey and Bea, and it was the best thing that ever could happen for Susan. Drop it, Junie Lee."

There were tears in Junie Lee's eyes as she walked away. She left just as Harry and Luke buzzed the door to be let in. She went to her room and closed the door.

Carrie laughed every time she heard the door buzzer. The story was that one of the residents had "run away from home," and the door was now locked all the time. The man, a New Yorker, thought he had been kidnapped. An attendant came and let Luke and Harry in.

After all the family celebration from the day before, their lunchtime was subdued. *I have so many things I want to ask him, but I won't ever have the time. It will be eight months till we see each other again, if then.*

Luke voiced the same thing. "Carrie, I'll remember your name if I never remember anyone else's. There is just so much I want to ask you. Even if I didn't have to go home, I doubt if we could remember everything we should tell each other. I am going to pray. Yes, me, Luke Harvey, is going to pray that I will live and be able to come back next June for the reunion."

"I was just thinking the same, Luke. We need to write to each other. Here is my address." She handed him a file card with her address and the phone number in the room and a blank one for him to write his. "My phone doesn't have an answering machine, but if you want to talk and I don't answer, try again later. I'd love to hear you on the other end. Here's an empty card for yours."

Luke handed the card to Harry. "Here, son. I have a phone, but I can't remember the number off the top of my head. I live at Legacy at Highwoods Preserve, Assisted Living, Tampa, Florida, but I don't recall the address."

"I've got it, Dad."

"Carrie, you would love it at Legacy. I have what's called, what is it, Harry? A regency suite. It's a private room. It's not their best, but it is fine for an old bachelor like me. We have couples there who have larger suites."

"Guess I'll stay here, little brother." *How I'd love to visit him there!*

Despite thoughts about unasked questions, neither of them delved into any of them. The lunchtime chatter was friendly but inconsequential. After lunch, Luke and Carrie went back to her room and visited, while Harry visited with the old soldier, Mr. Davis.

Carrie still did not have a new roommate, but the lady who was supposed to have come a week before had not been able to leave the Watauga Medical Center in Boone. She was expected to arrive later this afternoon.

Settled in her room, Luke asked what he knew was a touchy subject. "Carrie, maybe it is none of my business, but I am wondering about our niece's adoption."

"Oh yes. Susan."

"Yes. I assume you knew the identity of her birth mother. In the first place, why would our brother not want her to know she was adopted? And now, since she knows, why not tell her, if you know who the mother was?"

"Luke, it was Bea, not Harvey, who insisted that she was never to know. She looked enough like the rest of the family that it wouldn't be obvious. Bea's family weren't tall people, so Susan being short was no big thing. Her curls were different, but lots of other children, if not in the family, had curls. My Gerald has wavy hair. Bea and Harvey were so happy to have a beautiful, healthy baby of their own."

Carrie sighed, unsure of her answer to his second question. "Luke, I made a promise to my brother and sister-in-law that I'd not tell her, and I won't. That's it. But there may be at least one party who could ruin it for her and tell her. I think it would stir up a nest of rattlesnakes. I oppose it."

"So what if Susan decides to pursue it on her own and attempt to find her birth mother, living or dead?"

Oh, I hope Junie Lee doesn't grab Harry while he's wandering about out there. She's likely to stir up that nest! "Luke, that would be on her head, not mine. Let's just leave things where they are."

By two o'clock, both of the octogenarians were getting tired and needed naps. Harry came to take his dad back to Blowing Rock. After lingering hugs, mingling tears, and promises to write and call, Luke walked away from his sister with a low heart and a head held high.

Carrie stood in her doorway, watching them until they were out of sight. *Hope Junie Lee doesn't pounce on them before they get out the door.*

Chapter 40

Luke

Blowing Rock, North Carolina, October 2009

Junie Lee's door was closed as they walked by her room, and she was not in the hallway. Carrie's mind could be relieved. Luke napped most of the way back to the hotel and slept the remainder of the afternoon. They were to have dinner with Susan and Mac at their house. Susan had promised it would be a light supper after the huge meal at the homeplace yesterday. Chicken rice, she suggested.

Luke dreamed after he lay down on his bed in the hotel. He and Stella were old, but it wasn't really Stella. It was the lady who played piano at Legacy. They were eating at his house in St. Petersburg and talking about Susan. The lady was angry because Susan wouldn't tell her the name of her mother. Then the lady changed into Carrie. Luke woke up with confusion, calling out, "Stella!"

"You okay, Dad?"

"Had a wild dream. I didn't know where I was at first. Dreamed of your mother, but then it wasn't her. I forget what it was all about."

As they got ready to go to dinner, Luke kept trying to recall the dream, but it was gone; just disturbing.

Harry had packed up most of their belongings, except for what they would need until morning and their musical instruments, so they planned to stay with Susan and Mac until Luke was tired. The dinner was simple but delicious.

"Good-lookin', you are one good cook. My Stella would have approved."

"Thank you, Uncle. I would have liked to have known Aunt Stella."

"Hah. Never considered that she was your aunt. I dreamed about her today, but then it wasn't her. There is this lady at Legacy who plays piano. I think I was dreaming about her, too. What's her name, son?"

"Oh, your girlfriend, huh? I think her name is Lynnie Van Sant. Ms. Van Sant was a well-known concert pianist locally in Clearwater and Tampa. I know she taught at Creative Keys in Clearwater. I had forgotten about this when I met her at your place."

Mac laughed. "Girlfriend, huh. Guess you'll be glad to get back to her. Has she heard you play your fiddle?"

"I actually played my fiddle with her accompanying me. We played some old-fashioned songs and hymns. It was nice playing that way." *I'm not telling them I played the violin in my high school orchestra. Oh, I do know how to play. I just happen to like fiddle playing.* "I fiddled for her, too, and she played Beethoven for me."

"Ah, my father, the lothario."

"We all have things about us that even those closest to us don't know."

Susan looked thoughtful. "Yeah, but there are things we don't even know about ourselves, like who my birth parents were."

Luke's mind went back to his conversation with Carrie. *I don't understand why Carrie is so stubborn about this. I'd want to know. After my shock about Papa back those twenty years ago, I was happy to know about it. I only wish I had pursued it then. I would have gotten to know my brothers and sisters.*

"Susan, Carrie and I discussed it today. She says to let it alone. I'm not certain I agree with her. Would you attempt to find out?"

"You bet your gazoonie, I will. Mac and I will soon be hitting the road back to Macon for the winter, but every day until we go, I'm checking out courthouse birth records in every county around here. I might come up with something. No, I probably won't bother Aunt

Carrie anymore about it. She made a promise to Mama and Daddy that she'd never tell me. I respect that. But I will search."

"I hate to ask what a gazoonie is, but it doesn't sound like I'd win the bet. Go for it, good-lookin'."

By six thirty that evening, Luke was fading into the setting sun, but he hated to leave so soon. Harry must have noticed and asked if he'd like to go back to the hotel.

"I hate to leave. If I happen to nod off here by the fire, just keep on talking. I want this to last as long as possible. Like the old joke, 'I don't buy green bananas.' Each day is a gift. I read in the Bible that we are given 'three score and ten [Psalm 90:10], and if by reason of strength we make it to four score, anything else is one day at a time.' Don't reckon I quoted it exactly."

He presently nodded off, and the others talked around him. He dreamed again. He was wandering through the Willson graveyard, talking to Papa. Papa was telling him about the family. He told him about Harvey and why he chose Harvey as his last name. Then the dream went elsewhere, but Papa was there showing him the places he had visited in the High Country.

Harry let him sleep. "He can fall asleep at the drop of a hat, and then sleep all night long. He's amazing."

When Luke awakened after an hour's nap, he was a little mixed up. He asked for Papa. "Where'd he go? Where did Papa go? We were—"

He laughed at himself. "Guess I was dreaming. Did I miss anything?"

"Nah, just told 'em a bunch of lies about you, Dad. You think you can say so long so we can get out of their hair?"

"You know I hate to leave, but I know we can't stay forever. I'm just going to count the days until they either end up in June 2010 or they end. Thank you for a delightful week. The time has been filled with so much. I don't know if I'll ever process it all. But my heart is even fuller. Thank you, thank you, thank you."

He hugged Susan, shook hands with Mac, and as he did in leaving Carrie, he held his head high.

"I'll be down to see you soon. Maybe Christmas. How about it? Will you be around then, Harry?"

"Yes. I always come home and have Christmas with Dad and Gwen. We'd love to have you, and you may stay in our guest room. What do you think, Dad?"

Luke had already gone out the door. Harry found him standing by the car, looking for the moon. It was in its dark phase. *Hope I'm not going into a dark phase.* A chill coursed through his spine.

It was just a few moments past seven thirty the next morning when Harry woke up and saw his dad standing with the curtains open, watching the sun's reflection sending tendrils of light over the mountains and the valley below them.

"Morning, son. Just getting the last glimpse of heaven before we descend into—" He didn't finish. But he was thinking about the dark phase that disturbed him last evening.

"Harry, if I never get to come back here, at least I'm satisfied that I came. After I'm gone, keep in touch with our family. Scatter my ashes at Willson's graveyard. You'll do that, won't you?"

Harry put his arm about his dad's bony shoulders. "You know I will, Dad. How about some sunny-side up eggs and grits, and get down the mountain."

"Harry, she isn't my girlfriend."

The two laughed all the way to the car. They ate breakfast at Sonny Rock Eggs and Things and headed off the mountain.

CHAPTER 41

Susan

Mitchell County Courthouse, Bakersville, North Carolina, October 21, 2009

Susan saw nothing to laugh about this morning, and her breakfast eggs had not satisfied the emotional hunger to learn who she really was. She soon left on a drive to Bakersville, the first stop on her quest to find the identity of her birth mother. She shivered in the late October cool air. *Hope Uncle Luke won't catch a chill and get sick before they have a chance to get off the mountain.*

Despite the lingering beauty of the mountains, as she wove around curves on US 221 and then North Carolina 194, her thoughts were dark. With all the excitement of Uncle Luke coming to meet the family, she had put aside her anger at learning about her adoption. Last night, Uncle had stirred it up again. *No, I'm not going to straighten my hair and wear platform heels to look like a Willson, but I will scrape every smidgen of ink from birth records to learn who I am. Oh yeah, I'm a Willson, but who am I? Who was my mother? Who sired me?*

Why Bakersville? Mitchell County was not that far from Willson's Cove, although it wasn't as near as Newland. Any of the surrounding counties could have been her birthplace. She would search them all: Mitchell, Avery, Watauga, Ashe, and even Caldwell and maybe Burke, although they were in the foothills. The drive to Bakersville took her an hour and a half from home, but she arrived without incident. The office of records where she might find what she was seeking was open, and the clerk was helpful.

If it was a closed adoption, as she supposed, she couldn't look into adoption records, but she could find out if there were any female babies born to a Frampton or maybe a Vance on July 3, 1939. That was the focus of her search. It took her long past hunger, and when she finished, not finding what she was seeking, she looked for somewhere to replace the long-digested egg. Mammie's Kitchen sounded like a good spot, seeing she was looking for her mammie.

It was only one thirty after she finished lunch, so she still had time to go to the courthouse in Newland. Back on Highway 194, it took her another fifty minutes to get there. *Good. If I can get two courthouses a day, maybe Mac and I can get home to Macon by the weekend. I think he is more than ready. I feel sorry for him, having to put up with my snit about this. But he isn't the one who was adopted!*

Newland offered no more than had Bakersville, so she stuffed her notes into her huge purse and headed for Blowing Rock.

Her sweet Mac had supper ready for her.

"Oh, Mac! I wanted to find it so badly. I wanted to find it already the minute I talked to Aunt Carrie. I understand why she won't tell me, but don't you think, if the woman may still be living, she'd want me to know?"

"Shhh. Sweet girl, just get your mind on something else tonight and sleep. If you just relax tonight, let's watch a movie or something, make some mulled cider, and sit by the fire. If you can do that without fussing, I'll go with you tomorrow. How's that sound?"

She looked at him like a puppy who needed petting and nodded her head in agreement.

Wednesday morning wasn't as raw as the morning before, but it was still cold. At least there was sunshine as Susan and Mac made their way to the Boone courthouse. It must have been a trial day because there was little place to park. Of course it was always difficult to find a parking place in Boone, but this was worse. They ended up parking five blocks away and walking.

Mac shivered. "Glad for this coat today. That wind is mean, despite the sunshine."

"Oh, come on you flatland wimp! Enjoy a little fresh air. I'll treat you to some lunch if you stop complaining."

When they finally found the place where birth records were kept, they each began their search on separate microfilm projectors. With both of them working, it took them an hour. Neither one found anything close to their search: female; July 3, 1939; and Frampton or Vance.

It was too early for lunch when they finished, so they took off for West Jefferson. The beautiful Beaux Arts 1904 courthouse was an eye-catching change after the modern facility in Boone. As they ascended the steps, Susan had a positive feeling. *This is it. I'll find her here.*

She did not.

Susan was quiet, a disappointed quiet, as they left the courthouse and stopped at Hardee's for her to treat Mac to lunch.

"I know this is hard for you, Suze, but maybe you need to resign yourself to not finding anything. If you want to, I think we have time to make the courthouse in Lenoir. What do you say?"

With a mouthful of biscuit, she mumbled, "I'm in."

It took a little more than an hour down US 221 and US 441 to Lenoir, and they had plenty of time before the records office closed. Again each of them sat in front of microfilm viewers and scrolled through the 1939 birth records.

Susan heard her husband give a low whistle.

"What?"

"I don't know if this is what we're looking for or not, but it is not a pretty sight."

"What?" Louder.

"Look here."

Susan moved over to his viewer. She gasped. July 3, 1939; baby girl; mother: Jessy Vance, age twelve; father: none listed. "Oh my. No wonder Mama and Daddy didn't want it known. The poor child! She must have been abused!"

Tears flowed freely down her cheeks and onto her sweater, leaving tiny diamonds of moisture beading up on the blue wool. Susan reached for Mac's hand.

"Mac, I don't know if I should look for her or not. If she is living, she is probably not even around here. She would be eighty-two or three, depending on her birthday. Thank you for finding it, honey. Thank you." She gave him a bear hug.

They took the microfilm to the desk and got a printout. Susan tucked it safely into the bottom of her purse and grasped her husband's hand, and the two of them left the courthouse.

The search of records was over, but the search of Susan's heart was anything but done. She saw her need as one to know if her birth mother had overcome the horror of a childhood trauma and had gone on with her life as normally as possible.

It didn't hit her immediately, but when it did, she gasped. "Mac! I have been suspecting that Uncle Jeb's brother, Tommy, had probably gotten some Frampton girl pregnant. My mother, not my father, was a Vance! At least I can be rid of the dread that sweet old Tommy wasn't an evil fellow! And if Will is my first cousin, is Junie Lee Vance my mother? She was Uncle Jeb's sister. Junie Lee may be her nickname. Oh mercy! I like that little lady, but my mother? What am I to do?"

US 321 to Blowing Rock was a short ride taking half an hour. She and Mac talked it back and forth, but they were both more confused than when they didn't know. They got home in time to make a good supper and enjoy the evening in front of the fireplace. Mac caught up on his newspapers, while Susan searched the Internet for people named Jessy Lynn Vance, including obituaries. She came up empty. She made some notes in her journal and then got ready for bed. Tomorrow, she would go back to Banner Elk. She would confront Aunt Carrie.

CHAPTER 42

Susan

*Life Care Center, Banner Elk, North Carolina,
October 22, 2009*

Susan surprised her aunt. Thursdays were the days she usually had her hair washed. She had a difficult time doing it herself, so Gladdie would come to the home and do it for her. Her hair was still damp and hanging down around her shoulders. Gladdie had left only moments before Susan arrived.

"Well! I didn't expect to see you so soon. I thought you and Mac were headed back to Macon for the winter. Neither did I expect to see you with such a sour look on your face. And I can guess that you are still stewing about who your birth mother was."

"I'm sorry, Aunt Carrie, but I need to put this to rest, and I can't until I know the truth. I know now that her last name was Vance. At first, since I learned that your children were my first cousins, when the rest of the cousins were not, I thought the only scenario was that Tommy had gotten some Frampton girl in trouble. I was almost good with that until I decided to check courthouse birth records. I went to Bakersville, Newland, Boone, Jefferson, and found nothing. My last-ditch effort was Lenoir."

Carrie sucked in her breath but said nothing.

"I learned that a female was born to a Jessy Vance, July 3, 1939. Is Jessy the same as Junie Lee? Is that why Ms. Junie Lee is so attentive to me? Is Junie Lee my mother?"

"As I have said before, sweet girl, I could never tell you anything more than I've done told you. You were adopted. I will tell you no more!" She got that look on her face that said, "No more!"

"Aunt Carrie, I know you promised, but now I know this much, and it's tearing my heart apart."

"Yes, I promised. See Junie Lee. She's been pestering me to tell you, and I can't. See Junie Lee."

Both of them had tears in their eyes, but Susan gave her a hug and left. She would see Junie Lee.

It was not difficult to find the little woman. She was standing outside her own room as though she expected Susan.

"Hey, sweetie. Why don't you come in and sit a spell with me? I take it Carrie is being stubborn."

"Not stubborn, Ms. Junie Lee. She is committed to the promise she made seventy years ago. I have found out, uh, found out that… Oh, help me! Are you my mother?"

The little woman laughed, but it was not a joyful laugh. "No. I could only wish to have had such a lovely daughter."

"I don't understand. I found out with my DNA that Aunt Carrie's children are my first cousins, so that would make either you or Mister Tommy my parent. I did a lot of research, and despite the fact that it was likely a closed adoption, birth records with the mother's names are available." She repeated the same thing that she had said to Aunt Carrie about searching the courthouses. "I found a Jessy Vance with the right statistics. The only conclusion I could draw was that you are my mother."

"Lenoir. Susan, let me tell you a story. If it's difficult for you and for Carrie, it's very close to me. I was not the only girl in the family. I had a twin sister. We were identical. Yes, her name was Jessy. Jessy Lynn."

"My mother."

"Yes. When our parents died, we were young children. Tommy, the oldest, was only fifteen; Jeb was eleven; and we were seven. We, all four, were taken to Crossnore School, but the boys refused to stay. They went to live with an aunt until Tommy decided he wanted to strike out on his own. He and Jeb went back to the house where we had lived with our parents. We would come home some weekends and attempt to be a family again."

"But y'all stayed at Crossnore School."

"We did. We loved it there. I graduated from there. But Jessy Lynn didn't. We were in eighth grade, just starting our monthly thing a couple of months before, when this overgrown fellow, who wasn't quite right, started frightening the girls. His last name was Frampton. I don't recall his first name. I wasn't scared of him. It was more the other way around. I would tease him and egg him on. He'd turn tail and run."

"Frampton."

"Jessy Lynn had been doing some housekeeping for an older couple at a house up the hill back of the school, about a quarter mile away. It was getting dark, but she was fine walking the short distance. Evidently, according to Jessy Lynn, the Frampton boy thought she was me, and when she didn't act the way I usually did, he grabbed her. He had never actually grabbed any of the other girls, but he grabbed Jessy Lynn. She said she fought him, but he overpowered her, and he took her at the back of a building and violated her. She got away from him and ran back to our dorm. She was a mess, covered with dirt and blood. I cleaned her up and took her to Dr. Eustace Sloop."

"And he saw what the boy had done to her."

"Yes, but he said she was probably too young to conceive. She should stay at school. Jessy Lynn wanted to go home, so the school sent for Tommy to come and get her."

Tears swam in Susan's eyes.

"Susan, it is difficult to tell this story. I know your heart breaks like mine has been broken for more than seventy years! But I must go on. Maybe telling it will relieve my burden.

"Tommy was courting Carrie then, and he told her what happened to Jessy Lynn. She told him that Bea and Harvey wanted a baby. So when it was clear that she was going to have you, Tommy talked to Harvey and Bea. Bea had an old school chum in Lenoir who sometimes took in girls like Jessy Lynn. She wrote to her, and the woman agreed to take her. She'd never had one so young, but she was willing, so long as she behaved. She didn't want some little tramp at her place. Harvey and Bea took her to Lenoir and agreed to raise the baby as though she had been born to them. I don't know how they got the birth certificate clear. It may not have even been a court adoption, so far as I know. They had to have known someone who could fix it."

"Then maybe I was not legally adopted! Oh my. You know I didn't think of this before: I didn't have anything to question when I got my birth certificate for my social security. Oh my! So what happened to Jessy Lynn? Did she die?"

"That's is the heartbreaking part. The day after you were born, Harvey and Bea went to get you. They were planning to bring Jessy Lynn back to Crossnore. She would be there for the rest of the summer until school would start again. There wouldn't be so many other children there during the summer. It would be a safe place for her. The Frampton boy had been sent away, somewhere up north where he had relatives. When Harvey and Bea got there, the lady in Lenoir said that Jessy Lynn was gone. The woman was absolutely frantic."

"Did she leave a note or anything?"

"No. Nothing. She had been there the night before, supposedly resting after a difficult delivery. The next morning, she was gone. Most of her belongings were still there. They called the police to look for her, but it was as though she disappeared off the planet. No one ever heard from her again."

"Oh, my poor mother!"

"They said she probably drowned herself in the river. But her body was never found. I never believed she did that. I still do not believe she's dead. I think she found her way somewhere far away and changed her name. She would have done that."

"How can you be so sure?"

"We were identical twins. We thought together. We felt with each other, even when we were apart. I think I would know if she is dead. You may never know your mother, but you can know that you always have part of her with me. I hope your heart can rest now that you know."

"Thank you for telling me. She looked like you? I guess the rest of my life I will look at little white-haired ladies to see if I see you in them."

The two ladies hugged and cried in one another's arms.

When Susan had composed her emotions, she was able to speak again. With a twinkle in her eye, she said, "Aunt Junie Lee, when I grow up, I want to be just like you."

"You already are a lot like Jessy Lynn. She was a talented girl. We were both musical. We sang together and were learning how to play the piano, too. I gave it up after she left."

They embraced again, and Susan promised to write her often and come to see her when she and Mac returned to the mountains in the spring. "Mac and I are heading out to Macon tomorrow."

She left Aunt Junie Lee and went back to Aunt Carrie's room.

Aunt Carrie had fixed her hair by this time and was getting ready to go to lunch. "I can see that your Aunt Junie Lee has spilled the beans. I am relieved. Thank God!"

"Yes, thank God. I am satisfied, but Aunt Carrie, the rest of my life I'll be going around looking for Junie Lee's double. I'm glad she was the one who could tell me what I wanted to know. According to her, I wasn't exactly adopted. I was given to Mama and Daddy. The birth certificate was evidently fudged. Ha! Don't tell the IRS!"

"I don't know anything about that. Now walk me to the dining room. Promise to come and see me when you come back to the mountains in the spring."

"Well, of course. You are my double aunt. How could I neglect you?"

Chapter 43

Luke

Legacy at Highwoods Preserve Assisted Living, Tampa, Florida, late October 2009

Carrie would not be neglected. Luke would call, and Susan would write to her.

After arriving back at his place in Tampa, Luke was enjoying the balmy late-October weather and took the opportunity to be outside. Remembering his early years of gardening with Jesse, he had a little patio garden outside his room for some flowers. His nearly two weeks away had made the flowers look a little shabby. He apologized to them.

"Sorry I have neglected you. You look a bit sad. I'll see what I can do to cheer you up."

"Yes! I have definitely felt neglected, Luke! Where have you been?"

He looked at the plant as though it had actually spoken to him. "Uh, glad to have been missed, but I had some real plants to cultivate in North Carolina." He then turned around to see Lynnie on the sidewalk, laughing at him.

"I wasn't sure if you actually thought your plant was answering you. What is the plant? Looks like it used to be a geranium."

"Here, look. It is still definitely a geranium. It had lovely red flowers when I left, but for almost two weeks, it had to fend for itself. How are you, Ms. Lynnie? Come on up and sit with me for a spell."

"Did you say you've been in North Carolina?"

"Yes. I only learned a few weeks ago that I still have a half sister there. We had never met, and we both needed to correct that deficiency. I met twelve nieces and nephews and their spouses, went to the family church, ate more than I've eaten in years, and hated to leave. If it weren't so cold up there, I might consider moving there. It was the first time I've ever been in the area."

Lynnie was quiet for a while. Then she smiled and asked, "North Carolina. Beautiful state, especially the mountains. Where in North Carolina? Are you a Harvey from the area?"

"We stayed in Blowing Rock. No, Harvey is only my legal name. My mother and father had never legally married. She was a Lindsay from here, and he was a Willson from there. Harvey was his pseudonym. He used to come here in the winter, and I happened. There. I have admitted it to someone other than the family. The ghost is gone."

Lynnie furrowed her brow. "Men! But, Luke, I don't understand. Ghost?"

"Here's the short version. I didn't know about my unfortunate beginnings until twenty years ago, when I stumbled on some letters my Papa had written to my mother and her daughter, my half sister, Maggie. Maggie raised me from the time I was born because my mother died shortly afterward. In those letters, I learned about my North Carolina family. My niece, Susan, stumbled on more letters that told the story from that end. She facilitated a meeting between my half sister and me and then a wonderful family gathering at the homeplace."

Lynnie took a deep breath. "Glad they aren't real ghosts. Ha, ha."

"I don't mean to pry, but you sort of blurted out 'Men!' You have problems with our less-disciplined sex?"

"Let's just say, we all have a story. Now, I have missed our music. I've been playing almost every evening, and I'd like to hear you on your fiddle again. Give me a little break for a change. I can certainly see the North Carolina influence in your style. Your fiddle looks to be old. Where did you get it?"

"Ah. Papa made it. He was a fine luthier, making banjos, fiddles, and a few lap dulcimers. I had never really heard a lap dulcimer played properly until I was in North Carolina. Beautiful, but haunting. My one niece, whose name I can't recall without looking at the paper they gave me, played at our gathering, and I was hooked on the sound."

"Did you play with her?"

"Not just her, but we had two fiddles, two banjos, the dulcimer, a couple of guitars, a harmonica, and would you believe, a bagpipe?"

"Bagpipes? Ha, ha, ha."

"Yes, Mac. He didn't play a lot, but he did a drone for us on some of the tunes and joined in of some that were familiar to him. That was Susan's husband. Not a mountain boy. He's from Macon, Georgia. His best one was 'Amazing Grace.'"

"I can hear this in my mind, as a musician, that is. Speaking of which, I need to get back to my room and look through my music for something new to play this evening, unless you will consent to play instead."

"Not tonight. I just got back yesterday, and I need to recoup my strength. See you at dinner. Six?"

"Six."

I really like that lady. She is different from Stella. Stella was classy and could be snooty. I loved her like a young man loves a woman. Lynnie, how about that. I remembered her name. Lynnie is classy but comfortable. She sees me as an equal. Not certain I ever had that with Stella, and certainly not with her family. Hmmm. Harry called her my girlfriend. I wouldn't go so far to say she is my girlfriend, but I like her companionship. How's that for you, my son? Think I want to know more about this lady.

Chapter 44

Susan

Macon, Georgia, November 2009

Thanksgiving was just a couple of weeks away; Susan was helping Judy, her step-daughter-in-law, with getting the house in order. This would be Judy's first time entertaining the entire family and the first time she would be hostess in the McBride family home.

"Susan, you don't know how grateful I am that you are here to help and, as a matter of fact, even be able to consider this our home. You and Dad McBride getting married was such a shot in the arm for this family. I think we have all been a lot closer than we have been since Jack's mother died."

"I'm looking forward to it. Mac is so happy and relaxed."

"Yeah, even Jessica noticed, and that says a lot. She finally decided that you are for keeps!"

Susan got a good laugh about that.

"Dad says y'all are going to St. Petersburg for Christmas. The kids will hate that. Maybe we can have an early Christmas before you leave."

"We'll take that under advisement! That may not work out. Let me run something by you. I am considering going to North Carolina before Christmas and take my aunt to St. Petersburg to spend Christmas with her brother. We've told you this strange story of my family, and I'm thinking they need to spend as much time as their limited life expectations will give them. I realize that would mean cheating our grandchildren out of a chance to enjoy their grandfather, but I feel strongly about this."

"How old are the brother and sister?"

"She will have her eighty-eighth birthday right before Christmas, and he will be eighty-eight in June."

"Do it, Mom. The young'uns will survive. I would do it in a heartbeat."

Susan was pleased that Judy called her mom. Judy's mother had died shortly after she and Jack had married. "Good. I said something to Mac about it, and he wasn't against the idea. I will need to check with my cousin, Harry, to see if it would be feasible on the St. Petersburg end. I'll call him after supper. Haven't talked to him since we came home."

Later, hoping Harry was able to talk on the phone and not playing in some restaurant in Miami or Key West, she called. He picked up.

"Yessum. 'Bout time you called me. Did you do any research about your birth mother before you went to Macon?"

"Yes."

"Well?"

"Long story. Do you have time to talk?"

"Sure. I'm taking a breather tonight. What did you learn?"

She told him everything from the trips to five different courthouses, to her begging Aunt Carrie to tell her, to finally hearing the truth from Aunt Junie Lee. "You know, I thought at first that Tommy Vance may have gotten a girl with the last name Frampton in a family way. That was based on me being first cousin to Aunt Carrie's children. But when I found out the mother was a Vance, my only conclusion was that Junie Lee was my mother. She told me the entire story. Anyway, I'll be looking for Jessy Lynn Vance the rest of my life. My guess is that she is dead."

"Wow! Another Willson family saga! I guess you still consider yourself a Willson."

"Harry, I wanted to ask you how you would feel about me bringing Aunt Carrie along to St. Petersburg?"

"For Christmas? You betcha! She can stay in that big bedroom on the first floor. It is my other guest room, and it has a private bath. Perfect. You think she'll come?"

"All I can do is ask her. We would need to stop at least one night on the way. Mac and I don't even like to drive straight through anymore. I will call her tomorrow. Maybe call Gladdie first."

"Dad would be so pleased."

After a bit more chatting, the cousins cut off their call. Susan went ahead and called Gladdie.

"Hey, girl! How's it going? Guess you're glad to be where it's warmer."

"We are great. We have our chilly days. About January, we'll want to be even farther south. Speaking of which, do you think your mama would like to spend Christmas with Uncle Luke in St. Petersburg? Mac and I will come and get her and take her home."

"I'd bet my favorite pair of shoes on it. Want me to ask her?"

"No, I'll call her tomorrow. Harry was excited when I asked him. He has a good guest room with an attached bath on the first floor of the house. The only steps are a couple to get down to the walk from the street and a couple up onto the front porch. We can help her there."

"That will be wonderful. If she goes, how long will she be staying?"

"We can think about that later, but I'd say as long as she wants to stay. We would stay there, too, in another guest room upstairs. Gwen goes to school in the day and works at the hospital till midnight. Harry comes home for Christmas and then takes off again. But he has no schedule of places. He just takes his luck that resort areas will want to let him play. It wouldn't surprise me if he doesn't hang around St. Petersburg more."

"I'll be with her tomorrow to wash her hair. Why don't you plan to call after breakfast, say about nine. I want to be there when you call. Her hearing is bad enough that she might not get the picture. I can help."

"I'll do that."

"By the way, of interest, Mama and Aunt Junie Lee are getting along now. It was like day and night after Aunt Junie Lee told you the truth. Mama told the three of us then, but we aren't telling the other cousins about it. I never knew Aunt Junie Lee had a twin. Big surprise to all three of us. Mama thinks Aunt Jessy Lynn is dead. How do you feel about things now, since you know?"

"I'm glad to know. I can rest now. But I'll be looking for her in every little white-haired lady the rest of my life. Since they were identical twins, as least I have the model in my mind, Aunt Junie Lee."

"I'll be waiting for your call to Mama tomorrow."

Chapter 45

Carrie

St. Petersburg, Florida, Christmas season 2009

Carrie was beside herself with joy when she found out that Susan and Mac would come from Georgia and take her to be with her brother for Christmas. All she could say when Susan called her was, "Oh my!"

"Will you go, Aunt Carrie?"

"Oh my!"

In the end, Gladdie and her brothers talked her into it. So now she had decided to get some new clothes and shoes, get her hair done at the beauty shop, and have a nice present for Luke.

It would not be just any present, but a "dulcimore" that Papa had made. She had her old one stored away. It needed some work done on it, so she had Will call a friend of his who built dulcimers. The man, when he saw it, said, "It has good bones. I can have it good as new in a week."

Luke had been fascinated at the gathering when Lily May played her dulcimer. Carrie wanted him to have one of his own.

She had no idea how long she would be gone, not even how long it would take to get there or to come back. She remembered Papa saying that it took him three days by train to get from St. Petersburg to Johnson City. *It might take a whole week!* She had little conception of interstate travel, having never been any farther in her life than Charlotte or Johnson City.

By the time Mac and Susan arrived to take her on the "trip of her lifetime," as she termed it, she was more than ready, like a week ahead of time.

"Not excited are you, Mama," Gerald quipped, when he, along with Will and Gladdie, came to say so long the night before she was to leave. "You look mighty pretty. I'll bet one of those fellers at the place Uncle Luke lives will be swept off his feet by you. You be careful now. I won't put up with no shenanigans!"

"Oh posh! Where'd you hear of such things?"

Will had brought the dulcimer. It was perfect, and it played like a dream. Carrie could play a little, but not like Lily May. She strummed a tune and was satisfied that it was just what she had dreamed.

Saying farewell to her children before the trip was emotional for her. *Hope we won't be in a bad accident.*

Gladdie must have sensed her anxiety. "Mama, you are only going to Florida, not the moon! Relax and enjoy it."

So she was ready when Susan knocked on the door of her room. Aunt Junie Lee was there to bid her so long. "I never say goodbye to anyone, just so long. So long isn't forever."

Junie Lee had a tear in her eye as she whispered in Susan's ear, "It's the last thing I said to Jessy Lynn before she went away."

Partly to make her aunt feel better and partly from her own renewed beliefs that God is in control, she whispered back, "Auntie, your twin is in God's hands wherever she is. Trust God."

The trip, as Susan had surmised, would be cut up in three days. The first day, they made it to close to Charleston, South Carolina; the second day, to St. Augustine, Florida; and finally to St. Petersburg.

Carrie was a great traveler, surprising even herself. She wondered over everything she saw from the front passenger seat of Mac's SUV.

In the southeastern section of South Carolina, there were still some vestiges of cotton in the fields. She had never seen cotton growing, and that was a great wonder. She saw tall pine trees with huge cones on the ground, and that was a great wonder. She saw millions of semis zooming down the interstate, sometimes along six lanes, and that was a great wonder. She saw signs for adult shops, and even that was a great wonder, whatever that was. When they spent the night in a hotel, that was a wonder. She had Mac, the surgeon, in stitches 90 percent of the trip.

She was utterly exhausted when they finally pulled up to the white Craftsman house on Eighth Avenue NE, that her final great wonder was how they had ever made it in one piece.

It was Sunday, the twentieth of December, and despite the relative warmth of the air, it was filled with Christmas. Decorations graced all the homes, festive decorations hung from streetlights, bells could be heard jingling by Salvation Army volunteers in front of nearby stores, another great wonder.

Carrie Willson Vance was in St. Petersburg, Florida, and in the house where her papa had lived every winter from 1916 to 1929. Tomorrow would be her eighty-eighth birthday.

Chapter 46

Luke

Legacy at Highwoods Preserve Assisted Living, Tampa, Florida, Christmas 2009

If decorations on Eighth Avenue NE were festive, they were no less at Legacy. Doors to rooms were decorated as the resident wished, or if they had none of their own, the attendants did their best to put one on the door that would suit the occupant. The entire facility, inside and out, was adorned and bedecked in the most elegant manner, and a beautiful huge, real Fraser fir that was decorated was in the lobby, and another one in the dining room. There was a cheery, festive atmosphere everywhere. Carolers came and went, Christmas music was piped over the intercom several times a day, and residents joined Lynnie around the piano to sing favorites. There were cookies, holiday drinks, and little Christmas parties every day.

Luke didn't have his own Christmas decor, but Jasmine, his favorite attendant, had brought a musical door hanging especially for him. It was a swag of greenery laced through with holly berries, red ribbon, tiny violins, banjos, harps, and different-sized bells. It jingled whenever he opened or closed his door.

If Carrie had been excited about the trip and spending Christmas with her brother, he was no less excited. He had to tell his friend, Lynnie. It was right after breakfast when they met in the hallway leading to their rooms.

"I don't know how long she will stay, but she will be over in St. Pete at our house, the house where I grew up and where our papa lived every winter."

"Your papa, the luthier?"

"Yes. Lynnie, I need to get her a present. As a woman, what would you recommend?"

"You say she's in her eighties? I think women our age always like to have at least one more scarf. Luke, if we hurry, the van will be leaving for International Plaza soon. How about we go Christmas shopping? I need to buy some little gifts for some of the staff who help me and for the three girls who play Scrabble with me. Are you game?"

"Why not. I'll meet you here at the piano in five minutes."

Luke laughed to himself. *I think I just got asked out on a date!*

Luke and Lynnie joined five other shoppers going to the mall. They had two hours to shop and would have to return to the main entrance to be picked up again. The other five went their own ways, but Luke and Lynnie stuck together. Lynnie was a good shopper. She knew what she wanted, and she bought it without hemming and hawing about. *A lot easier to shop with than Stella, with her indecision and dissatisfaction with the choices.*

Lynnie then helped Luke find the perfect present for Carrie. "Luke, if you want something of good quality and don't mind spending an outrageous price, you can go to Neiman Marcus, but Dillard's will have something beautiful for less than fifty dollars. We're right here, so let's look."

They walked a short distance and found the right department. Lynnie suggested what she might choose for an older lady who was evidently simple and uncomplicated and lived in a colder climate. "Look at this one, Luke. Do you think this would go well with her?"

It was a muted gray plaid, with brighter strands of blue and maroon, and hints of emerald green and gold running through it. The texture was soft and warm.

"This will look perfect with her white hair and blue eyes. Thank you for suggesting it." He purchased the scarf and a sterling silver scarf pin to hold it in place. "This is for my sister. Today is her birthday and then Christmas. Will you gift wrap them separately for me? Please?"

While the clerk was wrapping Luke's gifts, Lynnie fingered a few other scarves, holding one up to her face and peering in the mirror. She smiled and put it back down. She started to walk away to a different part of the store.

Luke had noticed what she did, so he planned to return the next time the van was to come or perhaps talk Harry into bringing him back so he could buy that for Lynnie. He caught up with her and suggested a treat. "The van will not be ready to leave for another twenty minutes. I think we have time to get an ice cream cone. Are you up for it?"

"So long as it's chocolate."

Toting their packages and their ice cream cones, they headed to the main entrance. *I'm glad I have Lynnie to follow. I'd get lost here, even though I've been here fifty times!*

When Luke got back to his room at Legacy, his phone was ringing. It was Carrie.

"I'm here, Luke. We got here late last night. When will you be there?"

"It depends on when Harry will come and get me. I'd love to come this afternoon. Then I can hug the birthday girl."

"Hah! He said to tell you he will be there for you at three. You can get in a little nap before. Me too!"

Luke had contemplated bringing along his fiddle, but he decided not to this time. He just wanted to be with his sister. *None of this half sister or half brother business. She is my sister.*

When Harry arrived, Luke was sitting in the lobby with Carrie's birthday present, the silver pin, in his lap. He had taken special care with his attire, but this evening was a night of wanting to be the head of his own house again, if for only one evening. He wanted to look the part.

But he asked Harry if they had time to run an errand first. "I need to go to Dillard's at the International Plaza. Can you take me on the way, or should we wait till tomorrow? I need to get a gift for someone at the home."

"Your girlfriend?"

"Well, she isn't exactly my girlfriend, but yes. She helped me get presents for Carrie today, and I saw something she seemed to have wanted to get but didn't. I want to get it for her. I hope no one else bought it after we left."

"Let's do it."

It wasn't that much out of the way, and traffic for three in the afternoon was lighter than would be expected. Harry went in with him, and they found the scarf. "Good! Now I'm fixed."

"Do you need gifts for any of the attendants or staff at the home?"

"Never thought of that. That can wait for a day or so. I just wanted this before someone else had the same idea. Thanks, son."

"We'll work on that tomorrow. Don't get those packages mixed up and give Aunt Carrie your sweetheart's gift!"

"Sweetheart. Hmmm."

They headed to the house then, ready for an enjoyable evening.

Chapter 47

Blended Family

The house on Eighth Avenue NE, St. Petersburg, Florida, December 21, 2009

Gwen had no more classes at the university until after the new year, but she still had her full-time job at St. Anthony's. She and Susan made dinner. The first thing that Luke noticed when he walked through the front door was the aroma of meat loaf, his favorite. That meant mashed potatoes, too. The second thing he noticed was Carrie's big smile.

Carrie was smiling not only because she was seeing her brother again, but because meat loaf was her favorite, too. Gwen had asked.

"Since it's your birthday dinner, what do you want for us to fix for supper. I'm not the greatest cook, but with Susan's expertise in the kitchen, it will be fit for the queen you are."

Gwen had not been around many old women, except for sick people. Her grandmother, Stella, had died when she was a toddler. There were a few old ladies at her church, but she only saw them on Sunday mornings when she was able to go. With her job, that was not on a regular basis. Aunt Carrie was her "old lady" model, and she loved her. She had doted on her from the minute she got there the night before.

Carrie was easy to please. "How about meat loaf?"

Gwen would be off duty for a day or two, but she would have to work most of the week. She had the option of working either Christmas Eve or Christmas Day. She had decided on Christmas Day. She wouldn't have to go on duty until seven in the evening, but that meant working until seven in the morning on December 26. This way, she could be with the family both Christmas Eve and Christmas Day. Meanwhile, the birthday dinner preparation was underway, including a nice coconut cake. Gwen wasn't much for regular cooking, but she was what her father termed the Dessert Queen. This was a recipe from Grandma Maggie's cookbook.

Gwen showed Susan the recipe in Maggie's handwriting. At the top, she had written "Georgie's Coconut Cake."

Luke hugged his sister, but he didn't hand her the gift he carried. Instead, he put it beside her plate at the table, the place next to his seat at the head of the table.

"Oh good! Grandpa. I was afraid no one would get her a present," Gwen whispered to him, as they all came to the table. Luke held Carrie's chair for her before he sat down.

The evening was filled with lots chatter and filling in gaps between the two halves of the family. Luke's tales about growing up in the house as a boy in the 1920s and 1930s; Gwen's remembrances of Grandpa when she was growing up in the house; and Susan telling stories about Aunt Carrie and Grandma Zanny.

When the cake was served, Luke recognized it immediately. "That's Georgie's coconut cake! You did well, Gwen." Before it was cut, he made a toast to the birthday girl: "May each day ahead be as sweet as Georgie's coconut cake!" He handed her the knife to cut the first piece.

There were a couple of presents at the table besides the one Luke brought. Harry noticed when they were in North Carolina that she had pierced ears. He had told Gwen, who found a pair of earrings with a fiddle and a bow. She bought them and wrapped them originally as a Christmas present, but she decided to give them for her birthday. She'd get another Christmas present. Susan had found an old booklet of dulcimer songs. It had the words, melody, and dulcimer chords.

She opened the booklet first. "Aha! You remembered that I used to play the delcimore. Thank you." Then she opened Luke's present. "Oh, a pin! Isn't this pretty! I was wanting something like that this morning when I put on this old scarf. This is perfect. Here, Susan. Pin it on me." Then she opened the little box with the earrings. "Awww. Ain't they the cutest things. I might have to have you help me put them in. I had Susan help me with the ones I have in now. My hand isn't that steady now. Thank you all for a most memorable birthday."

Gwen saw that her aunt and grandfather were getting tired. "Grandpa, why don't you say so long to your sister and let me take you home. Dad can come back for you tomorrow."

"Good idea. I ought to sleep well tonight. How about you, Carrie?"

"I could sleep good every night in that wonderful room. Until tomorrow, Luke. Until tomorrow."

CHAPTER 48

Susan

St. Petersburg and Tampa, Florida, Christmas week 2009

Carrie and Luke both slept well each night and enjoyed either each afternoon or each evening together. Susan saw to it that both of them had a chance to go Christmas shopping two days before Christmas. Carrie was overwhelmed by the International Plaza, another wonder. Susan got a wheelchair at the entrance, and she pushed her auntie about, while Uncle Luke tagged alongside. Susan was amazed at his stamina.

"Who would have thought there were such stores anywhere, let alone all in the same place. I never—" She had little money other than what Gerald had given her before she left home. She bought little presents for her five great-grandchildren and a few other things she thought Susan, Mac, Gwen, and Harry might like. All in all, she spent thirty dollars or so.

Luke, on the other hand, had a good retirement from Jones Fish Company, as well as his social security. He had given Gwen power of attorney, but he still had access to a bank account where he could spend his money, if not liberally, at least within reason. He made several purchases, and had them all wrapped in the stores.

The mall was crowded, so they left as soon as they were done shopping; Susan took them to Doc B's Fresh Kitchen for an early supper.

As Susan drove back toward Legacy to drop Uncle Luke at home, she could see that both Aunt Carrie and Uncle Luke were exhausted.

"Okay if I drop you off at the front door, Uncle Luke? Looks like both of you could stand a little snooze. We'll both be back tomorrow for the entire evening."

"Thanks, good lookin'. Snooze it is."

Once she got Aunt Carrie back home and helped her into the house, Susan was ready to relax. She nearly bumped into Harry, just returning from a shopping trip with Mac. With Gwen gone to work and no need to cook, Susan and Mac went out to the back porch and enjoyed the stars.

"Not quite like sitting on the porch in Blowing Rock, but stars are pretty anywhere," Susan said.

"I was thinking about the 'Star of Bethlehem,'" Mac said.

"Yeah. We are going to sing about the star tomorrow night at Uncle Luke's place."

The next day, Christmas Eve, Gwen came in from work at eight in the morning, just as everyone else was getting up. She went straight to bed, with a farewell growl, "If I'm not up by noon, wake me."

That meant a quiet morning for everyone. But it would be good to gather around the kitchen table for breakfast, which Susan and Harry were already in the process of cooking. Then they would attempt a quiet decoration of the tree Mac had brought in yesterday. Harry had retrieved the decorations from the attic. Then after trimming the tree, wrapping presents to go under it. They could be quiet.

"So how do we keep Catastrophe from destroying our lovely tree?" Susan asked, as Harry topped it with a lovely crocheted angel his great-grandmother was said to have hand crocheted.

"Keep her on the back porch or in Gwen's room. Look at her eyeing it already," Harry said.

Indeed, Catastrophe was in the center of the floor, her gray fur rising in hackles, head down, and eyes zeroed in on the tree. She was in an attack mode. Aunt Carrie, nimbler than Susan had ever seen her, reached down and scooped up the beast and carried her into her room. Without using her walker! There was no way to laugh quietly.

"Shhh. Don't wake Gwen."

Catastrophe was happy to crawl up on Carrie's pillow and sleep the remainder of the morning, while Carrie sat in a rocking chair dozing, and the other three went off to their own little niches to wrap presents. It was a peaceful morning.

Once Gwen woke up, the house became alive once more. She fed her cat and put her out on the back porch. It was screened in, and Catastrophe would be happy watching the birds, getting her mind off the monster in the living room, a wicked Christmas tree.

But the big plan for the day was to spend the late afternoon and evening at Legacy with Uncle Luke.

Chapter 49

Luke

Legacy at Highwoods Preserve Assisted Living, Tampa, Florida, Christmas Eve 2009

The excitement Luke felt anticipating his family coming to celebrate Christmas Eve with him stuck out from him like the points of light on the huge Moravian star suspended from the ceiling in the main dining room. At breakfast, Lynnie had been eating with one of her Scrabble ladies, Millie, and they saw him come bouncing up to the breakfast bar like a schoolboy.

"Looks like your buddy, Luke, is wound up. What is he up to?" Millie asked.

"He told me last evening his son and some other family will be coming for the evening, having dinner here, and then they will be giving us a old-time music concert," Lynnie answered.

"I thought you would be playing."

"Oh, I will. I will do several of my own arrangements of Christmas music, and Luke and I will be playing a duet of 'O Holy Night.' Surprisingly, he plays the violin as well as he fiddles. He only had formal lessons in high school, sixty years or more ago. But I think his fiddling gives his classical, rich texture no violinist can achieve. I like it."

"You like him, period! Silly girl."

"Bosh! I'm a spinster and old maid, an unclaimed blessing."

"So let him claim you."

"Bosh."

Luke heard the "bosh" and looked in her direction, giving her a wink. Her face reddened, and she turned away.

When she got up and started for her room, he left the table and caught up with her. "How about joining our family this evening for dinner? You would like them. My sister, Carrie, is here and my niece, Susan, and her husband, Mac. Harry and Gwen will be here, too. Millie can join us, too, if she wants. The table pushed together will sit all eight of us."

"Oh, Luke, I don't know. I don't want to intrude. The other two ladies in our Scrabble quartet have gone to be with family. Millie and I thought we'd do our Christmas together, since we have no family. I can ask her, but she may be too shy. I just don't want to infringe on something that will be almost sacred to your family."

"The invitation is open, if you want. Your call, Lynnie."

I wanted to give her the scarf I bought for her at dinner, but maybe that isn't the right time. Since I'm going to be gone tomorrow, maybe I can give it to her tomorrow at breakfast. I'll make a date with her for breakfast. That's what.

She would like Carrie, and I know Carrie would like her. She reminds me of someone.

Luke's mind was loaded with all the drama of the family, so he lay on his bed and dozed off. When he got up an hour later, he was addled at first. The dreams always confused him. But once his mind cleared, he got out his violin and played "O Holy Night" over and over until he was satisfied.

When he went to get his lunch, he saw Lynnie. She motioned him to where she was seated. "Luke, I spoke with Millie. She said she wants me to join her in her room for dinner this evening. She wants that to be our Christmas celebration. I hope you understand. I will see your family when we gather for the entertainment."

"I understand, Lynnie. That woman who does the programs here stopped me on the way over here. It looks like a nice program is on the slate for tonight."

"Yes, Molly, the programs director."

"Right. She said several other families will be here in addition to my family. I don't remember his name, but an old Pennsylvania Dutchman is going to recite "The Visit of St. Nicholas" in his Dutchy dialect. She said he is hilarious. And that retired doctor who lives across from you will read the Christmas story from the Bible. I'm glad we can all be together tonight."

"Me too. I was afraid when I came here, I would not have any reason for playing again. Retirement hit me hard, Luke. But I am seeing that living here has given me another way to serve others. I don't know your beliefs, but Christmas means so much to me—the music—the joy. It is all because a Savior was born for us. I told you back some time ago that we all have a story. Mine may not be finished yet. But regardless, I trust God to direct it."

"Lynnie, I have never been a church person. Papa took me a few times when he would come here in January, but Mom didn't want to go to church. I never grew up with it. On the other hand, I believe as you do. I read my Bible and pray. I went to the little mountain church where Papa and my brothers and sisters are buried in the mountains of North Carolina. I came to a better understanding that Sunday of what God has done for me. I am adopted by God, not much different from the fact that my half family has adopted me, although I was not a legal son. If I never live beyond today, I will be with God."

Lynnie smiled. "I'm glad, Luke. That says we are brother and sister."

I wouldn't mind more, but brother and sister is good! Luke thought.

"Do you want to run through our duet this afternoon?" Luke asked.

"I think we should. What time will your family be here?"

"Four. How about right after we eat, and then I'll take my nap."

They sat together for lunch, and then Luke retrieved his fiddle from his room. The practice went well, and they parted ways. He barely hit his pillow till he was out. But before the family showed up, he was up and ready for the afternoon.

Chapter 50

Carrie

Legacy at Highwoods Preserve Assisted Living, Tampa, Florida, Christmas Eve 2009

Everything was still a wonder to Carrie. As the family showed up at Legacy, she expressed her great wonder at the opulence and beauty of the facility. Once inside, she had great wonder over the gigantic tree in the lobby, the lights, the greenery, the poinsettias everywhere, and the lack of nursing home smells. "Oh, the wonder of it! To think my brother lives here!"

Luke was in the lobby, waiting for them when they got there. Harry got a wheelchair for her to ease her from getting tired from walking. Luke guided them to his room mainly just to show Carrie where he lived. "It's not the best room in the house, but it is all I need."

"Must be good to have a room without a roommate. I never know who I am going to have in there next. The last one I had died, and the one before that went home. The newest one has 'old-timers,' so she isn't much company."

After they saw his room, Luke led them to one of the smaller sitting rooms where they could visit. Harry told him that he would be there in the morning right after breakfast. "I want you to spend the entire day at home, Dad. We have a tree, right where you and Mom used to have it. We will have a good ol' Harvey Christmas dinner, with a Willson flair."

"That's good. I tried to get my lady friend to join us tonight for dinner, but she is taking her meal with one of the other ladies at her room. I want you all to meet her, and you'll see her when we have our entertainment tonight. You did bring your banjos, didn't you?" He looked at Harry and Susan.

"You know we wouldn't miss a chance to play with you, Uncle Luke. Of course we brought them."

Carrie decided to bring Luke's Christmas present this evening, since there would be music. He would get his dulcimer. *Maybe he will try to play it. Maybe I can show him how.* She had given it to Mac to put wherever they were going to play music later.

Since it was Christmas Eve and at least half the residents had gone for the holiday to be with family, dinner would be served as a family meal at six, rather than from five to six thirty as usual. Tables had been set up to accommodate visiting families, and the table Luke's family had was set up for the six of them. Dinner was turkey with cornbread dressing, glazed sweet potatoes, green bean casserole, cranberry salad, and apple pie à la mode for dessert. The kitchen went all out to provide a delightful meal for residents and their families. Had anyone wished for wine, they could have had that as well. Luke declined for their table. He knew that Carrie disapproved of alcohol.

"Need to keep my head on straight," Luke whispered to the server.

As soon as the meal was over, they migrated to the area where the piano was. Chairs had been set up in a semicircle around the piano. Luke, Harry, and Susan got out their instruments and tuned them to the piano. Luke noticed that Lynnie was not there yet, but they were ready to play once they were tuned.

Carrie called Luke's attention to the big package next to the piano. "Little brother, I believe that package has your name on it."

"What? Huh? That by the piano?"

"Yes. Open it before folks show up to hear y'all playing."

He tore away the wrapping, opened the box, and found a long, narrow case. At first, he thought it was another fiddle, but when he opened it and saw it was a dulcimer, he gasped. "A dulcimer! Carrie, where did you get this?" Tucked into the f-hole was a goose quill pick, and lying beside it was a felt-covered piece of a dowel for pressing the strings. "Authentic."

"I used to play some. Not as good as Lily May, but I weren't half bad some years back. I'm not so good anymore, so I thought you should have it. Papa made it. I had some work done on it, so it'll be good."

"Can you show me how to play?"

"I'll try. Here."

He handed the instrument to her, and she checked the tuning. Despite bringing it the distance from North Carolina, it had held its pitch. She fixed it in her lap, picked up the quill, and began playing "Sourwood Mountain." For eighty-eight, she was good, but one song was her limit.

"Here, you try."

Luke was game. He knew the tune, so he tried. It wasn't as good as Carrie's rendition, and it would have made Lily May cringe. But yes, Luke was game.

"I can't think of any gift I could have gotten that would have pleased me more. I'm so glad to have it. I will take care of it like I have Papa's fiddle these more than eighty years."

"Papa gave this to me for my twelfth birthday, seventy-five years ago. It has been sitting in a closet at Will's for years. I decided it was wrong that it was not being played. It is yours, Luke."

People were beginning to gather, having finished their dinner. Molly, the program director, waited until everyone had their seats, and she began with announcing the events anticipated. Luke saw that Lynnie had come into the room and was seated on the back row. Luke's group would be first. He had told Molly that he called their group Papa's String Band, so she announced, "Let's welcome Papa's String Band, with our own Luke Harvey and his family."

They played for twenty minutes, playing mountain tunes. Luke even convinced Carrie to play "Sourwood Mountain" on the dulcimer. After the folk tunes, they ended the mountain program playing "Oh Beautiful Star of Bethlehem," with Susan and Carrie singing, and Susan ended with singing the old mountain tune of "Brightest and Best," a capella. It was a beautiful way to begin the celebration.

When Carrie walked back to her seat, she suddenly gasped and clutched her chest. She was pale. Was she having a heart attack? Susan got to her immediately and helped her to her seat. She brought her some cold water. "I'm okay. Just too much, I guess."

She was fine then and laughed with abandonment with the next one on the program: Ralph the dutchman. His rendition of "The Visit of St. Nicholas" was so funny; everyone's side was splitting from laughter. Then he added to the laughter by telling the story of Belsnickel, the loud, cantankerous guy dressed in furs and carrying birch switches. "He visits the children before Christmas to see if they have been naughty or nice, but he instigates fights, so the truly good ones will resist the naughtiness." For this, too, Ralph used his Dutchy accent to recite.

Once the audience had calmed down, Lynnie came forward and sat at the piano. She played her own arrangements of all the familiar Christmas carols: "Silent Night," "O Come, All Ye Faithful," "Joy to the World," and many others. Then she nodded for Luke to join her. What a surprise to his unsuspecting family when he played like a real violinist, vibrato and everything.

The next part of the program was Dr. Marshall, a retired cardiologist, reading the Christmas story from the Gospel of Luke. Molly turned the lights low, and then he read it with such feeling that Carrie felt she was there on the hillside with the shepherds and in the manger with Jesus.

As soon as he had read it, a woman stood at the back of the room and sang "Sweet Little Jesus Boy." It was Jasmine, Luke's favorite attendant. The hush in the room was palpable.

Carrie was stunned, but not only had the program affected her, but something else. *I feel as though I have hands about my throat choking me.* She grasped Susan's hand, who was sitting beside her. "Susan, wheel me over to speak to Luke's friend, Lynnie."

"Are you certain you feel up to talking? You had a bad spell there a few minutes ago."

"Just wheel me, dear."

Several of the visitors had gathered around Lynnie, and some around Luke. But when Lynnie saw Carrie coming toward her, she graciously dismissed the others and moved toward Carrie.

Both women seemed to be in an awkward situation, but Carrie broke the spell. "Your playing is magnificent. My heart was lifted to heaven. Lynnie, is it?"

"Carrie. I…I'm ready. Can you and your niece come with me to my room?" she said quietly. Carrie saw that her hands were shaking.

None of the three said anything as Lynnie led the way. Susan could see the questions on the faces of the rest of their family. She had no idea what this was all about.

Chapter 51

Susan

Legacy at Highwoods Preserve Assisted Living, Tampa, Florida, Christmas Eve 2009

Susan spied the three men and Gwen looking after them. She could see their lips moving and could almost guess the conversation: "What's Aunt Carrie going to do? Try to find out Lynnie's intentions on her brother?" *I have my own questions. Aunt Carrie is acting odd. She almost acts like she knows Lynnie.*

The three women arrived at Lynnie's room, what she termed a deluxe suite. There was a little kitchenette, one bedroom, a living room, a bath, and a walk-in closet. It was elegant, with many of her own things in the room.

"Please sit down, Susan. You have a beautiful voice, perfect for those haunting old hymns. And you truly know your banjo. You are very talented."

Susan wheeled Aunt Carrie in and sat in a rocking chair next to her.

"Susan, I believe your Aunt Carrie knows what I want to say, and this is very difficult for both of us. When I first met Luke, he told me about your role in finding his family, and in the process, you found out that you had been adopted. That must have been very traumatic to learn when you are older that the family you thought you had been born into was not your blood family. How much do you know about your adoption?"

Susan frowned. Suddenly it began to dawn on her what this beautiful and talented woman was saying. She gasped and rose suddenly from the rocker. It rocked back and forth after she stood. She grasped the arms and sat back down with a plop.

"Are...are you Jessy Lynn?" she whispered. Then with excitement. "You are! You are Jessy Lynn!"

"Then you know part of the story. Yes. I gave you birth."

There was silence in the room. Brief. Eerie. Yet it was an epiphany; an awakening.

Carrie was crying. She mumbled, "I didn't tell her, Jessy." Then in a normal voice, she said: "I took one look at you tonight and knew who you were right away. You still look like Junie Lee."

"Shhh, Carrie, it is all right. I am glad it's over. It was God's timing. Hiding for seventy years is over. Now, tell me what you know, Susan."

Susan grasped Lynnie's hand in one of hers and Aunt Carrie's in the other. Tears streamed down her cheeks. Gushed would be a better description. She told Lynnie about the DNA testing and learning that Aunt Carrie's children were her first cousins, but the rest of the Willson clan were not close relations. "I believed that Tommy had been my father. When I looked in the courthouses for birth records, I found a Jessy Lynn Vance as my probable mother." Then she told how Aunt Junie Lee had told her the truth and the story about what had happened.

"Junie Lee's still living! I knew it. Praise God!"

"You should call her tomorrow. I got her phone number here in my purse. She lives in the retirement home in Banner Elk where I live. That will be the best Christmas present she could ever have," Carrie said, recovered from her own shock.

Lynnie's tears joined Susan's. "Did she ever marry?"

"No. She says she is an unclaimed blessing," Susan said.

Lynnie laughed through her tears. "I told my friend Millie this morning that I was an unclaimed blessing."

"I don't know what to call you. But I am so happy, Lynnie."

"I think Lynnie is fine. Jessy Lynn no longer exists."

"Funny I did not see Junie Lee in you. I said I was going to look for her in every white-haired lady I saw until I found her…you. But seeing you at the piano tonight, I only saw a wonderful concert pianist!"

"Thank you. Susan, my story is very long, too long to tell you even if we should live another seventy years. I don't want to take your time away from Luke and the others, so I wonder if we can get together sometime tomorrow, Susan. All the family, if that would be appropriate. I want to tell my story. Please don't judge me by what I did at age twelve. I was desperate to get away from that boy. Although looking back, it didn't make sense. The only thing I could think of was to run away."

Susan looked Lynnie in the eye. "Lynnie, I would never judge you. It was a terrible thing that happened to you. I love you for what you have become."

"Thank you, Susan." Then she turned to her sister-in-law. Carrie, obviously, you married Jeb. I take it he has passed away. Tommy, too?"

"Yes, several years ago. Both of them."

"I'm glad to have lived to see this day, but there is the sadness that our family had to be apart. I live now for the eternal hope of seeing them all in perfection."

The three ladies remained in her room, oddly enough, speaking of inconsequential things, yet with this moment of revelation surrounding every word. They remained until the tears had dried and the hearts had settled back to normal rate and rhythm.

"I suppose the rest of your party are beginning to wonder what in the world is going on. Shall we join them and shock their socks off?" Lynnie threw out her hands in mock dismay.

Chapter 52

Luke

Legacy at Highwoods Preserve Assisted Living, Tampa, Florida, Christmas Eve 2009

When the three ladies rejoined the others, Gwen and Harry were looking at some of the artwork in the room and Mac was standing and talking to Luke, who was seated and putting on his socks. They all turned their heads at the approach of the ladies because they were looking at Luke and giggling uncontrollably.

Luke frowned. "What's so funny? You never see a feller put on his socks before?"

That drew another spate of giggling. All they could get out of them was something about shocking off socks.

Susan knew it would not be an appropriate time to share the wonderful news, so she made a decision. She was finally in control of her giggles. "I would like to ask if we might invite Lynnie to Christmas tomorrow. Any objections?"

Luke was holding one sock in his hand, and his face beamed ear to ear. "I was going to ask her anyway."

Gwen clapped her hands. "Yes! Hope you like ham."

"Love it."

"I'll be here for the two of you at ten in the morning. Will that work?"

What are these women cooking up? I think I know, and it has nothing to do with me. I've kinda been suspicious of something. They're about to leave, so I'll get to the bottom of this.

"Well, Lynnie, why don't we let these folks get back across the old bay so they can put some cookies out for Santa. Hugs, you all."

He looked Susan in the eye and understood that his hunch was right. She would tell the others in the car. As his family went toward the front entrance, he offered his arm to Lynnie. "Sit a few minutes with me?"

"Sure. I bet you know, don't you?"

"You're Susan's mother."

"Yes. What was your clue?"

"Gut feeling, but every time I have brought up North Carolina, Carrie's name, or Susan's name, I felt a certain restraint, maybe. Nothing overt. But at least a vibe. I put two and two together, and it hit me this evening. I glanced at you while she was singing. Lynnie is Susan's mother."

"I'm glad you know. Susan will likely tell them in the car or maybe after they get home. It was wise of her to not say anything here. It may have created an unwanted scene."

This is one strong woman!

"So if you had a clue, what do you think the others knew?"

"Ha! Harry decided Aunt Carrie was taking you to task and wanted to know your intentions with her little brother."

"Oh, for pity's sake!"

Luke wiggled his eyebrows. "So what are your intentions?"

"Men! My intentions are hopefully the same as yours: friendship and companionship. I like being with you, but I have no illusions."

He shot her an enigmatic smile and shook his private thoughts from his head. "Lynnie, I'm sorry I said that. After what you went through—and I'm aware of some of it—I understand your reluctance to be in anything more than a friendship relationship. You are right: I'm a man. Forgive me."

"No, Luke. There is nothing to forgive. I learned to forgive the boy who did that terrible thing to me. But not until one day many years later, when I understood about Jesus on the cross saying,

'Father, forgive them, they know not what they do' (Luke 23:34), I realized that boy didn't know what he was doing. He was not right in his head, and what he did was a feral instinct. I forgave him, when I accepted that. It took many years, but I forgave him. Look what happened: Susan was born and gave joy to Harvey and Bea Willson for the rest of their lives, and she gives us all joy now. Jesus forgave those who crucified him because of their incontrollable spiritual instincts. The result is our new birth. Luke, that is the only way I can look at this and survive each day."

"That is beautiful, Lynnie. I will never forget that analogy. Thank you. I'm glad you'll be with us tomorrow. I feel like we are all becoming the family we should be. The bad things of years gone by, whether done by us, our forebears, or done to us can be flushed down the commode."

"As far as the east is from the west, so far has he removed our transgressions from us" (Psalm 103:12).

"I've heard that before. Seems not only our own transgressions, but those that have been done to us. God takes them all away. Thank you, Lynnie, for your friendship and companionship. I see it as a gift from God."

The two friends parted, and Luke went to his room. He put his fiddle on the shelf, undressed, cleaned his false teeth and put them to bed, and took the little cup of pills the attendant had put out for him. Then he crawled into bed and dreamed of his friend, Lynnie.

Chapter 53

Lynnie

Home at Eighth Avenue NE, St. Petersburg, Florida, Christmas Day

Luke awakened as the sun was filtering through his window. It looked like it was going to be a beautiful day. It was cloudy, and there was a sprinkling of rain, but before he was ready to go to the breakfast bar, the rain stopped, and the clouds gave way to sunshine, matching the sunshine on his face. He ate his breakfast with Dutchman Ralph, as he was now called after last evening's performance. Ralph told him about Christmases growing up on a farm in Pennsylvania back in the 1930s, and Luke shared his memories of Georgie and Mom fixing the best Christmas dinners ever. As soon as breakfast was over, Luke went to his room and dressed. He wanted to look his best. Lynnie might just want friendship, but he planned to treat her like his special friend at the least.

Luke retrieved his packages of scarves for Carrie and Lynnie, and some little gifts he had gotten for everyone else; nothing significant, but purchased with the recipient in mind. He went out to the lobby to wait for Harry and to wait for Lynnie.

Lynnie awakened late. She had fallen to sleep for the first time in years with a clear mind. If she dreamed, there had been no nightmares to disturb her. The image looking back at her in the mirror was clear-eyed and at peace. The first thing on the agenda was to call her twin sister, even if she missed the breakfast bar.

She picked up her telephone and dialed the number.

"Hello and Merry Christmas!"

"Junie Lee? A very Merry Christmas."

"Who is this?" Her voice was trembling. "Jess? Jessy Lynn?"

"It is. I don't even know how to begin. Just know that all is well. Thank you for telling Susan the truth about what happened. We have met, and she knows." She told Junie Lee briefly about her being a friend of Luke's, living at the same retirement home, and meeting Susan the evening before.

There was silence on the other end for an expectant moment, and then the telephone exploded. Joy! Laughter. Words jumbled. "Oh, my sweet dear! I wish I could have been there."

"Junie Lee, I intend to come to North Carolina as soon as I can. I have no current plans, but I will let you know when I do."

The sisters talked for an hour, and yes, Lynnie missed the breakfast bar. She fixed her own in her little kitchenette and got ready for the day with the family.

At the same time that Lynnie was waking up, Susan woke up in Mac's arms, comforted, not only with his nearness, but also with a sense of nearness that her mother would be part of her life. She, too, was clear-eyed and lacking the turmoil of the last four months. She edged out of the bed so she wouldn't disturb her husband, but he said, "Boo! Good morning, sweet lady. I love you."

"I love you back. Merry Christmas. You reckon Santy came last night?"

While she pulled on her robe, she chatted with her husband. "It will be a big day. I'm so excited that Lynnie will be here. She said she'll tell us some of her story. I don't know how she could have remained so composed last evening at the piano and then when she had Aunt Carrie and me in her room. She was amazing."

Mac nodded, rustling the pillow with his messy hair. "You know she is a strong person. How could anyone have gone through what she did, gotten a good education, become a locally celebrated concert pianist, influenced many young folks on a university level, and managed to stay on her feet. She definitely is amazing."

"You are pretty amazing yourself, husband. Not every man would let some ol' hi'billy folk singer drag him to the altar!"

"I was more than willing. Go on, now. Let's get some Christmas breakfast."

All night long, Carrie had been restless; her mind reviewing the seventy years of family history and speculating the history of her newfound sister-in-law. Despite her lack of sleep, she was energetic and looking forward to a day with family. She met everyone at the table, looking serene and content.

Carrie laughed, pointing to the tree. "Look under the tree, and it looks as though Santa Claus brought some presents after all. I thought we'd been too naughty. Did someone go shopping last night after we got home?"

Harry was putting a big platter of scrambled eggs on the table. "Yeah. Gwen said we needed to get something for Lynnie, so she went out and got something. We all had things to put there, too. I'll bet there will even be something there for you, Aunt Carrie."

"Hope it's not coal. Another thing I hope is that Jessy Lynn, I mean, Lynnie, called Junie Lee this morning. Junie Lee is up and about every morning before sunrise. That would be the greatest present: hearing her sister's voice."

After breakfast, Susan and Gwen cleaned up the kitchen and began the major meal preparations. Harry went across the bay to pick up Luke and Lynnie.

Luke was in his glory, escorting Lynnie into his own home.

By eleven, dinner was in the works in the kitchen, with recipes from Georgie by way of Maggie's recipe book and Carrie's in-her-head recipes, with Susan, Harry, and Gwen putting them all together. It would be a true family Christmas meal. Once put in motion, the cooks gathered with the others in the living room around the tree. Mac was elected to pass out gifts. Lynnie had brought something for everyone. How she managed that, given that she had only been invited on Christmas Eve, she did not reveal.

"Did you suspect before our trip to the International Plaza that you would be included in our Christmas?" Luke whispered to her.

"You found me out!" she whispered back to him, as she opened the gift he had given her. "Ah! You really did find me out. I loved this scarf the minute I saw it. I didn't know you saw me pick it up and hold it in front of me in the mirror. You rascal!"

Carrie was more than pleased with the scarf he gave her. Other presents were equally appreciated, but Susan's and Lynnie's greatest gifts were one another.

"One question I have, Lynnie, is how come the name Van Sant? I understand the Lynelle, Uncle Luke told me, but Van Sant?" Susan asked.

"Interesting question, and I have an answer. I am legally Lynelle Van Sant. When I left Lenoir the day after you were born, I crawled beneath a tarpaulin in an empty watermelon truck headed back to Florida. The driver never knew I was there. I stayed there, only getting out when they were parked in a closed gas station lot so they could sleep. I would sneak out to go to the facility and crawl back in. But when we got just below the Florida state line, I had gotten out, but they left before I got back in. What to do?"

Carrie gasped. "Good grief!"

"It was a little town, and I saw a sign on a building, Van Sant's Bakery. I thought, Vance and Van Sant are close sounding. I will be Lynn Van Sant. I hung around until they opened. I hadn't had anything to eat for twenty-four hours, when I had eaten the last of the food I took from the house in Lenoir. I was starved. As soon as the bakery opened, I braved going inside and begging for some food. I was scared to death that they would call the police and I would be sent back, but I was desperate."

"What in the world did you tell them?" Luke asked.

"I said something to the effect that I was running away from a man that was going to hurt me. I was hungry, and my name was Lynn Van Sant, just like hers. The woman was very kind, and although she didn't believe me, she took me into the back room and gave me a glass of milk and some hot bread and butter. I had never tasted anything so good. She could see that I was in terrible shape. I'd just had a baby, and the effects were obvious. I had a little sack of personal belongings, so she allowed me to clean up, and then she sat me down for a motherly talk."

Susan edged her chair closer, as if to get into Lynnie's story.

"Mrs. Van Sant's motherly heart surmised my dilemma, and soon, I had told her my entire story. I begged her not to send me back. To my surprise, she told me I could live with her. She said she was a widow and no living children. She would claim me as her niece if I would stay and help her in the bakery. I would learn to make a lot of cakes and cookies. I could go to school there, too. The most wonderful thing to me was she had a piano. She could play, but she paid for me to have lessons. I owe my life to Florence Van Sant."

"So when did you change your name to Lynelle?" Harry asked.

"That was Aunt Florence's idea. If I was to disguise my past, the name would need to be different. I went to school as Lynelle. Funny thing, I was never asked for my birth certificate or any other identification for high school. Aunt Florence managed to have a bogus one made, and I used that for college and my social security card after World War II."

"Where did you go to college?"

"Aunt Florence decided I should go to a woman's college, so she said Florida State College for Women[13] in Tallahassee would be the one. She had made a decent living from the bakery, especially after the war, so there was money. I protested, but she said, 'Who else should spend my money?'"

"What about a driver's license?" Mac asked.

"I never had one. I don't drive. Never have."

Gwen interrupted. "Ms. Lynnie, I am amazed. Your life is so unreal that no one would ever consider writing it even as fiction! God has a great sense of humor to allow such a great story. But! If you folks want to eat anytime today, I will need help in the kitchen, Dad."

Harry shook his head and followed her to the kitchen, with Susan tagging behind.

The Christmas dinner was delicious but, in a way, was anticlimactic to Lynnie's story and, in fact, the entire Willson-Vance saga.

Susan, Aunt Carrie, and Uncle Luke told the family stories from different angles, and adding in Lynnie's story, all converged to the point that they were now one family.

But one member of the family was terribly indignant, unhappy, and hungry. Catastrophe had been banned to the screened-in porch. She set up a caterwauling that would have made proud a Carolina Catamount.

Now that dinner was over, Gwen let her in. "Just stay away from the tree, and I'll give you a meal to put you to sleep the rest of the evening, madam."

The food, of course, came before fulfilling the promise. She ate, crawled up on Aunt Carrie's lap, and fell to sleep.

Carrie made a suggestion: "Jessy Lynn—I mean, Lynnie, and that's going to take a bit of practice—why don't you come back to North Carolina with us? You can stay with Gladdie and stay as long as you want to. When you are ready to come back here, Gladdie will take you to Charlotte and fly you home."

"Oh, Carrie, I don't know! Winter in North Carolina?"

Susan voiced her idea. "Lynnie, would you like to go, visit with Junie Lee, and then come home? How would it be if you go with us to take Aunt Carrie home and then back with us to Macon? We will fly you back here whenever you want to come back."

Lynnie got down on her knees by Carrie's chair, stroked the cat and looked into Catastrophe's one open eye, and asked, "You think that would be okay, kitty?"

Catastrophe purred.

"Yes. I'd like that."

Epilogue

Willson's Cove, North Carolina, June 2010

Susan and Mac, when they brought Aunt Carrie home after Christmas, brought Lynnie to visit her only living sibling. Junie Lee was beside herself with joy. They spent two days catching up on what would truly take the remainder of their lives to process, let alone all the history they had missed from one another. Lynnie returned home to Tampa via the McBride's home in Macon and then a flight into St. Petersburg-Clearwater airport.

Susan and Mac returned to the mountains in late March, and Mac got busy on his first banjo, using Grandpa's original design and the pieces the old man had already cut. His talent as a surgeon was soon evident in his delicate work on the banjo. It would be finished by the reunion.

Early June in the mountains of North Carolina might be hot, or they might be cold. No matter the weather, the Willson family reunion would occur, rain or shine. Fifty to seventy-five people, more or less, would converge on the cove, bringing more food than would ever be eaten.

Letters and phone calls kept the multibranched family connected, and when it was time for the reunion in June, Harry brought Luke, Lynnie, and Gwen to the mountains in time for Luke's eighty-eighth birthday celebration. Both Lynnie and Luke would remain in the mountains for the summer. Lynnie stayed in Blowing Rock with Susan and Mac, and Luke at the family home in Willson's Cove with Mike.

One thing the family decided to do was to go in pairs to the attic and retrieve old relics, spray for bugs, and clean and straighten up. By the time they finished, it was the family museum Mike had always thought it was. But the letters, all of them from the attic and from the hidden stash in Grandpa's shop, went to Lily May for archiving before they would be returned to the attic museum. Harry and Luke also donated their collection; only retaining letters that had no bearing on the Willson-Harvey saga.

As promised, Susan had organized a Mountain Music Festival at Willson's Cove. It was scheduled for the Saturday after the big reunion, when some of the kinfolk from off the mountain would still be there. It was a huge success, drawing in musicians from around the five-county area and even from east Tennessee.

But the one thing Luke wanted to do more than anything else on this trip was to go up on Grandfather Mountain and walk across the swinging bridge. When he learned that the bridge had been built in 1952, he wondered if Lynnie even knew of its existence. She did, but she had never seen it. She told him, when she left the mountains, she purposely never read anything pertaining to them. He talked her into walking with him across the mile-high span.

Lynnie was not exactly thrilled with the idea of being suspended on a narrow swinging bridge over nothing but air between an eighty-foot connection to solid ground, but Luke held her hand, and she knew she was safe. They made it. On the great rock at the end of the bridge, he proposed to her. She accepted.

Author's Note

Banjo Man is entirely fictitious. There is no such place as Willson's Cove or the places associated with it. The local environs, however, are real: towns, cities, and restaurants. Any resemblance to real people, deceased or living, is totally incidental.

Handcrafted folk musical instruments were, indeed, made in the Appalachian Mountains from the late 1800s to current times. When Florida opened up as a tourist market, these craftsmen often would travel south to hawk their wares. An affair, such as told in the story of Luther Willson, may not have been too far-fetched.

The strict religion of the mountain people sustained them for their hard life without the conveniences available off the mountain. Little churches dotted every community so the worshippers could walk to their church. Often, preachers, even today, would supply more than one little congregation.

But these mountaineers were normal red-blooded men and women with all the human frailties the human race experiences. And the sins that plagued the cities plagued the mountain people, no matter how religious they were.

I hope you will read, not an exposé of wrongdoing, but a story of forgiveness, adoption, and emerging faith among the characters despite those ill-conceived actions, and that no matter how old we are, we can find that faith.

Endnotes

1. Jones House, Boone, North Carolina: Jones House is a historic home located at Boone, Watauga County, North Carolina. It was built in 1908 and is a two-and-a-half-story Colonial Revival or Queen Anne-style frame dwelling. Summer concerts are held on the Jones House lawn from June through August.
2. Scottish Highland Games, Grandfather Mountain, North Carolina: Highland games events have been held each year since 1956 at Grandfather Mountain, North Carolina. The event celebrates the history and culture of Scots in North Carolina. Competitions and displays take place in Scottish styles of piping, drumming, costume, dance, and traditional sports.
3. Legacy at Highwoods Preserve: A senior living facility in New Tampa, Florida, that includes assisted living and memory care in a resort-quality environment.
4. Augusta Memorial Hospital: A twenty-two-bed hospital built in 1910, adjacent to the current Bayfront Health at St. Petersburg, Florida. The facility remained as Augusta Memorial until 1923, when it became Mound Park Hospital, and eventually became the current Bayfront Health.
5. Brown Mountain Lights: A series of ghost lights reported near Brown Mountain in North Carolina. An early account in the *Charlotte Observer* goes back to 1913, "when a fisherman claimed to have seen 'mysterious lights seen just above the horizon every night,' red in color, with a pronounced circular shape."
6. East Tennessee and Western North Carolina Railroad: A narrow gauge railroad extending from Cranberry, North Carolina, to Johnson City, Tennessee, from 1882 to 1950.
7. The Larelle House Bed-and-Breakfast: A restored 1908 Victorian at the historic district of Old Northeast, St. Petersburg, Florida.
8. Life Care Center, Banner Elk, North Carolina: Both short-term and long-term care facility focusing on inpatient and outpatient rehabilitation, with twenty-four-hour skilled nursing care.
9. Ray's Weather: A daily local mountain weather forecast covering Western North Carolina. Local photographs, some humor, and Ray's unique golf forecast are posted.
10. The Crossnore School: Founded in 1913 by medical doctors Drs. Eustace and Mary Martin Sloop; first created as a boarding school for disadvantaged moun-

tain children, today it continues to serve children in need from North Carolina who need group foster care and community-based services. (Rag Shakin' is a reference to original thrift owned by Gilmer and Poppy Johnson, now the site of the Crossnore School Miracle Grounds Coffee Shop. The Blair-Fraley Sales Store across the street is humorously called the Rag Shakin'.)

11. Appalachian State Teachers College: Originally founded by Dr. Blanford B. Dougherty as Watauga Academy in 1899, became a two-year normal school and then Appalachian State Teachers College in 1929. In 1967, it became Appalachian State University.

12. Ben Long's fresco *Suffer the Little Children*: The ancient art of fresco is the masterful combination of the artist's hand, lime, sand, water, and pigment to form luminous, permanent images. One of only four master fresco artists in the world, Benjamin F. Long IV was born in Texas in 1945 and grew up in Statesville, North Carolina (Crossnore School website).

13. Florida State College for Women: On May 15, 1947, Florida State College for Women becomes FSU. Florida's governor signed an act making the Florida State College for Women coeducational and renaming it Florida State University on May 15, 1947.

About the Author

June E. Titus is a retired nurse, writer, poet, banjo picker, and artist. She lives with her husband, Ed, in the historic antebellum town of Thomasville, Georgia. Now a grandmother in her eighties, she remains active in her local church and is currently involved in a local book club. Her varied interests include history, literature, music, acrylic painting, and current social issues. June has been writing for several years. Her existing body of poetry numbers in the hundreds, going back some sixty years. Two short books of poetry, *Quiet My Heart* and *Finishing Well*, are available on a print-on-demand basis. June has always had a story roaming around inside her head. As a child, she had an entire imaginary family for her to create stories. In the past thirty years, she has written several fictional stories and discarded most of them. Two books about unplanned pregnancy have been self-published, *All Things* and *Soar Above the Yesterdays*. Both are now out of print. Currently, June posts a weekly inspirational blog by subscription and on Facebook entitled *Monday Musings*. Prior to moving to Georgia, she was a regular contributor to the *Watauga Democrat* newspaper and *All About Women*, a monthly magazine, both in Boone, North Carolina. Her family history and her own twenty years of living in the North Carolina mountains served to familiarize her to the High Country and its people and traditions for the inspiration for *Banjo Man*.

CPSIA information can be obtained
at www.ICGtesting.com
Printed in the USA
JSHW020525210621
15946JS00002B/10